CW01643353

# BLOOD IN THE GARDEN

By Chris O'Donoghue

A DI Sonny Russell mystery

First published in 2021 by Boghopper Books with PrintedWordPublishing
Copyright © Chris O'Donoghue 2021

Second edition printed 2023

The right of Chris O'Donoghue to be identified as the author of this work has been asserted by him in accordance with the Copyright Design and Patents Act 1998

All rights reserved. No part of this publication may be reproduced, transmitted, or stored in a retrieval system, in any form or by any means, without permission in writing from the publisher,nor be otherwise circulated in any form of binding or over other than that in which it is published and without a similar condition being imposed on the subsequent purchaser.

A catalogue record of this book is available from
The British Library
ISBN 978-1-91607-672-3

Typesetting in Minion Pro by Edward Sturgeon
Cover Illustration © Paul Harwood

Printed in Great Britain by Printed Word Publishing

PWP
PRINTED WORD PUBLISHING

*Other books by Chris O'Donoghue*

**The DI Sonny Russell Mysteries**

**BLOOD ON THE TIDE**
**BLOOD ON THE SHRINE**
**BLOOD ON THE STRAND**
**BLOOD ON THE CARDS**
**BLOOD ON THE DUNES**

# Dedication

*"All that is gold does not glitter,*
*Not all those who wander are lost;*
*The old that is strong does not wither,*
*Deep roots are not reached by the frost.."*
*– JRR Tolkein*

I couldn't have written this fifth book
in the DI Sonny Russell series
without the continuing support
of my sternest critic, editor-in-chief
and soulmate, Greer Harris.
Also thanks again to Paul Harwood
for yet another eye-catching cover.

*Seventy years before Alex Cupidi arrived at Dungeness,*
*Chris O'Donoghue's excellent, eccentric,*
*pint-supping Inspector Sonny Russell was travelling*
*the lanes of Romney Marsh in a police Wolseley,*
*solving all manner of crimes.*
*Out-of-the-ordinary and highly recommended.*
William Shaw – renowned author of
*The Birdwatcher, A Book of Scars, Salt Lane*

*I recommend this series of books.*
*Proper 50s police detective work*

*A really cracking read, so full of atmosphere*

*The writing is concise but vivid and authentic*
*– clearly carefully researched.*

*Like the best books in this genre you will not want to put*
*it down until all the loose ends are tied up.*

*A book that once you've started you will put off*
*all other jobs to carry on reading.*

# Chapter 1

## Monday evening

WPC NETTIE Sharpe was baffled. Her usually smooth brow showed several fine worry lines. Her hands were clasped behind her as she walked slowly round one of the vegetable patches in the walled garden, looking carefully at the ground. The plants were so neatly lined up in regimented rows that they looked like soldiers on parade. But something was wrong. The friable earth was rich and weed free but something about the vegetables just didn't look right. The plants round the outside were fine, but in the centre, in an area about six feet square, they looked sickly. The tops of the leeks flopped over and the feathery green leaves of the carrots drooped. She glanced around and spotted a couple of spades leaning against the side of a potting shed. After pausing to make sure she was still on her own she strode across the gravel path, grabbed one of them and returned to the vegetable patch. Taking a deep breath she made up her mind.

She knew she was going out on a limb; knew she could be jumping deep into hot water – if she got it wrong – but she had a strong feeling. And she had learned from DI Sonny Russell to follow her instincts. He had consistently come up trumps when following a 'feeling' and had encouraged her to do the same. So, stepping onto the earth, she made her way across the patch, careful not to tread on any vegetables around the outside. When she reached the centre she tugged tentatively at one of the sickly leeks and was surprised when it came up easily, the roots barely held by the soil. The same thing happened with a carrot. When she'd cleared a big enough space she started digging, heedless of the muddy state her shoes and stockings were getting into.

Soon a heap of soil stood piled up next to the hole and she'd found nothing. Nettie sighed. She wondered if she'd got it wrong this time. But it was too late to stop now and she decided to carry on digging. Suddenly the spade hit something solid. It was only a couple of feet down but she was certain she had been right. Getting down on her knees she leaned into the hole and started scraping the earth away with her fingers. They snagged on something – a piece of brightly-coloured cloth. Carefully she moved more soil until pink flesh was revealed. Gently stroking the earth away she revealed a hand. She sat up on her heels. It was just as she'd suspected but it still came as a shock. She stayed like that for some time – just thinking what to do next.

She was so engrossed in her thoughts that she didn't hear someone come up behind her. The blow she received knocked her out cold and she toppled to one side. Dropping the second spade her assailant grasped her beneath the armpits, dragged her roughly across the path and into the shed, then returned to the vegetable patch.

~O~

A neat cabin cruiser floated on the River Medway, secured to a wooden jetty. A figure lay on one of the bunks in the forward cabin, his hands clasped behind his head; his eyes closed. Lost in thought, he was thinking about his mother. He just couldn't understand why she had been so cold towards him. If she had reacted differently he would still be home, not slumming it, living in a boat, eking out a living, getting work where he could. He gave a great sigh. Perhaps it was time to do something about it.

# Chapter 2

***Vladimir Grigoryevich Tretchikoff****, nicknamed "The King of Kitsch" was an artist whose painting The Chinese Girl, popularly known as The Green Lady, is one of the best-selling art prints of the Twentieth Century.*

## Monday morning – 12 hours earlier

**DI SONNY** Russell had been called into Superintendent Vic Stout's office. The customary cheroot burned in the heavy glass ashtray. The large, polished desk was clear, apart from a folder lined up neatly in the centre. The equally large office window looked out on to the park, where the trees were in full leaf. The window was open and the sound of birdsong filtered in, mixed with the cries of children playing in the open space beneath the trees.

'You wanted to see me, sir?' Russell asked.

Stout waved to a chair. 'Sit down – sit down.'

This was a rare invitation. The Super must be in a benign mood. Russell sat and waited for him to speak.

'I've got a job – one that needs handling with tact. I think you may be the man for it.'

Russell cocked his head to one side. 'Sir?'

Stout leaned forward, placing his elbows on the desk and linking his fingers. 'It's a little sensitive – will need discretion.'

Russell was intrigued. 'You can count on me.'

'I'm sure I can.' Stout blew out his cheeks. 'It concerns an acquaintance of mine – well, more of a friend, really. One of my golfing buddies – Douglas McDonald.'

The DI nodded. *I thought as much*, he said to himself. Stout was always trying to curry favour up at the golf club. Russell knew that the Super would love to be a member but so far had failed to get the required nomination, however much toadying he undertook. Inwardly he smiled but out loud he asked: 'How can I help?'

Stout seemed to consider. 'Well, not to put too fine a point on it, he's disappeared.'

'I see. But I don't understand what I can do. Shouldn't it be handed over to missing persons?'

'Under normal circumstances, yes. But in this case…' His voice trailed off.

'I think you'll have to give me a bit more, sir,' Russell suggested.

Stout sat back and folded his hands across his ample stomach. He seemed to be weighing up how much to tell the DI. 'As I said, it's rather delicate.' He leaned forward again. 'Can I trust you to be discreet?'

'You know me, sir,' Russell said, a blank expression on his face.

'Mmm. I suppose so.'

Stout was taking so long to come to the point that Russell was beginning to feel the stirrings of impatience, but managed to keep it in check. 'Perhaps if you gave me a little more detail?' he said mildly.

'Yes, yes, of course.' Stout opened the folder and straightened the papers. 'I don't know for certain, but his disappearance may be to do with a woman – the wife of another member of the golf club.'

'I see.'

'They both vanished at the same time.'

Russell looked puzzled. 'If that's the case I don't see how I can help. They've probably run off to a love nest somewhere.'

Stout waved his hand dismissively. 'That's what I thought, but the woman's husband is also a friend and...' He let the words trail off.

'Who is it?' Russell asked.

'It's David Peters.'

'The horticulturalist?'

'Yes. That's right.'

Peters ran a nursery over towards Appledore, started by his late father-in-law. But it wasn't just any nursery – there were several acres of glass houses and growing beds. Chambers' Nurseries not only supplied plants to most of the corporation gardens in the south-east but also sent regular consignments, nationally by rail, to the Woolworth stores. Russell understood that he was a powerful man – not only in the horticultural community but the community at large. He also suspected that Peters was something high up in the local Freemason's Lodge – not a Grand Master but not far off. But Douglas McDonald, the missing man, was a different kettle of fish. He fancied himself as somebody important – somebody with clout – but that was, Russell suspected, because he suffered from small man syndrome. He didn't have a position of power – he was an accountant, or pursued some similarly dull occupation – but he still strutted about like a puffed up panjandrum.

Russell had been introduced to him at a function but hadn't been impressed. The man was a boor and as soon as they'd shaken hands his eyes were on the next guest, who just happened to be female. Russell cast his mind back. He thought he knew the woman from somewhere but couldn't place her.

'This is Peters' wife, Rose.' Stout took a photo out of the folder and slid it across the desk. Russell picked it up and studied the woman's face. She couldn't be described as pretty – maybe as handsome. He smiled. *She* was the one who had grabbed McDonald's attention. He recalled that she was a large woman who dwarfed McDonald although judging by the huge grin on his face, he didn't seem intimidated by her.

'A striking woman, sir.'

'She is that,' Stout agreed.

'So what would you like me to do?'

'First I want you to go and talk to Peters – get a feel for the relationship – see if you can find out why she went.'

Russell paused, looking thoughtful. Then: 'With respect, sir. Is this really a job for a Detective Inspector?'

Stout shifted uncomfortably in his seat. 'Hmm, possibly not, but, as I said, it is a little delicate, so I'm entrusting it to you.'

*And because he's a member of the golf club and you want to keep in with him*, Russell would like to have added. But he said nothing.

'After you've seen him, perhaps you could go round and talk to Douglas McDonald's wife, Heather. Find out if she has any idea where he might have gone.' Russell nodded and stood. He was starting to move towards the door when Stout spoke. 'Oh, I understand you're without your DC.'

'Johnny Weeks?' Russell said. 'Yes, he's taken some leave to study for his sergeant's exam.'

Stout nodded sagely. 'Hmm. Why don't you take that WPC?'

'Nettie Sharpe?'

'That's the one. She's keen and bright, isn't she?'

'Yes she is.'

'And it won't hurt to have a female in tow – especially when this is rather a sensitive case.'

Russell nodded. 'Yes, I'm sure you're right.' He was secretly pleased. WPC Sharpe certainly was keen and would make a good detective, if women were allowed to apply. One day, he hoped.

~O~

Stout had given him Peters' address. When he asked if the WPC would accompany him she couldn't keep the smile off her face. She was very fond of Russell – admired his abilities – and was glad to have the opportunity to spend time with him. 'I think I know where it is, sir,' she said. 'It's just north of Hurst Green on the A21.

'I think you're right. Come on, we might as well get on our way.'

They set off, Nettie driving and, after travelling north for half an hour, they saw the entrance to Sowsden Manor. Turning off the road, she drove the Wolseley past an ornate gatehouse and down a broad, gravel drive.

'Take your time,' Russell said. 'We might as well savour the view.' They passed a grass tennis court, then a thicket of shrubs and mature trees. He recognised the shrubs as Rhododendrons, the flowers long gone but the leaves glossy. This was followed by a billiard-table flat lawn, set out with croquet hoops. He looked away and the manor itself came into view. Russell whistled. 'Sowsden is certainly an impressive building.' Although not old, it was built in classical style, constructed in mellow sandstone, with mullioned windows and castellated battlements. The borders round the walls were lush with flowering perennials: *Rudbeckia* in burnt orange, *Echinacea* – shocking pink with a complementary bronze cone; the delicate, whirling butterfly-like flowers of *Gaura* and the electric blue spires of *Perovskia*.

In front of the pillared entrance there was a broad turning circle with a large circular fountain in the centre. Water bubbled out of a fish's mouth and cascaded down. To one side stood a utilitarian Land Rover. 'Park here,' Russell said. They left the car and walked up to the entrance. He turned towards the policewoman. 'Let me do the talking. You just observe and take notes. See if you spot anything.'

'Of course, sir,' she said.

Next to the wide front door was a bellpush set in a round, polished brass surround. Russell pressed the button and could hear the distant ringing within. He waited for a few moments then heard the sound of bolts being drawn and the scrape of a key in the lock. The door opened to reveal a small man, with a mass of curly hair and a bushy beard, peering at them through a pair of gold-rimmed, half-moon spectacles. He smiled warmly.

'Sorry for the delay; we don't use this entrance much and it's Mrs Floyd's day off. What can I do for you?' he asked cordially.

Russell reached into a pocket and produced his warrant card. 'I'm Inspector Russell and this is my colleague, WPC Sharpe.'

The man looked baffled.

'We've come about your wife.'

Realisation dawned. 'Oh I see. You'd better come in.'

They entered a small vestibule and were led through a pair of glazed double doors into a grand entrance hall. The room soared upwards through a galleried first-floor landing to a ceiling, maybe forty feet above, where an impressively ornate glass chandelier hung. A concert grand piano was dwarfed by the vast space.

'This is some place you have here,' Russell observed.

'Not bad, is it,' Peters agreed.

'Has it been in the family long?'

'Yes, but not mine. My wife inherited when her parents died.'

'I'm sorry.'

Peters waved his hand. 'Don't worry, they were quite elderly. She was, you might say, a late arrival. Anyway, I presume you've come here to talk about her disappearance.' He tipped his head to one side. The action put Russell in mind of a dog, awaiting its master's instructions.

'Yes, Superintendent Stout asked me if we would pop round.'

'That was good of him. Shall we have a cuppa while we talk?'

'Yes, that would be nice.'

'Follow me then.'

Peters led the way across the vast hall, past the Bechstein grand and through a side door. This led to another room, only slightly smaller, with a big, solid table in the centre. Along one wall was a wooden dresser with china displayed. Russell recognised the pattern – possibly Spode.

'Please, sit down.' They sat while Peters busied himself at the Aga. Nettie opened her bag and took out a pad and a pen. Russell studied the man while he was preparing the tea. The detective wasn't tall – five-foot eight in his shoes – but Peters was shorter and, surprisingly broader. His dress was at odds with the grandeur of the house – a baggy ginger coloured jumper with holes at the elbows and a pair of shapeless corduroy trousers. His feet were pushed into a pair of well-worn carpet slippers.

'I understand you're concerned about your wife.'

'Rosey?'

'Yes,' Russell said. Peters turned, holding a delicate bone china teapot in his stubby fingers. His baffled expression made Russell wonder if he'd misunderstood. 'Oh, have I got it wrong?'

'No, no. It's just not like her to go off without saying anything at all. She usually says something before one of her jaunts.'

'Right. How long has she been gone?'

'Let me see.' Peters considered. 'I last saw her on Wednesday morning.'

Russell did a calculation. 'That's five days.' Nettie wrote in her notebook.

'Is it?' Peters seemed perplexed but not bothered. 'Yes, I suppose it is.'

'Weren't you worried about her?'

'Hmm? No, not especially – at first.' He brought a tray over to the table and sat down opposite them.

'What do you mean – "at first"?'

'Well, I thought she'd gone off to see a girlfriend – have lunch or something.'

'Did she do that often – go off without saying where she was going?'

'Oh yes. She has her own car, you know.'

Peters had poured the tea. Russell lifted his cup and took a sip. It was Earl Grey, not his favourite but he was thirsty. 'When did you start to get worried?'

'Not until that evening.'

'What did you do?'

Peters took a drink. 'It was a bit late to ring round so I left it until the next morning.' He held the cup in both hands and peered over the rim.

'And in the morning?'

'Er, I rang round her friends.'

'Had anyone seen her?'

Peters' forehead crumpled into a frown. 'No, that's the odd thing. I thought she must have stayed with one of them but no one had seen her.' He held the teapot up. 'Another cup?'

Nettie shook her head but Russell said, 'Thanks,' and held his cup out. As Peters poured from the teapot he said: 'I can see that might have worried you. What did you do then?'

'I got in touch with Vic – Superintendent Stout, that is.'

'And what did he say?'

'He told me not to worry. She probably wanted a few days on her own.'

'I see.' Russell paused while he took a drink of tea. Putting the cup down carefully on the saucer he said: 'Had there been an argument?'

'What do you mean?'

'Had you had words?'

'Ah, I see. Well, to be honest, we did have a bit of a row.'

'What about?'

'Oh you know, the usual.'

'I'm sorry, I don't. Would you like to explain?'

'Me not paying her enough attention, spending too much time at work – that sort of thing.'

'I see. Did these rows happen often?'

'Hmm. I suppose lately they'd started to become more frequent.'

Russell changed tack. 'You said that she owned this house.'

'That's right.'

'Did that cause any friction?'

Up until then Peters' reactions had been casual. This question changed his response. 'What do you mean?' he snapped.

'Well. I wondered if there was any resentment.'

He snorted. 'Of course not.'

'What about the business?'

'The nursery?'

'Yes. Who owns that?'

Peters looked flustered. 'Well I run it,' he said defensively.

'But who actually owns it?'

'Oh, I see. Well… Rosey does. Family money, you know.'

'I wondered if that caused any problems.'

Peters visibly relaxed and shook his head from side to side. 'No. No problems there.' He gave a little laugh and looked down at the table. They sat in silence for a while, drinking tea.

Russell was happy for this to continue as, left alone, he thought the other man might divulge some more information. This technique had achieved some good results in the past. He flashed a look at the WPC. She gave a slight nod in return. The silence stretched until Peters looked up and spoke.

'Oh, she did leave a note.'

'Do you still have it?'

'Er, yes. But it's a bit of a mess. I was so cross that I threw it in the bin but took it out again later. Here it is.' He got up and walked across to the dresser. Picking up a piece of paper he handed it to Russell. It was indeed a mess – screwed up, flecked with tea leaves and stained with some other unsavoury fluids. He carefully flattened it as best he could. Peering closely he could just make out the spidery writing. It had been written with a fountain pen and the ink had run making the words almost indecipherable.

'Do you know what it says?' Russell asked.

Peters pushed his spectacles up on to the bridge of his nose and leaned forward. 'Yes, it says something like: "I need some time on my own – away from you. Don't worry; I've left food in larder so you won't starve. Just get on with your life – like you always do." I think that was the gist of it, anyway.'

Russell held the paper up. 'May we keep this?'

'Of course,' Peters said, with a dismissive wave.

'Did she take anything with her – clothes for instance?'

Peters' baffled look returned. 'Mmm? I don't know.'

'Could you have a look?'

'I could, though I doubt I can tell. She has so many garments.'

'Have a look anyway, you never know.'

'Right. Yes. Of course.' He got up from the table and walked towards the door they had entered by.

'Perhaps we could come with you?' Russell ventured.

Peters appeared unfazed by the suggestion. 'Oh, I don't see why not. Follow me.'

They made their way back to the entrance hall and Peters led them up a wide curving staircase to the galleried landing. From here Russell could see down into the hall. He didn't have time to linger as Peters scuttled along a corridor and through a panelled door which led into an enormous bedroom. Russell noted that there were twin beds with a considerable space between them. He shared a glance with Nettie but didn't comment. Instead he walked across to the mullioned windows. The view was stunning. Adjacent to the house was a lawned terrace, the grass manicured and emerald green. There was a meadow below a stone parapet, covering perhaps five acres and beyond, dense woodland. He stood and stared. Russell was unusual in his profession in having a social conscience. He wondered how one person could own all this – and keep it to himself, when so many had so little and were struggling to put their lives back together after the depravations of the war. Russell's reverie was broken by the other man's voice.

'Through here.' Peters led them into a room that was bigger than most bedrooms. 'This is her dressing room.' One wall was lined with floor-to-ceiling, wooden panelled doors. He opened the first one.

'I see what you mean,' Russell said. The wardrobe was filled with dozens of outfits; numerous pairs of shoes were lined up below the clothes.

Peters gave a wry grin. 'I don't think I could even begin to tell you what she took.'

'What about a suitcase?' Nettie ventured. 'Do you know if one of those is missing?'

'I could have a look.' He walked to the last door and opened it. Inside were several shelves, each with valises, trunks and cases neatly lined up. In the middle there was a distinct gap.

Russell pointed. 'Any idea what was there?'

'Let me think.' Peters cupped his chin with one hand and gripped his elbow with the other. Russell waited while the other man thought. The silence stretched. Finally Peters shook his head and said: 'I don't know. You see my problem, don't you?'

'I do, but perhaps we can look at this logically.' Russell had noticed that the luggage appeared to be colour coordinated. On the lower level were trunks in natural leather, lilac, cream, etc. Above each one, in the same colour, was a large suitcase. On the next shelf, a smaller case. Next a hat box and on the top shelf, a valise. Just to the right of centre was a column of burgundy coloured luggage, but two shelves were empty. On one there should have been large suitcase, on the other, a valise, judging by the adjoining shelves.

'Could they have been them?' Russell asked.

'I suppose so,' Peters agreed.

'At least we know that, then. It would be helpful if we also knew what clothes she had taken, but I can understand that it would be difficult to know.'

'Sorry I can't be more helpful.'

'Never mind. Perhaps we should go back downstairs.'

'More tea?' They were back in the kitchen that was big enough to swallow the whole of Russell's railway carriage home – with room to spare.

Again Nettie shook her head. Russell said: 'No thanks.' Two cups of Earl Grey were enough for one day. 'You said she has her own car.'

'Oh yes. It's an MGA sports car – the latest model, of course. She adores it. Bright red. See it coming from miles away,' he chuckled.

'Any idea of the registration?'

Peters considered. 'Afraid not. She hasn't had it long.'

Russell returned the frown. 'She must have a log book?'

'I suppose so. I might be able to find it, but I'd need to search. Is it important?'

'It could be.' He took his wallet out from an inside pocket, extracted a card and handed it to Peters. 'Perhaps you could give me a ring when you do. We'll be going now. Let me know if you hear from your wife, of course.'

~o~

After he had closed the door Peters leant against it and smiled. The detective and the attractive WPC had obviously been taken in by his bumbling performance. They could hardly know that acting was his first love. He frowned. If he hadn't got involved with Rose he might have been able to pursue his dream. Instead he had to appear to enjoy running *her* family business rather than make his name, treading the boards.

~o~

They drove slowly back up the drive. On the left were more ornamental shrubs including a huge tree he recognised as a giant Redwood. Someone had spent time and a great deal of money laying out the grounds in the past, Russell thought.

Nettie whistled. 'This estate must be worth a bob or two.'

'It must,' Russell agreed. 'If the money came from the wife, I'm surprised that Peters didn't seem more concerned about her disappearance. The only time he displayed anything more than a mild curiosity was when I asked if there was any friction over money.'

'I noticed that too, sir. But he didn't remain agitated for long.'

'No, he soon lapsed into his absent-minded default position. Either he really wasn't concerned about her or he is a jolly good actor.'

I doubt that, sir.'

'Me neither. The man probably lives in his own little world.'

When they reached the end of the drive the WPC asked: 'Where to now, sir?'

'Turn right and head towards Kilnhurst. We'll pay a visit to Heather McDonald. I've got the address here.'

As they neared their destination he recognised where he was. He shuddered.

Nettie noticed. 'What is it, sir?'

Russell took a deep breath. 'I don't know whether you remember but a couple of years ago there was a rather grisly case where ex-Nazis were being bumped off by a pair of German brothers.'

'Yes, I do. It was in revenge for the death of their brother, wasn't it?' she said, as they turned into an estate of neat, semi-detached houses.

The DI peered at the address written on a piece of paper. 'And this is the actual house where one of those murders had been committed. I wonder if the occupants know about it?' Nettie brought the Wolseley to a halt and they got out of the car. The garden looked very well-maintained, with a neatly mown patch of lawn behind a square-cut privet hedge, but was a long way from the grandeur of Sowsden Manor. They walked up the paved pathway and Russell knocked at the white-painted front door. They only had to wait a few moments before it was opened by a small, immaculately turned-out woman.

'Yes?' she said, staring at them suspiciously. She was delicate, almost child-like in stature, with neat facial features beneath a straight cut fringe, her hair, dark and lustrous. She wore a pale chocolate-coloured dress and fiddled nervously with a string of cream beads hanging from her neck.

'Mrs McDonald?' Russell enquired.

'That's right. You're not selling insurance, are you?' Her voice too was childlike – light and musical.

Russell smiled. 'No, we're the police.'

Nettie, who had been behind her boss stepped to one side and the woman saw the uniform. 'Oh!' Her dark eyes widened and her hand flew to her mouth. 'Is it about Douglas?'

'It is actually. Do you think we could come in?'

'Of course,' she said, flustered, and held the door wide so they could enter.

'In here?' Russell asked, indicating the first door on the right.

'Yes, please go in. Would you like some tea?'

The DI didn't need any more but thought it might help to settle the woman's nerves. 'That would be nice.'

'Take a seat,' she said, 'I won't be a moment,' then left the room.

Nettie perched on a chair but Russell remained standing, looking around. The layout was familiar from when he'd first met Soffit, the property developer of the estate, but the furnishings were completely different. 'As I recall,' he said quietly, 'the décor was muted, neutral, the furniture was chunky and deeply upholstered when I first came. Now look.' He held his arms wide.

The walls were papered with a busy, large geometric pattern in dove grey and yellow. A framed print of Tretchikoff's *The Chinese Girl* took pride of place, as it did in a thousand other suburban homes. The three-piece suite was modern, with spindly black legs and thinly upholstered seats – neither sturdy nor comfortable looking. Russell sat gingerly on one of the chairs, wondering if it would hold his weight without buckling.

Mrs McDonald returned with a tray, which she placed carefully on the coffee table. The tea service certainly wasn't Spode, more likely a set churned out by one of the myriad anonymous potteries in Stoke-on-Trent. She offered Russell a cup. The tea was pale and milky. He took a sip but made no comment. She perched on the sofa opposite them. Russell noticed the hand that was gripping the handle was shaking, making her cup rattle in the saucer. Russell decided the direct approach might be best.

'I understand your husband has gone missing, Mrs McDonald.'

The cup shook so violently that tea slopped into the saucer. 'Ye-es,' she stammered.

'How long since you've seen him?'

She answered quickly, her eyes flashing and her head bobbing. 'Five days.'

The two officers shared a glance. The same length of time as Peters' wife. Nettie made a note. 'And you've not heard from him?'

She put the cup and saucer down and held her face in her hands. 'Not, not a thing.'

'Has he gone off before?'

'Never,' she said, clasping her hands in front of her and shaking her head from side to side.

'I see.' Russell took another sip of tea – purely for appearance sake. 'Can I ask how long you've been married?'

She was taken aback. 'What? Oh, I see. Nearly fifteen years.'

'Any children?'

She looked crestfallen. 'No, we couldn't have any.'

'I'm sorry, I didn't mean to upset you.'

'That's all right. I've accepted it now.'

Russell gave an encouraging smile, hoping it would help to calm her. 'Do you work, Mrs McDonald?'

'*Me*?' She gave a little snort. 'No, I'm just a housewife.'

'No hobbies?'

'I do some sewing and a little embroidery.'

'Gardening? The garden looks well cared for.'

'What? No – Douglas looks after that. He's always out there. I'm not allowed to touch his precious plants.'

Russell felt sorry for her. Since the war had ended more women went out to work, which he thought was a good thing. But some husbands still clung to the old-fashioned idea that a woman's place was in the home. It seemed that this was McDonald's attitude. The spotless room – and probably the rest of the house – showed that she must spend a lot of time cleaning. It seemed strange that the man should disappear when he was so obviously well looked after. Russell decided to probe a little deeper.

'Are things all right between you?'

'What do you mean?' Her reply was swift and sharp. She sat upright. Russell had touched a nerve.

'Has there been a row? Have you had words?'

Almost immediately she started crying. Big fat tears rolled down her cheeks. Quickly Nettie leaned forward and handed her a white handkerchief. Mrs McDonald gave a nod and dabbed at her eyes. 'I'm sorry,' she said, between sobs. 'I think that's why he went away.'

'Could you explain?' Russell asked gently.

'I burned his chops.' This produced a further burst of sobbing. Her small chest heaved and her shoulders shook. Russell waited until the outburst died down.

'Is that all?'

She looked up, her eyes red-rimmed and sparkling with tears. 'Isn't that enough?' she asked miserably.

'It does seem a bit drastic – going off because of some burned chops.'

'You don't understand.' There was a plaintive crack in her voice. 'He's very particular about his food. He has a delicate stomach and if it's not just right he suffers. He's in pain for days.'

It sounded to Russell like the *man* was a pain, but he let it pass. 'I see. How has he been lately?'

'What do you mean?'

'Well, has he changed in any way – followed a different routine, perhaps?'

She shook her head. 'No, he still went off to work every morning – came home for his tea; spent the weekend in the garden or the shed.'

Russell paused for thought. The woman took a sip from her cup and looked at him over the rim. 'Did he take anything with him? A case? Clothes?' he asked.

'Yes he did. I know exactly what he took: A jacket, two pairs of trousers, two shirts, underwear and an overcoat. Plus his shaving things and a small leatherette suitcase.'

That seemed very specific but Russell suspected that the woman knew every article of clothing her husband owned. 'Anything else you can think of?'

'A tent.'

Russell was taken aback. 'A tent?'

'Yes. He bought it on a whim – said we could go camping somewhere nice.' She gave another snort. 'We never did though. It stayed packed up in the garage, along with a whole lot of camping equipment, which he took too.'

This was curious. If Douglas McDonald *had* gone off with Rose Peters, he couldn't imagine her roughing it in a tent. A woman living in what was tantamount to a stately home, with a cavernous walk-in wardrobe *and* a large selection of luggage, would expect a five-star hotel, not a campsite. Russell dismissed the thought for now and decided to press on with interviewing Mrs McDonald. Despite the woman's apparent delicate nature, he felt he had to broach the subject of the horticulturist's wife's disappearance at the same time.

'Did you know that David Peters' wife is missing?'

Mrs McDonald started, as if touched by an electric current. 'That *hussy!*'

'Yes, Rose.'

'I can't see that's got anything to do Douglas's disappearance.'

'It's rather a coincidence, don't you think?'

'What do you mean?' she replied sharply.

This was proving trickier than he'd expected. But he ploughed on. 'I wondered if your husband is having an affair with Rose Peters.'

The woman shot to her feet. Her knee caught the edge of the table causing it to lift a few inches off the ground. The jug tipped over and a pool of milk flooded the tray. She hardly noticed. '*How dare you!*' she spat.

Russell remained calm. 'So you don't think it's likely?'

'NO!' she said emphatically, then looked down. Nettie had already risen and righted the jug and was mopping up the milk with a napkin. Heather looked at Russell, her eyes narrowed and her breath coming in quick bursts. 'How can you suggest such thing?'

'It was just a thought.'

'And rather a cruel one.' She snatched the napkin from Nettie and threw it down. She stared the policeman in the eye. 'I think it's time you left. I don't want you here – with your nasty accusations. Please leave.'

Russell quickly revised his opinion of a henpecked housewife. He wondered if she was more of a harridan. 'Very well, madam. He gave her a card. 'Please get in touch if you do hear from your husband.' They were just walking out through the front door when Russell turned and said: 'You don't happen to know what car your husband drives, do you?'

Mrs McDonald let out a snort. 'That blessed thing! Cares more for it that he does for me. It's a Morris Oxford – his pride and joy.'

Just as she was closing the door Russell asked: 'I don't suppose you know the registration?'

'Of course I do. AKE 746.' With that she shut the door, forcefully.

As they drove back to Collinghurst, and the police station, Russell said: 'Tell me what you think, Nettie. Both Rose Peters and Douglas McDonald have been missing for several days. That is certain. Talking to David Peters, it seems that his wife's actions are in character – she sounds like a woman of impulsive gestures so could easily have gone off on a whim for a while. She'll probably turn up, completely oblivious of any fuss she might have caused. However, McDonald's disappearance is different. My first thoughts were of a domineering husband and a submissive wife, but the way she reacted towards the end has made me think differently.'

'What if she had driven him into the arms of another woman?' Nettie asked.

'It's possible. But what sort of woman? Heather is attractive, in a mousey sort of way, but from what I remembered of the brief meeting I had with her husband, he's no Adonis.'

'I met him when we went to investigate a break-in at the golf club. A weedy little man. And as for Rose Peters being attracted to him…' She shook her head. 'It just doesn't add up. From what we've learned about them I really can't see McDonald and Rose going off together.'

'No, nor can I. Then there's the tent and camping equipment,' Russell said. 'Maybe McDonald wouldn't mind roughing it but I'm pretty certain Rose wouldn't be seen dead within a mile of a campsite, judging by her lifestyle.' They drove on in silence for a while. Then Russell spoke again. 'No, the fact that they have both gone off can only be a coincidence.' He sighed. 'I suppose I'd better report to what little we've found out to the Super when we get back. Then I can get on with some proper police work.'

~O~

'Look, Sonny,' Stout said, ''I understand your reservations but I really would like you to pursue this case further.'

Russell frowned. This *wasn't* a case in his book. Just two people, who, for whatever reasons, had gone away for a few days. He would have liked to give voice to his thoughts but decided to tread carefully. He'd upset his boss in the past and wasn't ready to repeat the exercise.

'But they are adults, sir,' he suggested.

Stout dismissed this with a wave of his hand. 'I know, but they are missing persons and *I* think we need to take this seriously.'

'What would you like me to do then?' Russell's tone was resigned.

'Go and talk to the people McDonald worked with and pay a visit to the golf club. Find out if anyone has seen him. Oh, and get someone to go back to his house and get a photo of the man. We'll circulate it with a description.'

'Right, sir.' Russell turned to leave.

'And remember, please treat this seriously.'

After Russell had closed the door he shook his head. Stout had used the word seriously twice. He was obviously desperate to get that nomination for membership of the golf club. Russell walked back into the main office and stopped at the WPC's desk. 'Do you fancy driving me again this afternoon, Nettie?'

She glanced her wristwatch. 'Er, I was just going off for lunch, sir.'

'I'm popping home first. I'm sure I can rustle something up.'

Nettie smiled as she rose from her seat. 'In that case…'

# Chapter 3

***The curved sword or Scimitar** was widespread throughout the Middle East, from at least the Ottoman period until the age of smokeless powder firearms relegated swords to dress and ceremonial functions.*

**ISOBEL BAILEY** had done enough for the morning and decided to treat herself to lunch at *Miss Smollett's Teashop* next door. She'd locked away the diamond bracelet she'd been repairing in the safe and tidied her tools. She was just crossing the shop when the door burst open with such force the bell was nearly catapulted across the room.

'Izzie! You've got to help me!' Duncan Fountain's customary pale complexion had turned a ghostly white. His eyes were large behind his over-sized spectacles, the dilated pupils magnified.

'Duncan, calm down.' Isobel walked past him, shut the door and turned the sign to *CLOSED*. 'Sit down and tell me what the problem is – slowly.' She went to the sink in the corner and came back with a glass of water.

They had been friends for some time, drawn together by antiques – she as a jewellery restorer and he as high-class dealer. She'd always considered him a confidant but it looked like the tables were about to be turned.

Fountain took a gulp of water and swallowed noisily, his prominent Adams apple bobbing. 'I don't know what to do,' he whined. This was the most miserable she'd ever know him.

'What's happened?'

'It's terrible…'

'What is? If you don't hurry up and tell me I won't be able to help.'

'There's a body.'

'What?'

'I said, there's a body.'

'I heard that. Where?'

'In my car.' He put his head in his hands.

'*What*! How did it get there?'

'I don't know,' he said miserably. 'I parked in my usual spot…'

'In the derelict warehouse, near your shop?'

'Yes.' He'd let go of his head and was wringing his hands, turning one over the other at fast speed.

Isobel reached forward and placed her own hands on his, stilling them. 'Where is the car now?'

'It's outside.'

'Well let's go and have a look.' She gripped his hand and pulled him to his feet. 'Come on.'

The blue Morris Minor Traveller was parked at the kerb. Fountain shook so much as he tried to fit the key into the lock that Isobel had to take the key from him. She opened the back doors to reveal an ancient looking carpet.

'Look.' He pulled the corner of the carpet back. The pale face of a man was exposed, his eyes closed and his skin as ashen as the dealer's.

Isobel's hand flew to her mouth. 'Oh my God!'

'What should I do?'

'You need to tell the police.'

'Yes, but after that business with those stolen antiques I was asked to fence...'

'That's completely different. This is much more serious. I can't see how they'd think you could be involved with this.' She quickly flipped the carpet back, covering the dead man's face.

'But what if they don't believe me?'

'Look.' She gripped his arms and turned him to face her. 'Drive over to the police station – it's only round the corner – and ask to speak to Sonny Russell. He'll keep an open mind. If not, I'll have words with him!'

'You're right. Best get it over and done with.'

'Do you want me to come with you?'

Fountain took a deep breath. 'No, it's okay, I need to face up to it on my own.'

'If you're sure...'

Fountain just nodded, calmer now. He shut the back door and locked it.

~O~

'So you claim that the body was there when you opened the car?' DI Bonnie Parker had a habitual Capstan Full Strength dangling from the corner of his mouth as he spoke – ash peppering the grubby lapel of his jacket. 'It's a bit strange though,' he said, frowning.

'What is?' Fountain asked.

'That the body was found in your car and covered with your carpet.' Parker sat back and folded his arms.

'No listen. I came here in good faith. I wanted to talk to DI Russell.'

'But he's not here. You've got me.' Parker affected a Cheshire cat smile and sat silently for a minute or two.

Fountain had come into the station asking for Russell, only to be informed that he was out of the office. He didn't want to talk to anyone else and was about to leave. Wickstead, the desk sergeant, sensing the matter might be serious, persuaded him to wait and talk to another DI. So, without wanting to, he found himself in a dingy interview room, sitting across the other side of a battered table from Parker, regretting his reluctant decision to stay.

Parker leaned forward. 'Look, let's assume for the time being that I believe you.'

'But it's the truth,' Fountain said miserably.

Parker held up both hands. 'Whatever you say, sunshine.'

'What happens to me now?'

'Well, if you are telling the truth, you'll be free to go.' Fountain started to rise from his seat. Parker put his hand on the dealer's chest and pushed him down. 'Not so fast. The flash and dab boys are having a decko at the body – and your car. I'm sorry but you're going to have to wait and see what they've got to say.' His sickly grin suggested he was a long way from actually feeling sorry.

Lewis, the forensics man, and John Crooks, the pathologist, were indeed busy with the car. The body had been lifted out of the back of Fountain's Morris Traveller and laid carefully on a stretcher. 'Is there any doubt about the cause of death, John?' Lewis asked.

'I shouldn't think so, judging by the amount of blood. Poor blighter was stabbed. A broad blade up under ribs and straight into the heart. Death would have been nigh on instantaneous.'

'You say a broad blade?'

'Yes, wider than a Bowie knife, for instance. Something like a sword.'

'Time of death?'

'How long ago did he shuffle off this mortal coil, do you mean?' Crooks puffed out his chest and clasped his hands across his ample stomach.

'I wouldn't have put it quite like that.' The pathologist's direct sense of humour didn't faze Lewis.

Crooks rolled his eyes upwards. 'I'd say he's been dead for between 12 and 24 hours.'

Lewis blinked. 'Crikey, John, that's a bit vague, even for you.'

'Cheeky!' the pathologist said, wagging his finger. 'I'll give you a more accurate estimate once I've got him in the lab.'

'Fair enough.' Lewis grinned and turned back to the car. He had looked carefully around the floor of the Traveller after the body and the carpet had been removed but there was nothing else that was obvious. 'Now,' he said. 'If I'm not mistaken, the spare wheel is stowed here.' He crouched down and opened a wooden flap beneath the floor, reached into the void and pulled the wheel out. Next came the jack and wheel brace. Kneeling on the ground he thrust his arm in up to the shoulder. 'Hello, what's this?'

Crooks heard a note of excitement in Lewis's voice and turned to see him drawing out something wrapped in a greasy rag. Carefully unfolding the fabric the forensics man revealed a large knife with a wicked looking curved blade. 'Well I'll be…' he said.

~O~

Russell's home was in a pair of old Victorian railway carriages, close to the beach. Although compact, the set up contained everything a batchelor could need. However, since he'd been seeing Isobel Bailey he'd started wondering whether it was time to move to something more conventional, sad though it would be to do so. However, the goldsmith he had fallen for seemed charmed by his unusual dwelling. She had her own beautiful period cottage in Nottery Quay and, for the past few months, they had spent some weekends in her beamed cottage and others in his home. He supposed that until the relationship was made permanent this happy situation could continue.

With Nettie driving, the Wolseley bumped down the stony track and came to rest outside Russell's railway carriage. There had been no rain for several days and dust swirled round the car. 'It's warm enough to sit outside,' the DI said, as he pushed the gate open and walked up the stepping-stone path. 'Make yourself at home. I'll see what I can find.'

Nettie took off her tunic jacket, and sat on the wooden bench outside the carriage. She knew her boss loved his little garden. He'd told her that he was not a natural gardener but he'd become fascinated by it. Although the ground was mainly shingle, he had worked hard, adding compost and soil and researching which plants would not only survive but thrive in coastal conditions. At this time of year it was full of colour. The rich pink of Rock Rose, *Cistus purpureus*, jostled with the yellow buttons of *Santolina chamaecyparissus*, cotton lavender. Majestic spires of Cardoons, *Cynara cardunculus* thrust their electric blue, thistle-like flowers skywards. On his walks along the beach he'd collected large pale-coloured stones of uniform size and she could see he'd carefully placed them in circles round his flower beds. Her reverie was disturbed by a little bundle of brindle fur tearing out into the garden. 'Aggie!' she cried, and crouched down so she could ruffle the terrier's wiry coat. The dog was closely followed by Russell, carrying a tray which he placed on the little wooden table.

'I'm afraid it's only bread and cheese.' He gave a rueful grin.

'That's fine. I was only going to have a sandwich anyway.'

In actual fact he was being modest. In addition to a crusty loaf and a slab of mature cheddar there was tomato, sliced cucumber and a jar of homemade pickle. Also on the tray was a jug of fresh lemonade and two glasses. 'Sit down. Let's eat and we can forget about the "case" for a while.'

They ate in companionable silence. Nettie surreptitiously slipped Aggie a piece of cheese under the table which the terrier took gently in her mouth – a shared conspiracy. When they had finished eating Nettie spoke.

'Where are we going first, sir?'

'I think our initial port of call should be the golf club. Get that out of the way.' He took a drink from his glass. 'You said you'd been there.'

'Just once – after the break-in. What a strange place.'

Russell chuckled. 'I agree. I'm with the man who said that golf is "a good walk spoiled". Never seen the point of it. Aggie and I would much rather go for a stroll without the burden of a bag of sticks.' He leaned back and stretched his arms. 'I suppose we'd better get going although I'd rather spend the afternoon here.' He got up and started putting the things back on the tray.

'Can I give you a hand, sir?'

'No, you stay put, I can manage.'

# Chapter 4

*A* ***golf links*** *is the oldest style of golf course, first developed in Scotland. The word links comes via the Scots language and refers to an area of coastal sand dunes and sometimes to open parkland.*

**THEY ARRIVED** at the golf club and Nettie parked the Wolseley between a silver Alvis TA21 and a two-tone Bentley Continental. The dusty police car looked decidedly shabby next to these two gleaming limousines. Nettie whistled but Russell remained unimpressed. He didn't own a car and had no interest in them apart from being a means of getting about. His DC, Johnny Weeks, lived near to his home and usually drove him, or he borrowed a car from the pool at the police station. At his suggestion, the DC was sitting for his sergeant's exam in a few weeks so was currently involved in studying for the tests. Russell missed him.

They had been involved in a number of interesting, but difficult, cases in the past and worked well as a team. He had no doubt that his companion would easily pass the exam and was pleased for him, but knew he would be likely to move on and wondered who his replacement would be. Meanwhile, he was happy to have Nettie's help. As a female constable, she was not permitted to join the detectives but she could still assist and did so more than ably. They walked up to the club house.

As they entered a man wearing an Argyle sweater and a pair of plus fours and holding a bag of golf clubs looked them up and down. He said, rather imperiously: 'Can I help you?'

'We'd like to see the club chairman,' Russell answered, his manner matching the man's.

'You want Robert Mould.' He swung the golf bag over his shoulder and started walking towards the door. Just before disappearing from sight he turned and said: 'You'll find him in the bar, I daresay.'

'It's this way, I think, sir.' Nettie said, and led the way into an airy room overlooking the course. A handful of members sat around in easy chairs while a couple propped up the bar. Most affected indifference to the strangers while one or two looked up briefly then carried on with their conversations. Russell approached the pair at the bar.

'I'm looking for Robert Mould.'

A large man with a shock of white hair and a ruddy complexion spoke. 'I'm Robert Mould.' Russell held out his warrant card. The man gave it a cursory glance 'What can I do for you?' His voice was deep and cultured.

'We'd like to talk to you about Douglas McDonald.'

'Oh – him.' Mould sniffed and put his tankard to his lips.

'I understand he's a member here.'

'Well he was.'

Was?'

'Yes. Up until a few weeks ago.'

'Oh, what happened?'

'His cheque for his green fees bounced.'

'Is that all?'

Mould took another drink. 'Not really.'

'What else then?'

'We could put up with that. He assured me that he'd settle his account at the end of the month. It was his attitude, mainly.'

'Would you care to explain?' Russell asked.

The club chairman drained his tankard, pushed it across the counter and nodded to the steward who was standing behind the bar, polishing a glass. 'Certainly. Would you like a drink first?' His upper-class drawl oozed charm but there was no warmth in it.

Russell made a show of pulling his cuff back and looking at his wristwatch. 'It's a bit early for me, sir.'

In reply Mould just shrugged and took a draught from his refilled glass. He smacked his lips and said: 'I suppose you could say he became a liability.'

'What do you mean?'

Mould sighed. 'The man had begun getting tetchy with the other golfers. Didn't like it if a four held him up on the links. Started marching up to people and demanding that either they got on with it or got out of his way. We put up with it for a while. Then the complaints started multiplying and I had to speak to him.'

'How did he react?'

'He didn't take it well. Went off in a huff.'

Nettie was making notes on her pad. 'How long had he been like it, sir?' she asked.

'What? Oh. A few weeks.'

'How had he been before?'

'Mostly he was fine. A bit bolshie at times, but I put that down to little man syndrome.' He laughed. 'D'you know what I mean?'

Russell ignored the remark. 'Why do you think he changed?'

Mould shook his head. 'I don't really know. Trouble at home perhaps? I understand his wife is a bit of a harridan.'

The two officers exchanged a glance. 'When was he last here – at the club?' Russell asked.

Mould was lost in thought for a moment, then spoke. 'Probably three weeks ago – give or take.'

'And you haven't seen anything of him since?'

'Not a thing.'

'His wife said he'd taken a tent when he left. Is there anywhere he could have set up camp?'

The chairman guffawed, his shoulders heaving with laughter.

'What's so funny, sir?' Nettie asked.

'You know the expression, "to have two left feet"?'

'Yes.'

'McDonald had two left hands as well.' He laughed again. Doubt if he'd know which way up to pitch a tent.'

'That seems a bit harsh, sir.'

'Maybe. Let's be generous and say that the man is not the most practical.' It was Mould's turn to look at his watch. 'Well if that's all, I have a match in five minutes – rather an important one.' He looked questioningly at Russell.

The DI nodded. 'That's all for now, sir. But if you do hear from him, perhaps you'd be kind enough to get in touch.' He held out a card.

'Crikey. I think oleaginous describes that man rather well, sir,' Nettie said as they walked back to the carpark.

'Yes, he certainly has an oily manner.'

'And it didn't sound like there was any love lost between him and McDonald.'

'Quite.' They had reached the car and the WPC was opening the driver's door.

'Do you fancy a walk in the dunes?' Russell asked. 'Aggie could do with a run.'

Nettie smiled. 'Why not?' She enjoyed going out with the DI.

Crossing a fairway, empty of players, they made their way towards the beach. After walking for perhaps half a mile, Aggie dashing in an out of the Marram grass, chasing lots of new scents, Russell stopped, hands on hips and looked towards the sea. The tide was a long way out and there was a huge stretch of flat sand. To the left they could see groups of holiday makers with umbrellas and windbreaks. But here, there was just a solitary figure with a large black Labrador, walking by the water's edge.

'Right, time to head back,' he said and turned. He whistled for his dog. She had gone on a further twenty yards or so and was barking. 'Come on Aggie. We've got to go now.'

'You don't hear her bark very often, sir,' Nettie observed.

'No, she's generally quiet. Must have seen a rabbit or something.' He whistled again. After a few moments, the terrier appeared, running hell for leather and panting. Russell bent down and patted her head. 'There's a good girl. Let's get going.'

If he'd taken the time to go and see what she had been barking at he might have been surprised. An area of sand between the clumps of Marram grass had been flattened. Next to it were the remains of a campfire, charred sticks round the outside and a faint wisp of smoke rising from the ashes.

# Chapter 5

***The $64,000 Question** was an American game show broadcast from 1955 to 1958. Contestants answered general knowledge questions, earning money which doubled as the questions became more difficult. The final question had a top prize of $64,000.*

**'WHERE TO** next, sir?' Nettie asked.

'I suppose we'd better go to where he works.'

'Where's that?'

Russell took out his pocket book and flipped through to the relevant page. 'It's a timber merchant in Nottery Quay apparently. Called Staggs.'

Nettie started the car. 'Oh. What does he do there?'

'His title is *accountant* but I suspect he's just a glorified bookkeeper.'

Thomas Staggs was situated adjacent to the quay. As they drew up in the car they could see a small coaster unloading baulks of timber. Two crew members were deftly using a derrick roped to the stubby mast, swinging lengths of wood out across the gunwale and lowering them on to a four-wheeled trolley. On the quayside two more men were busy guiding the timber into place. When enough pieces had been loaded one of them shouted and held up his hand. The ship's crew stopped and jumped ashore. With two pulling and two pushing they manoeuvred the trolley slowly through the open doors of a warehouse.

'That looks like hard work, sir,' Nettie said as they got out of the car.

'I bet McDonald never got his hands dirty though,' Russell replied with a grin.

They walked into the warehouse. The air was filled with fine sawdust, swirling like dust motes. The deafening screech of machinery cutting wood made conversation nigh on impossible. Russell walked up to one of the workers with the trolley, cupped his hands and hollered: 'We're looking for the manager.'

The man pointed towards a doorway and mouthed: 'Through there.' With the DI leading, they went through the door. Nettie closed it behind them and the noise diminished slightly.

'Up here do you think?' She pointed to a wooden staircase. Russell nodded and began climbing the stairs. At the top there was a landing with three doors leading off it.

One said *staff room,* the second, *accounts* and third had a sign on it saying, *R Staggs – Manager.* 'I think this must be it then.' Russell knocked and pushed it open.

The office was not large. Along one wall were shelves with ledgers and files stacked up, while set in another was a large, dusty window, looking down on the workshop below. A man stood up from behind a desk, placed at right angles to the window. 'Yes, can I help you?'

The detective held out his warrant card. 'I'm DI Russell and this is WPC Sharpe. We're here to talk about Douglas McDonald.'

'Oh, him.' The man sat again. He was fairly young, perhaps in his mid-thirties, but prematurely balding. He'd obviously tried to cover it by combing long strands across the top, but had only succeeded in emphasising the lack of hair. 'You'd better sit down.' He gestured to the two wooden chairs across from the desk. They sat.

'Can you tell me when you last saw him, Mr Staggs?'

The man turned to look at a calendar on the wall behind his desk. He lifted a page. 'It was the twenty-fifth of last month.'

Nettie did a quick calculation. 'But that's nearly three weeks ago.'

'That's right.'

'Hasn't he been into work since?' Russell asked.

Staggs snorted. 'I should think not. He was sacked.'

'Oh!' Russell was taken aback. 'Can I ask why, sir?'

'He was fiddling the books. Had been for some time.'

'Why didn't you inform the police?'

The man blew out his cheeks. 'Didn't want a fuss. It was only petty cash.'

'But it's still thieving.'

Staggs gave a non-committal shrug.

'Have you any idea where he might have gone?'

'Home, I suppose.'

Nettie looked at Russell and frowned. 'Could he have looked for another job?' she asked Staggs.

'Might have, but he didn't ask for a reference – not that I'd give him one anyway.'

'I see. Might one of your workers know where he's gone?'

'Doubt it. He wasn't popular.'

'Who does the accounts now?' Nettie asked.

'I bloody do,' Staggs said, obviously disgruntled.

'Why haven't you employed another bookkeeper?'

'No bugger wants the job.'

'Really?'

'Look. You've seen the dust and heard the noise. Would you want to work here?'

'I see your point, sir.' Russell paused, then said: 'Seeing the initial on the door, I assume you're not *Thomas* Staggs?'

'I can see why you're a detective.' He gave a wry smile. 'No, that was my old man. Left this to me.' He opened his arms in an all-encompassing gesture.

'I take it you don't enjoy it much.'

'Enjoy it? I preferred being in the Army. Didn't have to make decisions.'

'So you don't like running your own business?'

'No I don't. If I didn't feel some sort of loyalty to the old boy's memory I'd have packed it in long ago.'

Russell rose from his chair. He handed Staggs a card. 'Perhaps you'd let me know if he does get in touch.'

'I doubt if he will.'

'Oh, and I think you should report the theft of the money. You may be able to get it back – *when* we find him.

~o~

'Well that puts a different complexion on it,' Russell said, when they were back in the police car. 'Heather McDonald obviously doesn't know her husband as well as she thinks she does.'

'Very true, sir. I wonder where he's been going, when he was supposed to be at work?' Nettie asked.

'Certainly not to the golf club.'

'No, the chairman, Robert Mould, made that obvious.'

'It sounds like his world has been falling down around him. Not surprising that he's gone off.'

'But where, sir?'

'Ah, that's the $64,000 question.'

'So where do we go from here?'

Russell turned towards the WPC. 'To be honest, Nettie, I really don't know – I'm at a loss.' He sighed. 'I suppose I'd better go and report back to the Super – see what he wants me to do.'

~O~

Nettie started the car and they headed off to Collinghurst. Russell was slumped in the passenger seat looking idly out of the window. They had travelled no more than half a mile when he cried out; 'Stop!' The WPC stamped hard on the brake, the car skidded to a halt and Russell had to brace himself against the dashboard, just stopping his head from connecting with the windscreen. Luckily Aggie was in the footwell so didn't have far to go.

'Sorry, sir,' she said, bashfully.

He gave her a rueful smile. 'That's all right. Just back up. I think I saw something.'

She put the gear lever in reverse and, looking over her shoulder, backed the car up the road.

'There!' he said, pointing. Tucked in a narrow lane off the road was a car.

'It's a Morris Oxford, sir.'

'I don't know much about cars but that's what I thought too. What did Mrs McDonald say the registration was?'

Nettie reached into her bag and retrieved her notebook. 'AKE746.'

'That's it. That's McDonald's car. Come on, let's take a look.' When they reached the vehicle Russell tried the driver's door handle. 'Locked.'

'Same here, sir,' Nettie said from the other side. They peered through the windows. 'Looks like a tent and camping equipment on the back seat,' she said.

'You're right.' Russell looked around. 'No sign of McDonald though. Better radio in and get someone out here who can open it up.'

He got back in the car and called up the station. Wickstead, the duty sergeant, answered. 'Hello, Sonny. What can I do for you?'

'We've found the car we think belongs to Douglas McDonald. The Super has asked me to look into him. Trouble is the car's locked. Can you send someone out with a bunch of keys – see if they can get inside?'

'Certainly. Beaumont and Lees are kicking their heels in the station. I'll get them to have a look. Tell me where it is.' Russell explained the location and was just about to ring off when Wickstead said: 'Oh, by the way. A chap called David Peters rang in with a message for you.'

Russell smiled. 'That's someone else Stout is interested in. What did he say?'

There was a pause while the sergeant checked his notes. 'Apparently Mrs Peters stayed with a friend for a couple of nights. Does that mean anything to you?'

'It does. Who's the friend?'

'Er, her name is Felicity Valour.'

'Do you have an address?'

'Yes, it's Honeycomb House, St Mary in the Marsh.'

'Thanks, Sarge. We'll go over there now. No point in waiting for the others to arrive.'

'Before you go, Sonny, someone came in the station looking for you.'

'Oh yes?'

'Remember that antique dealer, Duncan Fountain?'

'I certainly do. He was mixed up in that case involving the

Nazi plunder, the one where Isobel got shot.'

'That's right. He was lucky to get off with a fine.'

'What about him?'

'Apparently he's *found* a body in the back of his car.'

'*Really?*'

'So he says.'

'Do you need me back at the station?'

Wickstead chuckled. 'No, it's all right. Bonnie Parker has got it under control.'

'Oh God.'

'Don't worry, Lewis and John Crooks are involved too.'

'That's something I suppose.'

'I'm sure you'll hear all about it when you get back.'

'I dare say. I just hope Parker manages to sort it out without making his usual blunders. I'll see you later.' He finished the call and turned to the WPC. 'Do you know where Honeycomb House is, Nettie?'

'I know St Mary in the Marsh. Edith Nesbit is buried in the churchyard there.

'That's right. She wrote *The Railway Children.*' Russell grinned. 'I don't live in an old railway carriage for nothing.'

Nettie reversed the car into the lane, indicated then drove east. When they got to Lydd she turned left on to Dennes Lane. 'Looks like you know your way around the Marsh,' Russell said.

'I used to cycle round here when I was younger. I know most of the lanes.' In ten minutes they arrived at Old Romney, crossed the A259 and drove past the charming, early-Norman, St Clement's church. Continuing along Five Vents Lane until they reached a junction Nettie turned onto New Sewer. It wasn't long before Russell pointed and called out: 'There it is.'

Standing just back from the road was an elegant, Georgian-fronted, mellow brick farmhouse. They were just about to turn into the drive when a silver Mercedes coupé with the roof down pulled out and Nettie had to stamp on the brake again. A blonde woman wearing sunglasses gave a cheery wave as she powered off up the lane. 'Mrs Peters certainly has some nice friends,' Russell said.

'Who live in nice houses,' Nettie added, manoeuvring the car carefully into the drive.

Russell knocked on the door. They waited for a while and when nothing happened he knocked again. This time, after a brief pause, it was opened to reveal a slight, dark-haired woman. She was wearing a short white sleeveless dress and white plimsolls. She was flushed and slightly breathless. 'Sorry!' she said. 'I've been playing tennis with Lottie Verbs. That was her driving off. How can I help?' After Russell introduced them her eyes widened. 'Oh!' she exclaimed, apparently taken aback. 'Has something happened?'

We've come to talk about Rose Peters,' Russell explained.

'Oh, I see.' Her colour deepened. 'You'd better come through.'

She led them along a passageway. Russell slowed when he noticed a large display of photographs on the wall. Many of the pictures were obviously family groups but a number showed a large man wearing hunting pink – several of him sitting astride an equally large horse. The woman saw him looking. 'That's my husband – he's the MFH.' When Russell looked blankly at her she added: 'Master of the Foxhounds – he hunts.' Russell just nodded. He didn't agree with the so-called sport but kept his counsel and they continued through the house and out on to a terrace overlooking the garden. The bed in front of them was filled with colour. Russell could see it was a rainbow palette starting with a purple smoke bush at one end, swirling through red Fuchsia and Monarda, orange Helenium and pink Sedum blending into white Cleome and Hydrangea and finishing with a vivid blue Ceanothus.

'What a marvellous garden,' he said.

'Do you like it? Davey Peters designed it. He's a friend, you know.' Her colour had almost returned to normal but she blushed, reddening again. 'W-would you like a drink – some lemonade perhaps?' she stammered.

'That would be nice, thank you.' She bustled back indoors and Nettie and the DI sat in two easy chairs.

'Does she seem nervous to you, Nettie? She was rather pink.'

'She does rather – or perhaps it's the result of a vigorous game of tennis.'

'Possibly. Let's see what she has to say about Peters' wife.'

They sat quietly, looking out across the garden until Mrs Valour bustled back with a tray. 'Here you are,' she said brightly, putting it down on a side table. Glasses were handed round and she sat on another chair. 'Now, what did you want to ask about Rosey?'

Russell took time sipping from his drink before replying. 'Nice lemonade, thank you.' He put the glass down carefully. 'I understand Mrs Peters spent a couple of nights with you.'

'Oh – yes,' she answered quickly.

'Which nights would that be?'

'Which nights?'

'Yes.'

'Umm, let me think.' She rubbed her chin. 'The end of last week – possibly?'

'Can you be more specific?'

'Friday and Saturday, maybe.'

'So not Wednesday or Thursday?'

'I don't think so. Does it matter?'

'Mr Peters said he last saw her on Wednesday morning.'

Felicity looked flustered. 'Really? Then I suppose it could have been Wednesday and Thursday. The days just fly by don't they?'

Russell took a breath. 'Let's assume it was Friday and Saturday. That means she left you yesterday.'

'Oh, you're right, it must have been earlier. She wasn't here yesterday.'

'Right. Have any idea where she might have gone after she left you?'

'Back to Sowsden Manor?'

'No, I did say that David Peters hadn't seen her since last Wednesday.' Russell was trying to keep his patience but the woman was sorely trying it.

'So you did.'

'Could she have gone to another friend's?' Nettie asked.

Felicity furrowed her brow, thinking. 'I suppose so,' she said finally.

'Can you suggest a name?'

Her face lit up. 'Jo!' she said.

'Joanna Stone. She lives in Appledore.'

'Do you have an address?' Russell felt it might be easier to pull teeth than get a straight answer out of her.

'Orchard House. You can't miss it – right in the middle of the High Street.' Nettie made a note.

'Thank you.' Russell handed Felicity a card. 'Perhaps you'd be good enough to let me know if you hear from her.'

Just as they got back into the car the radio crackled into life.

'Sonny?' Sergeant Wickstead's voice came over loud and clear.

'Yes?'

'Bad news I'm afraid. When Beaumont and Lees turned up the Morris was gone. Sorry.'

'Not to worry. Can't be helped. Thanks for letting me know.' Russell broke the connection and said to the WPC: 'That's annoying. He couldn't have been far away. I wonder where McDonald's headed now?'

# Chapter 6

***Euphorbia characias**, the Mediterranean spurge, is an upright, compact evergreen shrub growing up to four feet tall and wide. It is valued as an ornamental plant for its ability to survive long periods of drought.*

**DI BONNIE** Parker was slumped in a chair, feet up on the office desk, ankles crossed, his scuffed brogues in need of new soles and a good polish. He was snoring gently, the remains of an unlit fag stuck to the bottom lip of his open mouth. The atmosphere in the room was fetid with the smell of stale cigarette smoke and sweat. A rap on the door made him start.

'What? Who?'

The door opened to reveal the dapper form of Lewis, the forensics man. He grinned. 'Sorry to disturb you Inspector, but I thought you'd like to hear what I've found out.'

Parker coughed, slipped his feet off the desk and sat up. 'I was just resting my eyes.'

'Of course you were.' Before the DI could react he went on: 'I've come to talk to you about the body. You remember Fountain was mixed up in that Nazi bullion affair a while ago?' Parker nodded as he lit a fresh cigarette. 'We had his prints on file from that case. And guess what?'

'Go on, tell me.'

'His prints were on that scimitar we found in his car.'

'Scimitar?'

'The knife with the curved blade.'

'Oh, that. No one else's dabs?'

'Nope, just his, although they were faint and smudged.'

Parker sat up straight. 'Got him. We've got him bang to rights.' There was a gleeful gleam in his rheumy eyes.

'Possibly.'

'Possibly? I'd say *definitely.*'

'We-ell…' Lewis sounded hesitant.

Parker's eyes narrowed, and not from the plume of grey smoke rising from the cigarette in his mouth. 'What is it you're not telling me?'

Lewis pulled up a chair and sat opposite the DI. 'It might not be so cut and dried.'

'How do you mean?' Parker growled.

'I've been back through the records. It seems that Fountain reported a break-in at his shop, a few weeks ago.'

Parker took a long drag on his cigarette. 'What's that got to do with anything?' he asked, as he exhaled.

'He gave us a comprehensive list of what had been stolen.'

'Don't tell me. The sword was on the list?'

'I'm afraid so.'

'But there aren't any other prints?'

'No. Whoever killed the man was very careful not to leave any.'

Parker frowned, then his face brightened. 'But what if the sword hadn't actually been stolen and Fountain had reported it, to cover himself. *He* could have done it.'

'I should think that's most unlikely. He'd hardly leave a blood-stained knife with his prints all over it *and* leave it where it could be easily found, would he?'

'Maybe... Unless he was surprised, shoved it under the shelf in the back of the car and forgot about it.'

Lewis shook his head. 'Hardly likely.'

'But possible.'

'I suppose so,' Lewis was reluctant to agree.

'I think it's time for me to have another word with our dealer friend – put some pressure on him.'

~O~

Felicity Valour had been correct. Orchard House was easy to find – slap bang in the middle of the main street running through Appledore. A high wall separated it from the pavement. A solid looking wooden door was set in the brickwork with the house name painted clearly on a plaque. The door opened into a small front garden. A low hedge separated the path from a pond surrounded by stone chippings. Expensive-looking terracotta pots had been strategically placed, some overflowing with *Euphorbia characias*, others with lush-leaved Hostas and grasses, gently waving in the breeze. 'More of David Peters' work?' Russell wondered.

'Very likely, I should say.' Nettie knocked on the front door. It was opened almost immediately by a tall, startlingly beautiful woman. She had ash blond hair, swept up in an elegant chignon and was wearing a simple silk dress in shimmering peacock blue. She took in the WPC's uniform at a glance and said: 'Sorry, I was just going out. Can you be quick?'

'We'll try not to keep you – Mrs Stone.' Russell answered.

'If it's about the bump I had in my car last week...'

'No, it's about Rose Peters.'

The woman's carefully defined eyebrows shot up. 'Oh! Has something happened to her?'

'Not as far as we're aware, it's just that she hasn't been at home for several days and her husband is worried about her.'

'Is that all?' Joanna Stone laughed, a delightfully musical sound. 'She's always gallivanting off without telling Davey where she's going.'

'He said she'd been staying with Felicity Valiant, over in St Mary in the Marsh. We went to see her and Mrs Valiant said she'd stayed there for a couple of nights.'

'I'm surprised at that.'

'Why?'

Joanna lowered her voice. 'I might as well tell you – it's not much of a secret. Davey's been having a thing with Flick – Felicity – for some time now.'

'Do you mean *an affair*?' Nettie asked.

'If you want to call it that.'

'Did Mrs Peters know?'

Joanna laughed again. 'Either she didn't know or...didn't *want* to know.'

'Why do you think that is?'

'Because she and Flick were good friends.'

'I see. Mrs Valiant suggested that Rose Peters may have come to stay with you. Did she?'

'No. Haven't seen her for a couple of weeks. Now, if that's all, I really must be going – sorry!'

~O~

'What do you make of that, Nettie?' They were back in the Wolseley.

'I don't really know, sir. If David Peters *was* having an affair with Mrs Valiant is seems odd that his wife would spend a couple of nights with her.'

'My thoughts, too. But then again, if she didn't know, or chose not to, for sake of their friendship...'

'It's all a bit baffling.'

'You can say that again. And the way the women keep referring to Peters as "Davey" it makes you wonder how close they are.'

'He does seem an unlikely lothario, sir.'

Russell chuckled. 'There's no accounting for taste. Nettie. Ah well. Better get back to the station – report our findings to the Super and see if he's got any proper police work for us.'

# Chapter 7

*__Paisley pattern__ is an ornamental textile design of Persian origin, using a teardrop-shaped motif with a curved upper end. It became very popular in the West in the 18th and 19th centuries. The English name for the patterns derives from the town of Paisley, in the west of Scotland, a centre for textiles where the designs were produced.*

**NO ONE** saw it coming – no one could have predicted it. DI Bonnie Parker certainly had no idea that he would start an unstoppable chain of events when he sent his sidekick, Clyde Barrow, out of the interview room on a mission to fetch mugs of tea. It all began in the most mundane manner.

The two detectives had walked into the interview room where Duncan Fountain had been forced to wait for much longer than he had expected. While sitting there he had gone through a kaleidoscope of emotions. From initial disbelief to indignation; frustration to anger and now he waited, sulkily resigned. Parker and Barrow sat down opposite the dealer. The DI took time lighting up then pushed a clear plastic bag across the table. Inside was the scimitar that had been found in the Morris Traveller. Fountain's eyes widened behind his glasses.

'That's mine! Where did you find it?'

'Where you put it,' Parker answered simply.

'But it was stolen from my shop.'

'A likely tale.' The DI's voice was acid with scorn.

'It was. I reported it, along with the theft of several other items.'

Parker gave a snort. 'That was just a clever ruse. One that I've seen clean right through.'

'What do you mean?'

'You said you'd had a break-in to throw us off the scent.'

'You've got to be joking.'

'No, sunshine. I'm deadly serious. You've had it hidden away all this time – then you used it to kill.'

Fountain shook his head – a stunned look clouding his face. 'I can't believe what I'm hearing.'

'You'd better believe it. The evidence is stacked against you, I'm afraid.'

Fountain leaned forward and placed his arms on the table. 'I came here in good faith to report a dead body that had turned up in my car – not to be accused of murder.'

Parker too leaned forward, mirroring the other man. 'That was another cunning ruse – one that took us in – for a while – but not for long.'

Fountain sat back – speechless.

'That shut you up, didn't it?'

Fountain just took a deep breath, folded his arms and remained silent. For the next ten minutes or so Parker tried to draw him out – make him react, but the dealer refused to rise to the bait. He just sat there, resolutely unmoved. Finally, after exhausting his repertoire of leading questions, he said to Barrow: 'For Christ's sake go and get some tea. Perhaps that'll loosen his tongue.'

As soon as the DC had left the room Fountain spoke. 'Look,' he said. 'You can keep me here as long as you want to, and ask me as many inane questions as you like, but it's not going to make me confess to something I haven't done. Get that into your thick policeman's skull – okay?'

'Why you…' Parker half rose from his chair and leaned across the table. 'For two pins I'd…'

'You'd what? Beat a confession out of me?'

'Don't tempt me,' Parker hissed.

'You'd love to have the excuse, wouldn't you?' Fountain was relishing goading the policeman. 'I remember you from last time. Incompetence personified.'

'What are you saying?' The DI was beginning to sound dangerous.

'I heard you'd tried to falsify evidence on your last case.'

'You're treading a dodgy path, matey.'

'Obviously the only way you can get a conviction.'

'I'm warning you.' Parker was now standing fully upright, wagging his finger furiously.

'You can warn all you like, but you'll struggle to trump up a charge against me this time.'

Instead of the assault Fountain was anticipating, Parker stood stock still, his eyes bulged, his breath came in huge gulps and his fists clenched then unclenched. He appeared unable to reply and at first Fountain smiled as he thought he'd silenced the man. But when the DI began to shake and his colour turned from puce to ashen grey, he started to get alarmed. Then Parker clutched at his chest with both hands, sank to his knees and crumpled forward. Fountain watched with rising horror as the policeman's head crashed against the edge of the table, bounced off and he fell backwards onto the floor. At first Fountain was stunned. It took him a few seconds to react, then he leapt out of his chair. He rushed round the table and bent over the prone figure and fumbled to loosen Parker's tie and undo the top button of his shirt. That was where DC Barrow found him when he returned with the tea.

The mugs went flying as Barrow launched himself at the dealer. 'Leave him alone, you little toerag!' he yelled. Flinging his arm around the man's throat they rolled across the floor.

With his windpipe constricted Fountain struggled to speak but managed to croak: 'Get off me!'

'How dare you attack him!' Parker lay still next to them.

Fountain was fighting for breath. 'I didn't attack him.'

'I saw you. You had him pinned to the floor.'

'I didn't! I was trying to help him.'

'You were trying to kill him!' Despite Fountain's best efforts to throw him off, Barrow wasn't going to let go.

'What the hell!' Russell and Nettie stood in the doorway, trying to make sense of the situation. After only a couple of seconds they looked at each other then rushed forward. The DI went to the two men and tried to loosen Barrow's grip while Nettie knelt next to Parker, trying to find his pulse.

'He's still breathing,' she said. 'But I think he's in a bad way. We need an ambulance – fast.' She got to her feet and dashed off to find a phone.

Russell grappled with the DC and managed to prise his grip from round Fountain's throat. Barrow tried to fight back but Russell wrenched his arm up behind his back. 'Easy lad. Let's calm down and assess the situation.'

'But he was trying to kill him!' he yelled.

'I don't think so,' Russell replied calmly. 'Your boss is not a well man.'

'What do you mean?'

'Look at his colour. I reckon he's had a heart attack. If he doesn't get help soon…' Russell left the sentence unfinished. As much as he disliked Parker, he didn't wish him dead.

Nettie returned with Wickstead. They made Parker as comfortable as they could and Nettie dabbed at the blood on his forehead with a damp cloth.

Fountain was sitting with his back against the wall, nursing his throat. 'I didn't do anything to him,' he croaked. 'He collapsed and banged his head on the table. I was trying to help.'

'I know. Are you okay?'

'I think so.'

'As for you…' Russell said, and wrenched Barrow's arm up a little higher, which made him squeal.

'Get off! You're hurting me.'

'I'll let you go if you promise to remain calm.'

'All right – I promise.'

Russell slowly released his grip and pushed him away. The DC rubbed his shoulder and glared but didn't move. There was quiet in the room while they waited for the medics. It was only a few minutes later when two ambulance men came in. Quickly, and without a fuss, they got Parker on to a stretcher and out into their waiting vehicle. The mood they left behind was subdued.

'I think you'd better go back to your desk,' Russell said quietly to Barrow. 'You'll need to report to the Superintendent later.' The DC slunk out of the room, his shoulders hunched and his head held low.

'Shall I go and write up the notes on the missing couple, sir?' Nettie asked.

'Yes, please do that.' He turned to Wickstead. 'Can you send someone in to mop up this mess, please?' He pointed to the broken crockery and the puddle of murky liquid, cooling on the wooden floor. 'And bring some more tea. I'm going to have a chat with Mr Fountain.' When they'd gone he sat down and gestured for the dealer to do the same. 'Now, tell me what happened – how you came to be here and the chain of events that led to DI Parker going out on a stretcher.'

Without interrupting he let Fountain explain in his own words, just nodding occasionally. The antique dealer's voice was croaky, a result of having Barrow's arm clamped across his windpipe. At one point he'd taken off his spectacles and dabbed at his face with a large Paisley patterned handkerchief. When he put them back on Russell could see his eyes magnified and red-rimmed. After a few minutes Fountain's voice tailed off and he looked down at his hands, clasped on the table.

'You definitely know nothing about the body in the back of your car?'

'No. It was a complete shock. Isobel said I should report it – actually she said I should come straight to you.' He gave a sob. 'I wish you had been here.'

'Me too.' Russell's reply was heartfelt.

'Then I wouldn't have to go through all this – with that buffoon, Parker and his idiot sidekick, Barrow.' Russell said nothing. Fountain looked up and a slow smile crossed his face. 'Is it true they're known as Bonnie and Clyde?'

Russell smiled back. 'I couldn't possibly comment.' Just then the door opened and PC Beaumont entered carrying a mop and a bucket, followed by PC Lee bearing a mug of tea. 'Right, I'm off to see the Super. Look after this chap will you?'

Fountain looked alarmed. 'Am I under arrest?'

Russell turned as he reached the door. 'No, you're helping us with our enquiries. Drink your tea and I'll be back shortly.'

Russell knocked on the Superintendent's door.

'Come!' The single growled word sounded less of an invitation – more of a challenge. Russell entered the smoke-filled room. A haze of blue coils hung below the ceiling. The heap of cigar butts in the ashtray spoke volumes. Stout stared at him. 'Oh, it's you. About time someone told me what all the rumpus was about. I was trying to have a telephone conversation with the Chief Constable and could hardly hear myself think.'

'It's DI Parker. He's been taken to hospital.'

Stout banged his fist on the desk. 'I knew it. I bet that bloody murderer attacked him.'

'Sir?'

'The antique dealer.'

'Fountain.'

'That's the one.'

'You've got the wrong idea.'

'What?! Stout's piggy eyes glittered above his bloated cheeks. 'Explain yourself.'

Russell sat in the chair opposite his boss and took his time getting comfortable. Stout sat glaring at him but said nothing. Finally Russell said: 'He's not a murderer and he didn't attack Parker. In fact he tried to help him.'

'So who did attack him?' Stout looked baffled.

'No one, sir. He's had a heart attack.'

'My God! Is he going to be all right?'

'We don't know. He hit his head when he fell, which might complicate things.'

'That's all we need. Just as he was getting somewhere with this murder.' The Super looked down and shuffled some papers on his desk. After a moment he looked up again. 'I assume you'll want to take over?'

'The thought had crossed my mind.'

'I don't suppose you've made any progress with finding Peters' wife and McDonald?'

'We haven't found them, no. But I think we've made some progress.'

There was a light tap on the door. 'Who the hell is this? Come in,' Stout said, his voice scratchy with irritation.

The door opened and WPC Nettie Sharpe appeared, holding out a sheaf of papers. 'The report on the two missing persons, sir.' Stout snatched the papers and dismissed her with a wave of his hand.

'Right, Inspector. Leave me to look over this. You go and get a conviction.'

Russell stayed put. 'It's not as straightforward as that.'

'What do you mean? You've got the evidence. Fountain obviously did it.'

'I don't think so. I've got a feeling…'

Stout cut him short and held his head in his hands. 'Oh no. Not one of your feelings.' He sighed. 'Go on. Tell me.'

'I've spoken with Fountain,' Russell said quietly. 'I don't think he did it.'

'But the knife – it had his fingerprints all over it.'

'He admits that it's his, so it would have. But it was stolen a few weeks ago.'

'So he says.'

'I believe him.'

'You would.'

Russell ignored the slur. 'He came into the station in good faith. It was unfortunate that I wasn't here and Parker got hold of him.'

'What are you suggesting?'

'Well you know how he tends to jump in with both feet without thinking.'

'You might have a point,' Stout agreed, grudgingly. 'But who did kill him then?'

'We've still got to find that out – and who the victim is, for that matter. But I'm certain it's not Fountain.'

'I'll trust you on that one. You'd better let him go with a caution, if you're sure.'

'I am, sir.'

Stout reached for his cheroots and Zippo. 'You'd better get on with it then.' He tapped the papers Nettie had given him with the lighter. 'I want you back on this as soon as possible.'

# Chapter 8

***Teddy Boys** were a British subculture started among teenagers in London in the early 1950s. They were strongly associated with American rock and roll music and adopted Edwardian-era fashion which Savile Row tailors had attempted to re-introduce in Britain after the Second World War.*

**RUSSELL FOUND** John Crooks where he expected to – in his lair. The mortuary was part of a forbidding looking, austere, red-brick building housing the hospital, on the edge of Collinghurst. The façade had the scale and proportions of a stately home but not the gravitas. Something about its bulk rendered it utilitarian and everyday, not special. The approach to the mortuary was down a long corridor, painted two-tone: dull institutional green below the dado rail and bilious beige above. At the end was a plain door marked PATH LAB – ONLY AUTHORISED PERSONNEL TO ENTER. Within there was a small, plain anteroom containing just a row of filing cabinets and a pair of straight-backed chairs – a bleak space for those unfortunate enough to be waiting to identify a body. Russell knocked then pushed the door open at the far end of the room.

'Ah, my favourite detective,' Crooks voice boomed across the room. 'Come and look at this.'

Russell walked across to Crooks, standing four square and wearing a long rubber apron. Next to him, covered with a green rubber sheet, was a body lying on a stone slab. 'Is that the victim that was found in Fountain's car?' he asked.

'The very same. But look. There's something curious about him.'

Russell moved in closer and leaned towards the slab. 'What is it, John?'

The pathologist lifted the sheet to reveal the man's right hand. 'See these marks?' He pointed to the wrist. The flesh was reddened with deep abrasions.

'Looks like he's been tied up.'

'Yes, but not in the usual fashion – with rope or wire.'

'What then?'

'Chain!' Crooks said, a note of triumph in his voice. He was always delighted with a new find, however macabre. 'But no ordinary chain…'

'So what was it?'

'A bicycle chain!' He sounded even more jubilant. 'Look closely and you can see distinctive marks where the links are held together.'

Russell looked more closely. 'Yes, you're right.'

'I know I am.'

'Do you think that's significant?' Russell asked.

Crooks appeared to ponder. 'Not on its own. But see here.' He moved to the end of the slab and peeled back the sheet. The man's face was revealed, pale but serene in death. Russell was constantly amazed at how peaceful those who had suffered violent deaths looked. If he didn't already know the details he would have thought that the man had died naturally. The pathologist gently turned the head to one side. 'What do you make of that?' On the left-hand side of the face, just below the hairline, there was a large bruise. 'Have a look with this.' Crooks handed the DI a magnifying glass.

Russell peered at the enlarged image. 'Close up it looks like three or four individual marks,' he said.

'But very regular.'

'Very. Any idea what caused it?' Russell was pretty sure the pathologist would have a theory. But he went one better than that.

'One of these!' He had put his hand into a pocket beneath his rubber apron and produced a strange looking cast metal object. It consisted of four connected circles with a curved bar below them. Crooks fitted his chubby fingers in the holes and made a fist round the bar.

'A knuckleduster!'

'Correct. Beloved of Teddy Boys. But not this one. This is my own.'

Russell grinned. 'So that, along with the chain...'

'Also one of their weapons of choice.'

'...Makes you think this could be the work of a gang?'

Crooks gave a non-committal shrug. 'That's for you to find out, Sonny. You're the detective, after all.'

Russell was thoughtful for a few moments. Then he said: 'I can't say I've seen many Teddy Boys around here.'

The pathologist guffawed. 'Me neither. Most of them are in and around London.'

'So what's he doing down here – in the wilds of Sussex?'

'As I said, you're the detective.'

'But it wasn't the blow with the knuckleduster that killed him though, was it?'

'Certainly not. That was the blade shoved into his chest. But take a look at this.' He turned the head fully to one side. 'Here.'

He pointed to the back of the skull where there was a large gash.

'A blow from a blunt instrument as well then?'

Crooks folded his arms across his chest, resting them on his ample stomach. 'Possibly, but I'm not so sure. We found traces of gravel, dirt and a few splinters in the wound. My suspicion is that he fell, or was pushed, and bashed his bonce. Whatever happened, he didn't stand a chance of survival.'

'Thank you, John. I don't suppose you've found any form of identification on him? We still don't know who he is.'

'I'm afraid not. Although the clothes we found him in might provide you with a clue.'

'Go on, tell me what he was wearing.'

'A drape jacket, drainpipe trousers and brothel creepers.'

'As worn by Teddy Boys.'

'Precisely.'

'Which ties in with the marks you showed me.'

Crooks nodded sagely.

'Hmm. The plot thickens.'

'It certainly does. But I'm sure you'll get to the bottom of it – you usually do.'

~O~

Russell wasn't so sure. There was very little to go on. He sat in the police Wolseley without starting the engine. Aggie was curled up on the passenger seat, oblivious to his dilemma, her paws twitching as she chased rabbits in her dreams. Russell smiled – then frowned. He was pretty certain that Fountain had been telling the truth and really didn't know how the body had turned up in his car. After all, encouraged by Isobel, he'd brought it to the station in good faith. And why had the body turned up? It seemed bizarre that the murder weapon was a knife that had been stolen some time before. It was almost as if someone was trying to frame the dealer. But why? And the association with Teddy Boys that was suggested by the use of a bicycle chain and a knuckleduster – how did that fit in? If it was a London gang, what could be the connection with a country antique dealer? The more he thought about it the more puzzling it became. If it did involve thugs from the capital he would have to investigate further afield than usual. His corner of East Sussex didn't see much in the way of national crime – and he preferred it like that. He supposed that he would have to inform Superintendent Stout, which would undoubtedly complicate things, so he decided to leave keep his theories to himself for the time being.

He ruminated for a while, random thoughts and ideas rolling round his head. Then he sat up. Of course, Dickie Merriman! His old army pal was a DCI in the Met. He would be the one with the knowledge of London gangs. Inspired, he started the car and headed back to the station. He had a couple of phone calls to make.

~O~

'Sonny! How good to hear from you. Are you coming up to see me?' Merriman was pleased that Russell had contacted him. It had been too long since they'd had a good catch up.

'If that's all right, I'll come up this evening. I need to pick your brains about Teddy Boys.'

'I'm intrigued. Will you drive?'

'No, I think I'll come on the train. Then we can go out to dinner.'

'Fine. Let me know which one you're catching and I'll pick you up from the station.'

His second call, a rueful one, was to Isobel.

'Sonny. There's no need to apologise. When I started going out with a Detective Inspector I knew I wasn't taking up with a nine-to-five sort of chap,' she said, with a note of mirth in her voice.

'You're very magnanimous. I'll make it up to you when I get back.'

'You'd better.' Isobel giggled. 'And say hello to that handsome Dicky Merriman from me.'

Before he left he found the WPC at her desk. As usual it was neat and tidy. 'Nettie. Would you mind having Aggie tonight?'

A grin lit up her face. She was nearly as fond of the little terrier as Russell was. 'Of course. I'd be delighted.'

Russell grinned back. 'I hoped you might be. I'm going up to London to get some background from DCI Merriman.'

'I know who you mean. You were in the Army with him.'

'That's right. Well remembered.'

'He's the one you went to see when we were investigating that Nazi contraband case.' She looked thoughtful. 'Fountain was mixed up in that too, wasn't he?'

'He was.'

'So is it about him, sir?'

'No, not really. I think his involvement is incidental. I'm pretty sure this case is to do with Teddy Boy gangs.'

'That's interesting. Have you had any more thoughts about Peters' wife?'

'Not really. I think she's just gone off on a jaunt. She'll come back wondering what all the fuss is about.'

Nettie frowned. 'I'm not so sure. There's something niggling at the back of my mind...'

He looked at his wristwatch. 'Can we talk about it in the morning? I'd better get going or I'll miss my train.' He settled his trilby on his head. 'I'll see you tomorrow and let you know what I've found out.'

~o~

It was only a short walk to Collinghurst station. Russell was carrying the overnight bag he kept in his office and was looking forward to a peaceful hour on the train with the most recent Agatha Christie novel, *A Pocketful of Rye.* He found a window seat in an empty non-smoking compartment and put his bag up on the luggage rack. Just as he'd settled, there was a jerk and the train set off.

~o~

As the train pulled into Charing Cross station Russell realised that he'd slept through much of the journey. The book lay open in his lap, just a few pages into the story. Yawning, he gathered his belongings, made his way along the corridor and stepped out of the carriage. He strode along the platform, his mood buoyant and as he presented his ticket he could see the smiling face of Merriman standing on the other side of the barrier.

'Welcome to the big smoke, Sonny.' They shook hands and Merriman led him to his gleaming Jaguar Mark 1 saloon. 'I've booked a table at a little Indian place I know, but thought we could have a drink first. Then you can drop your things at the hotel. I assume it's the usual one?'

Russell smiled. 'Organised as always. I remember that from our time together in Asia.'

'And I remember you scuttling off to spend time with those Buddhist monks. I presume you're still a vegetarian?'

'I am. Not likely to change now. Anyway, there's no need to

go to the hotel first. They're expecting me and they stay open late.'

'Fair enough.'

'I'm looking forward to having a meal that I haven't had to cook.'

Merriman swung the steering wheel and turned the car into Catherine Street. 'That's why I chose the Indian. Bound to be something you can eat there.' He pulled up outside the Opera Tavern. 'But first, they do a good pint here. Often you can see a famous face or two.' He pulled back the cuff of his jacket and looked at his wristwatch. 'Might be a bit early for the theatrical types though.' Reaching across he opened the glove compartment set in the walnut dashboard. He took out a card and placed in clear view of the windscreen. 'That should stop the local bobbies getting suspicious.' Russell read the lettering: ON POLICE BUSINESS and smiled.

They settled in a booth with two pints of Young's bitter. Merriman took a long drink, smacked his lips then put the glass down on a beermat. 'So, my friend, what made you come away from your sleepy little corner of Sussex? I'm sure it wasn't just to spend time in my company.'

Russell gave a grin. 'Straight to the point, as usual. Of course I'm happy to spend time with you but I want to pick your brains about something. Something which seems unlikely in my "*sleepy little corner of Sussex*". But something I'm sure you'll know a bit more about.'

'Go on. I'm intrigued.'

'Teddy Boys.'

'Well I wasn't expecting *that*.' He raised his eyebrows. 'What do you want to know?'

Russell proceeded to tell his friend about the body in the car and John Crooks's conclusions about how it had received injuries antemortem. Merriman listened quietly, occasionally sipping from his pint. After Russell had finished talking he too took a drink. 'So, what do you think?'

His companion sat back, folded his arms across his chest and pondered. 'I'm as mystified as you are as to why the body ended up down there. It seems like your antique dealer may have upset someone. But from what you've told me he's not aware of who, or how – if he's telling the truth, that is.'

'I think he is. I've met him a couple of times with Isobel and he seems pretty straight. Oh, she sends her regards, by the way.'

The DCI nodded his thanks. 'Okay. Assuming it is the work of Teds, we need to find out if there's some sort of warfare going on between two rival gangs. Do you remember, a year or so ago, the film *Blackboard Jungle* was being shown at cinemas?'

'Yes, I do, but I didn't go to see it – not really to my taste.'

'Nor mine. But when they showed it at the cinema at the Elephant and Castle there was a riot. They ripped up seats and caused all sorts of damage.'

'I remember. Didn't it spread to other parts of the country, when the film was shown?'

'That's right. Incidentally, do you know where the Teddy Boys came from?'

'Not really. But I'm sure you're about to tell me.' Russell knew of old that his friend, like John Crooks, amassed nuggets of knowledge, the more obscure the better.

Merriman drained his drink and held it out. 'Let's have another and I'll fill you in.' When Russell returned from the bar with two brimming glasses he began.

'Believe it or not it all started with a shortage of fabric after the war.'

'Really?'

'Yes, tailors were struggling to make a living using the limited supply of cloth they could get hold of. Then someone had a bright idea. If they started a particular fashion maybe they could persuade officers returning from the war to buy their creations. The thing was that the bright idea was to make clothes based on Edwardian fashions – long drape jackets with contrasting collars, that sort of thing. As you probably know, it didn't catch on with the target audience so they ended up with a lot of clobber they had to sell off cheap. Now, for the first time, with war over and things looking a little rosier, there was a movement among disaffected youth, bored, and looking for some entertainment. I believe someone has coined the word *teenager* to describe them.'

Russell smiled and nodded. 'My DC, Johnny Weeks, seems to have missed that stage. He's actually studying for his sergeant's exam.'

'Good for him. He's a bright lad. Anyway, where was I? Oh yes, teenagers. These lads were very influenced by American youth culture. You remember zoot suits?'

'Popular with musicians and gangsters in the Forties.'

'That's right. Well, our English lads started buying the drape jackets but pairing them with drainpipe trousers and brothel creepers – suede lace-up shoes with thick crepe soles. Their hairstyles are elaborate too – swept up into a big quiff at the front and brushed into a duck's arse at the back, using liberal dollops of Brylcreem. They also embraced American musical acts – Bill Hailey and the Comets, Little Richard, Jerry Lee Lewis and so on. They had money in their pockets to spend in cafes and milk bars but were easily bored. That's when the violence began. It started, as I said, when the *Blackboard Jungle* was shown. I believe it had just one song by Bill Hailey but it was enough to cause a riot. And it has continued, spasmodically.'

Russell had been listening with growing interest then asked: 'But what about gang warfare?'

'I was coming to that. They started getting banned from cinemas and cafes so had to find some other outlet for their frustrations. Gangs formed, defined by geographical location, and took great delight in beating seven bells out of each other. Or, and worse than that, they targeted black people. There have been a number of serious injuries but so far no fatalities, although I suspect it's just a matter of time, unless something is done about them.'

'I presume you've come across some of these gangs.'

'Unfortunately, yes. There are two particularly nasty ones: *The Fireballs* and *The Blades*. The first lot, I presume, are named after Jerry Lee Lewis's *Great Balls of Fire*. The other lot, after something much more unpleasant.'

'Tell me.'

'They think it's clever to embed razor blades in their brothel creepers. It makes a kick from one of them nastier.'

'Ouch!'

'Quite.'

'Where are these gangs located?'

'Not surprisingly the first lot are centred around the New Kent Road in the Elephant and Castle. The other lot, the Blades, are from neighbouring Bermondsey. I've got a nark, a snout, I've had for a long time, who lives down there. We could go and see him tomorrow.'

'That would be useful – maybe get a bit of background… find out if there's a Sussex connection.'

'I'm sure there'll be something, or how else did your stiff end up down there?' Merriman looked up at the clock behind the bar. 'Drink up, it's time we got going.'

The journey took only a few minutes but required navigating several small streets. Russell lost count of the number of turns his friend made before they pulled up outside the Punjab restaurant in Neal Street.

A very smart Indian, wearing traditional dress complete with turban, greeted them with a deep bow. 'Good evening Mr Merriman, I've saved your usual table.'

Russell grinned as they entered the dimly lit interior, an evening Raga playing softly in the background. 'You're obviously a regular.'

'I've been a few times. I think you're in for a treat.'

As promised the menu had plenty for Russell to choose from: onion bhajis, pakoras and samosas to start with vegetarian thali to follow and pistachio kulfi to finish. All washed down with India Pale Ale. At the end of the meal he felt pleasantly full and when Merriman suggested a nightcap, he didn't object. It was getting on for midnight before he was dropped outside the small hotel he stayed at when in London. Just before he closed the passenger door his friend leaned across. 'I'll pick you up at eight and we'll go and see my "friend".'

~O~

Nettie Sharp blinked several times. She tried to look round but found it difficult to focus. Her head was splitting, her whole body ached and she felt powerless to move. She tried to speak, to cry out but her tongue and lips wouldn't work. It was all too much of an effort. She closed her eyes and drifted back into unconsciousness.

~O~

Russell slept surprisingly well, considering that he was away from home and in a strange bed. Maybe it was the brandy, the exceptionally well-cooked food, the company or a combination of all three, but he felt rested as he washed and shaved in the morning. Even the breakfast – scrambled egg with wholemeal toast plus a pot of fresh coffee – went down well. He was feeling contented and relaxed and looking forward to his trip across the river. Unhappily this was all about to change when the waiter approached his table.

'There's a call for you, sir. The telephone is at reception – I'll show you.'

He put down his napkin and followed the waiter. Picking up the receiver he said: 'Hello, Russell here.'

'Sonny!' it was Merriman. 'Bad news I'm afraid.'

'Oh?'

Your Chief Super is on the warpath. Wants you to return.'

'Have you spoken to him?'

'No, the message was passed on by the desk sergeant, Wickstead. He seems a nice man.'

'Yes, he is. Does Stout want me back straight away?'

'So it seems. Something about being short-handed. Wickstead said he needs you back to find some missing persons.'

Russell breathed out noisily. 'No surprise there. With Bonnie Parker in hospital and Johnny Weeks on his sergeant's course he would think that.'

'Yes, Wickstead mentioned them. Apparently your WPC hasn't turned up for work either.'

'That's strange; she's usually very punctual.'

'That's what Wickstead said. So I'm afraid your little jaunt is off.'

'So it appears. It's typical of Stout – never seems to see the bigger picture,' Russell stated.

'You did warn me about him. Apparently he thinks it's more

likely to be the work of someone local.'

'I'm not convinced.' Russell paused. There was crackling on the line. 'Will you still go to see your contact?'

'Of course. I'm sure I can find out what you want to know. I'll give you a ring later.'

Russell's earlier carefree mood had evaporated and a cloud hung over him as he made his way to Charing Cross station. The train was on time and it was an uneventful journey back home. He felt too down even to read, and just stared disconsolately out of the window at the passing scenery. He had been really looking forward to finding out more about the Teddy Boy gangs. He felt sure that there was a connection with the body found in Fountain's car. It just seemed to be too much of a coincidence that a knuckleduster and a bicycle chain had been used for it to be a local job. Stout and his bloody missing persons. Russell was sure that his only interest was in keeping in with the respective spouses so he could join the golf club.

His thoughts returned to the non-appearance of Nettie Sharpe. He saw her as being just too bright to remain a humble WPC – he would like to have her as a *bona fide* detective constable. But the current rules in the police force, were such that women were not permitted to join the ranks of the CID. More's the pity, Russell thought. Maybe one day it would change but for now he would have to make do with her assistance as a uniformed officer. And then he remembered... She was looking after Aggie. What had happened to the little terrier? Hopefully they'd both be okay. Finally the train slowed as it entered Collinghurst station. Russell stood and retrieved his case from the luggage rack, took a deep breath, and steeled himself for the meeting with his boss. He knew he was going to have to control his temper.

# Chapter 9

***HM Coastguard** was established in 1822, the successor to the Preventative Water Guard. Its primary objective was to prevent smuggling, but it was also responsible for giving assistance to shipwrecks.*

**RUSSELL WASN'T** in a hurry to see Stout so stopped and had a chat with Wickstead. The sergeant's face was downcast; his grey moustache drooped, giving him the appearance of the Walrus from Lewis Carroll's poem. 'I'm worried about Nettie,' he said.

'It does seem strange,' Russell agreed.

'Her mother rang earlier.'

'Oh, really?'

'Yes. Apparently she didn't go home last night.'

'Perhaps she stayed with a friend.'

'That's what I suggested. Her mother agreed – until this morning. Apparently they'd had a problem with their phone yesterday so she assumed Nettie hadn't been able to get in touch. But when she hadn't heard from her daughter this morning, she was concerned.'

'I can understand that. Nettie is a very sensible girl. She wouldn't alarm her parents unnecessarily.'

Wickstead nodded sagely. 'Hopefully she'll turn up with a perfectly good explanation.'

'Fingers crossed. Presumably she's got Aggie with her?'

'Oh. I didn't realise. I shouldn't worry though, they'll look after each other.'

'I hope so.' Russell sighed. 'Stout has summoned me. Ah, well, better go and get it over and done with. Can't put it off any longer.'

Stout was in a typically tetchy mood. 'Russell, you've done it again. Gone off on an excursion without letting me know, when you should have been here.'

'But I was hoping to get valuable evidence on the case of the body in the back of the car.'

Stout put his head in his hands and leaned his elbows on the desk. 'Another of your wild goose chases. It's pretty obvious that whoever did it comes from round here.'

'I'm sorry but I disagree, sir.'

'You always do. But in this case, I think you're wrong. I'd rather you limited your enquiries to the local area.'

'If you say so.' Russell turned to go before he said something he would regret.

Stout called him back. 'I haven't finished yet,' he growled. 'I want you to concentrate on tracking down Rose Peters and Douglas McDonald.'

'But what about the body in the car?' Russell was incredulous.

'I've brought someone in from County to deal with that.'

'What? Who?'

'DS Pollard.'

Russell couldn't believe it. Peter Charles Pollard wasn't just old school it was if he hadn't even been to school. If Bonnie Parker was a bumbling incompetent he was still an intellectual giant in comparison. When Pollard was a humble bobby he acquired the nickname, PC Plod – P C Pollard sounded like that when said quickly. And the name stuck. Somehow he made it to Detective Constable then, after a considerable delay, Detective Sergeant. He wasn't far off retirement but was unlikely to make the rank of Detective Inspector. And now he was here.

'But surely the case should be handled by someone with a higher rank?' Russell suggested.

'There isn't anyone available,' Stout said firmly. 'Besides, I've known Pollard since we were bobbies on the beat. Rest assured *I'll* keep an eye on him. Oh, and he's brought his own DC with him.' He looked down at a paper on his desk. 'Murray Gordon.' He looked up again. 'Your DC is studying for his sergeant's exam, isn't he?'

'Yes.' Russell wondered what was coming.

'So you can have DC Barrow while Parker is in hospital.'

'I don't think that's a very good idea, sir.'

Stout furrowed his brow. 'Why's that?'

'We had a bit of an altercation yesterday.'

'Well you'd better make it up.' He picked up the papers and tapped them on his desk. 'Now get on with it. I want those two found.'

Russell wasn't to be dismissed so easily. 'Talking of missing persons, what about Nettie Sharpe?'

'Who?'

'The WPC.'

'Why, what's happened?

'She hasn't come in to work this morning.'

'Oh yes, that's right. I'll be having words with her when she deigns to turn up.'

'But what if something's happened to her?'

Stout made a show of selecting a cheroot from the tin on his desk and rolling it between his fingers before he spoke. 'Probably stayed with a boyfriend and overslept.' He lit the cigar with his Zippo, inhaled and blew out a column of smoke. 'If that's all?'

Russell realised he wasn't going to get any further and left the office without another word.

After the positive feelings he'd had the day before he was feeling decidedly downhearted. Not just because the more interesting case had been snatched away – and given to a buffoon, but because of the uncharacteristic absence of Nettie Sharpe. Plus he was worrying about his little dog. And now he was going to have to put up with the company of Clyde Barrow. Although not as inept as his usual boss, Bonnie Parker, he could be an annoying little squirt. Before he could go and tell him the good news Wickstead called out:

'Sonny, Douglas McDonald's car has been found.'

'Where?'

'At Pett Level.'

Russell walked up to the counter in the entrance foyer. 'Who found it?'

The desk sergeant chuckled. 'An irate fisherman rang up. He wanted to launch his boat and the car was blocking the slipway. He was all for ramming it with his truck but noticed some clothes on the beach and it spooked him.'

'Right. We'd better get down there then.' He put his head round the door of the general office. 'Barrow? Get a car and meet me out the front.'

The only car left in the pool was the Ford Pilot, the very car that his usual DC, Johnny Weeks, hated and avoided using like the plague if he could. Perversely Barrow had no trouble with the column change and moved smoothly from first to second then up to third without grating the gears. The journey took barely half an hour, mostly in silence, Russell just uttering directions to the sulky driver. They arrived at Pett Level. Barrow turned the car up past the old battery store, now consecrated as a chapel. The Morris Oxford, AKE 746, was sitting on top of the ridge. It was indeed blocking the access to the beach. Half a dozen locals had gathered. Russell walked up to them.

'Who rang the station?' he asked.

A thin man with a wispy white beard stepped forward. 'It was me.'

'How long ago did you find it?'

'About an hour, I guess.'

Another man joined in. He was holding a piece of rope tied to the collar of a mangy looking mongrel. 'It weren't here when I walked the dog past at half eight,' the man said.

Russell looked at his wristwatch. 'Hmm. It's 10.45 now. So it may have been left around 9 – 9.30?'

'Sounds about right,' the bearded man said. 'I found the clothes too.'

'Oh really? Can you show us where please?'

He led the two detectives down the shingle to the high tide line and pointed. 'There.'

Russell crouched and examined the pile. There was a checked shirt, a pair of corduroy trousers, and a sleeveless Fair Isle jumper, all neatly folded on top of a pair of old, but well-polished brogues.

He looked up. 'You didn't find anything else, or see anyone?'

The man shook his head. 'No, nothing.'

Standing, Russell addressed Barrow. 'Take these back and have a chat with those people. Find out if anyone saw anything. I'm just going to take a look around.'

He stood for a moment, staring out to sea. He knew this area well. His own railway carriage home was only a couple of miles away. Here the tide was a long way out, maybe a quarter of a mile.

The area between the bottom of the shingle beach and the distant water was a maze of rock pools dotted with the remains of a submerged forest, interspersed with large areas of glutinous mud. He calculated that there was still an hour to go before low tide so all this would have been uncovered well before 9am. It would certainly have been a perilous journey for a bare-footed man to make, if he was trying to get to deep water. Still thinking, he made his way back up the beach. The small crowd had dispersed and Barrow was standing by the Morris. Russell tried the door handle. It wasn't locked and opened easily. As he'd expected the interior was as neat as a new pin. It still smelled showroom fresh.

'Look sir,' Barrow said, enthusiasm overcoming his sulky mood. 'The keys are still in the ignition.'

'Well, well. The mystery deepens.'

'Do you think he came here to drown himself?'

'It's possible, although I'm not so sure. Why would he?'

'Maybe things were getting too much for him.'

'Could be.'

'He'd lost his job. He owed money to the golf club. He'd fallen out with his wife…' Barrow was really quite animated now.

'Possibly. But it seems rather drastic, don't you think?'

'Who know what someone would do if things looked that hopeless?'

Russell opened the car's back door. He reached in and pulled out a small leatherette suitcase. It weighed very little. Resting it on the seat he flipped the catches and lifted the lid. Inside there was just a pair of Y-fronts, a string vest and a pair of woollen socks but no other clothing.

'Strange,' Russell said. 'I've heard of travelling light…'

Barrow, who had been standing next to him, started. 'I think that's the radio, sir.' He trotted over to the police car and answered the call. Russell waited. The DC came back after a couple of minutes, looking excited. 'That was Sergeant Wickstead. He says someone's reported a Ford Popular dumped down a farm track off the Pashley Road.'

Russell was baffled. 'I don't see how that's important to us.'

'You will when you hear who owns the car.'

'What do you mean?'

'It's Johnny Weeks' car – your DC.'

'What on earth is he doing over there?'

'He's not! He got a lift to County Headquarters to swat for his sergeant's exam.'

'So why's his car there?'

'Wickstead said WPC Sharpe borrowed it yesterday.'

'Really?'

'Yes, he said she went off after her shift finished.'

'And she hasn't been seen since. This is rather alarming. We'd better get over there.'

'What about McDonald?'

'Hmm. I suppose he might be coming back.'

'But the clothes we found on the beach?'

'I'm not convinced they're significant.'

'Sir?'

'I need to think about it a bit more but something's not quite right.'

Barrow dug his heels in. 'Shouldn't we notify the coastguard and the lifeboat?'

Russell was surprised at the DC. He was normally meek and subservient, kowtowing to Bonnie Parker. 'I'm not sure that's necessary.'

'But what if he's out there somewhere?'

'Are you questioning my authority, constable?'

Barrow pulled himself up to his full height, actually towering over Russell by a few inches. 'Sir. I think you should consult with Superintendent Stout. You know what a stickler he is for protocol.'

Russell took several deep breaths. He wasn't used to having his authority questioned. He made a decision. 'I still don't think it's necessary, but you could be right. Get him on the radio and I'll speak to him.'

'Yes, sir.' Barrow waited until he'd turned away before a smirk crossed his face.

'But I'm not so sure that McDonald *has* gone into the sea.' Russell said when Stout came on the radio.

'That's as maybe. But if we don't send out search parties, and he has, there'll be hell to pay.'

'I suppose so. I just wonder if it will end up being a waste of time.'

'Listen.' Russell could hear the Super's mood turning sour. 'This is my decision. I'll pass you back to Wickstead and you can organise it between you.'

'Before you go, sir, I understand that the car WPC Sharpe was using last night has been found.'

'Oh, I believe I heard something about that,' Stout said casually.

'I think I should go over and check – she may be in trouble.'

'But then again she may not [illegible] might just be having a day off.'

'Even so…'

'Very well. But organise the search for McDonald first. I'll hand you back to the sergeant.'

~O~

The DI gave Wickstead his instructions. The coastguard was notified to keep a lookout along that stretch of the coast and the lifeboats from Hastings and Dungeness were instructed to set out and search the area. There was little he could do now and he was itching to get over to Pashley Road. As senior officer he knew he should really stay but he just couldn't take the absence of one of Stout's cronies seriously.

'Listen,' he said to Barrow. The DC's pugnacious attitude had deserted him and his sulky mood had returned. 'Do you think you can stay here, keep an eye on things, just in case McDonald turns up?'

'I suppose so…sir. What are you going to do?'

'I'm going to drive over to take a look at Weeks' car.'

'But what if I need to get in touch with the station?'

Russell sighed. 'There'll be a telephone in the pub. You can ring from there.'

'I suppose so.'

'And if you ask nicely I'm sure they'll give you a sandwich and a drink.'

~O~

Russell quickly found out why DC Weeks disliked the Ford Pilot so much. He was used to a gear stick poking out of the floor and found the column change baffling. There was very little tolerance between the gears and he lost count of the number of times he crunched them, producing an alarming grating sound from the gearbox. He was sweating with the effort and had to wind the window down to let some cool air in. It was with some relief that he finally turned into the track where Wickstead had said the car could be found. He changed down into first – another grating crunch – and bumped along the rutted unmade road. At first there was a wooden fence and meadow grass on either side with sheep grazing, but ahead was an area of scrubby woodland. As he entered, the sun was blotted out and the air coming in through the open window was distinctly cooler. The track turned to the left, the trees thinned out and there, parked to one side was Weeks' Ford Popular. Russell's stomach clenched. He had a nasty feeling about the situation, but didn't know why.

He switched off the engine. The only sounds were the rattling alarm call of a magpie and the cooing of wood pigeons, somewhere in the trees. He opened the door and got out. Walking across to the car he peered in through the driver's window.

Nothing.

The same in the back.

Why was he feeling so uneasy? He circled the vehicle looking for any obvious signs of a scuffle but there were none. He stood, rubbing his chin, baffled. Something was amiss – he knew it. Stout referred disparagingly to his 'feelings' but so often they proved to be correct and led to concrete conclusions. He was just about to try the driver's door, to see if it would open when he had a thought: the boot.

Walking round to the back of the car he twisted the handle. It wasn't locked. He lowered the boot lid and gasped.

'*Christ!*'

His mind shot back to the description of the body in the back of Fountain's Morris Traveller. To his horror, he saw a jumble of blue uniform with a tangled mane of blonde hair spread over it. The material was dark around the collar and there was a distinctly metallic smell. Russell leaned in, trembling. Gently, he brushed the hair away to reveal Nettie's face. Dried blood streaked her throat and face. He put his hand to her neck and touched it gently with his fingers. There was the faintest flutter of a pulse. He let go of the breath he'd been holding and stood motionless for a few seconds. Then shuddering, as if coming out of a dream, he dashed across to the police car. He radioed the police station and, although the signal wasn't very good, he managed to tell Wickstead what he'd found and impressed on him the urgency of calling an ambulance.

When he'd finished he went back to Nettie. He didn't want to move her so he crouched, holding her hand. This was how the ambulance crew found him when they arrived fifteen minutes later. In a daze he stood and watched as they carefully unfolded her limbs and lifted her out of the boot and on to a stretcher.

'Will she be okay?' he asked.

'Hard to say, at the moment,' one of them replied. 'She's got a nasty gash on her head and has lost an amount of blood.' Seeing Russell's frightened concern he added: 'Don't worry, we'll get her to the hospital as quickly as we can and she'll get the best treatment possible.'

# Chapter 10

*During her time at Rye Harbour the* ***Mary Stanford*** *lifeboat was launched 63 times. 47 launches were exercises and 16 were shouts. From these 16 shouts, 10 lives were saved. Her last launch was the night of 14 November 1928 in a south-west gale. All 17 crew were lost and the station was closed.*

**DOUGLAS McDONALD** was finding it hard going. The straps of the haversack were cutting into his shoulders and the kettle and primus stove hanging from it kept banging against his legs. He thought the walk along the beach at low tide would be easy but the patches of flat sand were interspersed with uneven rocks. He found he had to deviate frequently to avoid the rock pools but had still managed to soak his feet and ankles – the army boots he was wearing weren't as waterproof as they'd once been. Plus there were patches of very sticky mud, invisible until he'd stepped in them. He stood, leaning forwards, his hands clutching his thighs, while he caught his breath. He stared at the gently lapping water, a few yards from his feet, and realised with mild alarm that the tide appeared to be coming in. He looked back the way he had come but could see only the rocky outcrop that he had passed sometime before. Staring the other way he could just make out the distant cliffs that he hoped were the outskirts of Hastings. Turning again and looking inland it appeared that there was some sort of inlet. He could just make out a path winding steeply up through gorse and scrub. Perhaps he should give up on trying to reach the seaside town and find somewhere to camp. Yes, that would be a good plan.

Despite his discomfort he liked to think that he had put the police off his scent. He reckoned that leaving the clothes on the beach had been a stroke of genius, although he was annoyed that he'd had to leave his best pair of brogues behind. Still, it was a small sacrifice if it meant he was able to begin a new life. He was slightly less bothered about the car though. He *had* cherished it, cleaning and polishing the bodywork regularly every Sunday; making sure the oil was always topped up and that the tyres were kept at the correct pressure. But the finance company would soon take it back – and the house. He'd never liked that house. Something about it always made him feel uneasy. He had felt more relaxed and comfortable in the garden and had spent as much time as possible outside. Maybe it was the way Heather had insisted on buying modern furniture and making him decorate the rooms with fashionable wallpaper that he found ugly. But somehow it seemed more than that. He shuddered. Anyway, it wasn't his concern any more. He had a twinge of guilt that Heather would be made homeless when the house was repossessed, but the feeling didn't last long. She'd been a thorn in his side for a long time and she could go back and live with her mother. He smiled. They deserved each other. With that thought, his mood lifted and he turned inland.

~O~

All Russell wanted was to follow the ambulance to the hospital and sit by Nettie's side, even though he knew she would receive the finest care when they arrived. But he was duty bound to wait with Weeks' Ford until Lewis arrived to go over it forensically. However, he was too keyed up to sit in the police car and wait so he started walking along the lane. It was thronged with wild flowers in full bloom: frothy umbels of stately cow parsley, delicate Rosebay willowherb in regal purple and bright yellow buttons of ragwort, home to Cinnabar moth caterpillars, sporting chocolate and brown striped jerseys.

He walked for a few minutes until a farm came into view – presumably owned by the man who had raised the alarm. Russell decided to see if he was at home and could offer any information. He walked down to the tidy collection of farm buildings: an oasthouse, its twin conical roundels neatly roofed with Kent pegtiles with a white weatherboarded cowl perched on each, twisting gently in the breeze; a Dutch barn, half-filled with bales of straw and another lower barn, perhaps used as a grain store. In the centre of a concreted yard was a green Field Marshall tractor, its single-cylinder diesel engine thudding rhythmically. As Russell walked towards it a man emerged from the barn, ducking beneath the low door lintel. He was wearing corduroy trousers, tied at the ankle with baler twine, and a faded checked shirt. His rubicund complexion told of a life lived in the open. Over his arm was a shotgun, broken at the breech.

'Can I help you?' he asked. Although his voice was raised to be heard over the thumping of the tractor's engine it was neither menacing nor welcoming, just matter of fact.

The DI took his warrant card out of his pocket and held it towards the man who peered at it. 'Was it you who reported the abandoned car?' he asked.

'It was. Don't often get strange vehicles down here.'

'Can you tell me anything about it?'

The man realised that Russell had been staring at the shotgun while he spoke. 'This?' he said, pointing towards the weapon. 'It's for rats – in the barn.'

Russell nodded his understanding.

'And to answer your question,' the man said. 'All I know is that the car was there early this morning. I decided to keep my distance and came back here and rang the police station.'

'So you didn't know there was someone in the boot?'

Alarm crossed the farmer's face. 'Christ! No I didn't. Who was it? How long had they been in there?'

'It was a WPC. She hadn't been seen since yesterday afternoon.'

'God. So she could have been in there all night?'

'It's possible. She's in a pretty bad way.'

'Why, what happened?'

'I suspect she'd been hit hard on the head.'

The man raised his bushy eyebrows. 'That's terrible. Who'd do such a thing?'

Russell shrugged. 'I don't know, but I'm going to find out.' He took a breath. 'Anyway, I'd better get back; my colleagues are arriving shortly. Could I have your name?'

'Yes, it's Clements.'

'Thank you. I'll send someone up to take a statement, if that's okay.'

When he got back to the car the forensic man's bottle green Morris J-type van was parked neatly behind it. As the DI approached, Lewis got out of the van and spoke. 'So sorry to hear about the girl, Sonny. She's one of the best.'

'She certainly is. When I catch whoever did that to her…' Lewis sensed that Russell's normally easy-going demeanour had been replaced with one of barely contained anger. Eventually he reined in his feelings and said: 'I can't help but feel guilty.'

'Why's that?'

'If I hadn't gone gallivanting up to London she might not have got herself in this mess.'

Lewis rested his hand lightly on Russell's arm. 'Come on. You can't blame yourself. I wouldn't say she was reckless but she was pretty strong-willed. Whatever led up to this was bound to be as a result of something she was pursuing.'

Russell sighed. 'I suppose you're right.' There was the sound of an engine and a police Wolseley appeared. It pulled up behind the Morris and two uniformed officers got out. 'Ah, Lee,' the DI addressed the driver. 'Go and take a statement from Mr Clements, the farmer. See if he can tell you any more than I found out. 'Beaumont,' he said to the other PC. 'Have a good look around the car. You never know, whoever dumped it may have left something behind.' He turned to Lewis. 'Now you're here I'd better get back to Pett Level. Clyde Barrow is bound to be wondering where I've got to.'

~O~

Russell drove on autopilot, unaware of anything but his concern for the WPC. Subsequently he was surprised when he arrived back at the beach to see that McDonald's car was still sitting at the top of the sea wall but there was no sign of DC Barrow. The same man with the mongrel on a rope came walking towards him. 'You looking for that young detective?'

Russell nodded. 'Any idea where he is?'

The man pointed towards the pub. 'Reckon 'e's in The Smuggler. That's where the coastguard goes when 'e's stood down.'

Russell made his way to the pub and pushed the door to the entrance hall open. The odour of beer and tobacco smoke wafted out. A further door let him into the bar where the smell grew stronger. Three men seated on stools at the bar turned to look at him. One wore the uniform of a coastguard, another, the white rollneck jumper, navy serge trousers and seaboots of an old salt. Between them was Barrow. He saw Russell looking at the half-empty beer tankard on the bar and had the decency to blush.

'I've only just come in, sir,' he stammered.

'It's all right lad. I was longer than expected. Get me a pint and tell me what's happened.'

The coastguard moved aside so Russell could perch on the stool. He was the first to speak. 'Me and my colleagues 'ave been keeping a weather eye out along the coast from the harbour entrance to the cliffs, t'other side of Fairlight.'

Russell took a deep draught from his glass and put it back down on the bar. 'And?'

'Nothin'.'

'As I thought. How about the lifeboats?'

'The Dungeness boat is back,' Barrow said. 'They didn't see anything – reckoned the sea was so calm that a body would show up easily.'

'What about the Hastings boat?'

'Still lookin',' the coastguard said, elbow leaning on the bar. He shook his head. 'Don't reckon they'll find anythin' today neither. If 'e did go in the sea an' was still alive they'd 'ave found 'im by now. If 'e's drownded 'is body'll probably wash up further along the coast.'

'When's that likely to happen?' Russell asked.

'Dunno. Could be tomorrow or the next day. Maybe never.'

'Really?'

''Appens more often than you think. Some poor blighter falls overboard from a fishin' boat – never seen again. You wouldn't think so but these are treacherous waters round 'ere.'

The old seadog who had been listening while contentedly puffing on his clay pipe, spoke up. 'I remember the Mary Stanford disaster in '28. Terrible, it were.' They sat and waited while he took his time knocking out his pipe into a tin ashtray on the bar and refilling the bowl from a leather pouch. Putting the pipe back in his mouth, he struck a Swan Vesta, lit the tobacco and sucked hard. Soon there was a cloud of blue smoke rising to add more depth to the nicotine coloured ceiling.

'I was a deckhand at the time on *Moonshine*.'

Russell pricked up his ears. '*Moonshine*? Wasn't that old Ted Spencer's boat?'

The seadog nodded. 'That's right.' He scowled. 'Sold it to those two Germans.'

'Wolfgang and Ludwig.'

'I remember that case,' Barrow said. 'Weren't they bumping off Nazis?'

'Correct,' Russell said. 'Ludwig was arrested escaping from an old brickworks near Collinghurst. Wolfgang got away but we caught up with him in St Valery in Northern France. Johnny Weeks managed to save the man he was trying to hang but Wolfgang disappeared. It wasn't until sometime later that he was finally caught. Both are inside now.'

The old boy harrumphed. 'Anyhow, this was before all that nonsense.'

'Sorry, carry on,' Russell encouraged.

'It were November. We was fishing out of Compass Point, the day before it happened. Plenty of herring in them days. But we weren't out for long. It was obvious that the weather was changing. "There's a nasty sou-westerly coming," Ted said. "Best if we call it a day and head for home." With that we pulled in the nets though there weren't much in them. He put the helm over and we set off back. Even then, before the gale really got going, it weren't very nice. The sky had gone almost black and there was a nasty fetch on the waves. We was glad to get back in the shelter of the river, I can tell you. Anyway, we got tied up before the weather got really bad and headed off to the pub.'

'The Shipwrights Arms?' Russell asked.

'That's right. Alf had just taken over then. His missus was still alive too.'

Russell was surprised. 'Oh, I didn't know he'd been married.'

'Nah, he never talks about her. Anyhow, we was in the pub and the storm was raging outside. Wind kept blowing down the chimney, filling the room with smoke. After an hour or so I'd had enough and went home to bed. Couldn't sleep though, for the noise of the storm. Must have dropped off eventually cos the next thing I know is the maroons went off. It was pitch black, about five in the morning, and the weather was worse than it had been the night before. I tumbled out of bed and looked out the window. I could see men carrying torches making their way down the street. I knew it would take them a good half an hour at a trot to get to the lifeboat house. They'd have to go across shingle and scrub and fight against the wind and rain to get there.

'I heard later that it took them three attempts to launch the lifeboat – it was low tide and the wind was so ferocious. They must have been soaked to the skin before they even set out. In them days they didn't have an engine – had to row the boat out before they could get the mast and sails up. They hadn't gone far when the message came from the coastguard that they weren't needed, the crew of the ship they were going to had been rescued. Those on shore tried to signal to let them know but there was so much rain and spray they didn't see and carried on.

'Nobody really knows what actually happened but when it

was light the boat was washed ashore – upside down and everyone on board – all 17 of them was drowned.'

No one said anything for several minutes, each lost in his own thoughts. The silence was broken by the ringing of the telephone. The barman picked up the receiver and listened intently, then said:

'I'll tell them, thanks.' He looked at the four men 'Apparently the Hastings lifeboat has been stood down. They'll pick up the search again tomorrow at first light.'

~O~

Russell and Barrow had drunk up, thanked the coastguard and gone outside. 'What shall we do about McDonald's car?' the DC asked. 'We can't leave it there, blocking the slipway.'

'I suppose not,' Russell agreed. 'I expect Lewis will want to go over it when he's finished with Weeks' car.' His stomach gave a lurch as he remembered finding Nettie in the boot. He needed to get to the hospital to find out how she was. 'Did you say that the keys were still in it?' he asked.

Barrow put his hand in his pocket. 'I've got them here,' he said, flourishing them.

'Well go over and move it away from the slipway, but not too far. I'll wait in the police car.

~O~

The journey back to Collinghurst was spent mainly in silence, but it was more companionable than on the way out. Russell got the DC to drop him at the hospital. 'I'll walk back. You go and see Superintendent Stout. Tell him what's happened and that I'll see him later.' Suitably instructed Barrow drove off and Russell mounted the steps. Inside he went up to the desk where a receptionist was sitting, intent on some paperwork. 'Can you tell me where they've taken Nettie Sharpe, the WPC who was brought in earlier?'

The woman looked up. Her hair was backcombed into an elaborate beehive and she was wearing fashionable spectacles, with upswept 'wings'. 'I think she's been taken to the theatre.'

Russell was alarmed. 'The operating theatre?'

'I believe so. Can I ask who you are?'

'Yes, sorry.' He showed her his warrant card.

'Oh, I see, Inspector. Something to do with the head injury she received.'

'Why, was it bad?'

'I don't know the details. You'll have to ask the surgeon.'

'When's he likely to be available?' Now Russell was really concerned.

'That I can't say. I'm afraid you'll have to wait.'

Russell was torn. He knew he should really get back and report to Stout but he wanted to know if Nettie would be all right. He took a breath and decided to turn on the charm. He put his hands on the front of the desk and leaned forward, smiling. 'Listen. I wonder if you would do me a huge favour. I've got to go back to the police station but could you possibly let me know when there is any news about WPC Sharpe's condition? She's a rather special girl.'

It worked. The woman beamed. 'Of course. I'll let you know the moment I hear anything.'

Russell handed her a card. 'Thank you. Here's my number.' He smiled again and left the building.

# Chapter 11

*Prior to the mid-19th century the combination of the window tax and the glass tax put* ***glasshouses*** *far beyond the reach of the average person. The construction of large glasshouses, designed by the likes of Joseph Paxton, was strictly for the social elite, and their commissioning was a powerful expression of wealth and status.*

**IT HAD** been a real struggle to clamber up the bank. From the tideline it had looked an easy climb but when McDonald had finally negotiated the mud and rock pools he discovered that what had looked like a gentle upward slope turned out to be an almost vertical incline. So it had come as a huge relief after the mammoth task of ascending the bank to find an almost level area of rabbit-clipped turf. He'd taken off the accursed knapsack like a lizard shedding its skin and lay on the grass, panting. After a while he sat up, pulled the stopper out of his flask and took a deep draught of water. Although, by now, it was tepid, it tasted like the nectar of the gods. He looked around, thinking this might be a good spot to make camp. Then his eyes fell on a heap of ashes and charred sticks. Someone had lit a fire, and not very long ago by the look of it. Also, a rectangle of grass had been flattened and was yellower – apparently a tent had been pitched there too. This would not do. He had no intention of being discovered so soon. Standing, he heaved the pack back on his shoulders then looked around for a more suitable campsite.

The grassy clearing was surrounded by gorse, its spiky foliage covered with buttery yellow flowers which filled the air with the scent of coconut. As he looked around he could see the only exit suggested a continuation of the upward slope so he steeled himself for another climb. And indeed it was an almighty struggle, much of it conducted if not on hands and knees then leaning forward on hands and feet. The path was lined for several yards with impenetrable thickets of gorse and by now he was mightily sick of the stench of coconut. After struggling for a breathless ten minutes the wall of shrubs to one side seemed to thin and he saw a narrow gap. He pushed through, rewarding himself with scratches on his arms and cheeks which immediately began to bleed. But to his delight he saw it opened into another, almost flat, area of scrubby grass, smaller than the first but with no sign of human occupation. With even more relief than before he shrugged off his pack and started getting out his camping equipment. After his long-winded experiment with erecting the tent in the dunes near the golf course he now understood how the various components went together. Soon, the tent was erected, albeit on a slight slope, and the kettle was bubbling away on the primus stove. He hoped he'd be safe here from prying eyes.

~O~

To his credit, Barrow had done a good job of explaining the situation regarding McDonald's disappearance. Stout was in a fairly benevolent mood and even invited Russell to sit.

'I understand that you're not convinced that McDonald *has* tried to drown himself,' he said.

'That's right.'

'Convince me then.' The Super sat back in his chair and linked his fingers across his stomach.

'Well,' Russell began. 'For a start, the tide was out.'

'Go on.'

'There's about four-hundred yards of rock pools and slippery seaweed before you reach the water's edge, not to mention hidden mudholes. I just don't see that a man, intent on taking his own life, would willingly choose to cross that obstacle course in bare feet.'

'Ah, but what if he was wearing boots or shoes?'

'Then why leave a perfectly serviceable pair of brogues on the beach along with his clothes?'

Stout nodded in agreement. 'True... true.'

'Plus, if he made it that far he would still have had to wade through the shallows for quite some distance before he reached deep water.'

'I see that too.'

To Russell's amazement it appeared that he was winning Stout over. He pressed on. '*If* McDonald really was intent on committing suicide it seems an awfully cack-handed way to go about it.'

'Tell me, how *should* he have done it?'

Russell frowned. 'As we don't know the state of his mind, it's difficult to say. But if he was serious, he would have found it easier to go to the beach at high tide, when he would only have a few yards of shingle to cross before getting into deep water. I reckon he was just trying to put us off the scent and is holed up somewhere inland.'

'What makes you think that?' The Super seemed so intrigued that he hadn't even reached for his tin of cheroots.

'Mrs McDonald told us that he'd taken camping equipment with him. When we first came across his car, not far from the golf course, we could see it quite clearly on the back seat. But there's no sign of it now. All we found in the car was a small suitcase containing some underwear.'

'So you think he's gone off with it?'

'Almost certainly. I suggest that we should be searching along the coast. I reckon he's set up camp, somewhere off the beaten track.'

'Fair enough. I'll go along with that. But what about Rose Peters?'

Russell snorted. 'If you want my opinion, her disappearance has nothing to do with his. I just don't see them going off together.'

Stout looked thoughtful. His heavy brow was furrowed and his piggy eyes almost disappeared into the folds of skin around them. 'With what I've heard I'm starting to come round to your way of thinking. But where is she?'

'It seems she's in the habit of taking off without telling her husband where she's going. I wouldn't be surprised if she turns up, oblivious to the fuss she's caused.'

'You could be right. Let's give it another day or two and see if she returns.'

Russell spoke earnestly. 'Sir, I know you want me to pursue this but I'm much more worried about WPC Sharpe.'

'Why's that?'

Russell explained about visiting the hospital and his concerns about the young woman's condition. 'I think we'd be better served if I try to track down whoever did this to her.'

'Yes, quite right. I dislike it when something like this happens to one of ours. You do what you think is necessary. Meanwhile, you'd better let the lifeboat people know that the sea search is off but get some uniforms to start looking along the coast for McDonald.'

The DI was just rising to leave when he thought of something.

'What's happened about Fountain and the body in his car?'

Stout waved his hand dismissively. 'No need to worry about it. Sergeant Pollard has got that in hand.'

~O~

Russell left Stout's office in a better frame of mind than when he'd entered it but, as he approached the front desk, that was about to change.

'Sonny,' Wickstead called out. 'I've got two messages for you. Your pal from the Met rang. He said he'd call you back.'

'Okay, thanks. What's the other one?'

'It was the hospital. Bad news, I'm afraid.'

'About Nettie?'

'Yes, she's not good.' He looked down at a paper on the desk. 'The blow to the head has caused a subdural haematoma.'

'Bloody hell!' Russell exclaimed. 'That sounds serious. What's that in layman's terms?'

'A blood clot on the brain, apparently.'

'Is it treatable?'

'Yes, they do something called trepanning, apparently.'

'I've heard of that. I think they temporarily remove a section of the skull.'

'That's what they said.'

'What are the chances of success?'

They didn't say, but because she's young she stands a better chance than if she was elderly.'

'Well that's something, I suppose.'

I'm really sorry, Sonny. I know you're fond of her. We all are.'

'I am. What must her parents be going through?'

'They're with her now, the hospital said.'

'I'll go over later and see how she is. Let me know if you hear any more.'

~O~

Russell walked to his own office almost as if he were in a trance. He quietly closed the door – he didn't want to be disturbed – and sat heavily in his chair. He couldn't help feeling it was his fault. He'd always encouraged the WPC to follow her instincts and he was pretty sure that had led to this terrible situation. But what *had* happened? And where was Aggie? Nettie was obviously his major concern but the little terrier, as his constant companion, was almost as big a worry. There was a light tap on the door. Russell didn't want to see anyone at that moment but reluctantly said: 'Come in.'

The door opened and he was relieved to see that it was Lewis. He really like the man – admired his thoroughness – but the news he brought wasn't good. He took time sitting down in the visitor's chair. 'Sonny. I'm just back from going over Weeks' car. Whoever did that to Nettie was very careful – must have been wearing gloves. The only prints we found belonged to her and Johnny.'

'I thought that would be the case.'

'But there's something else.' His face was stiff with concern.

'What's that?'

'We found this.' He held out a length of rope, one end neatly spliced into a loop.

'Oh God! It's Aggie's lead,' Russell exclaimed.

'That's what I thought.'

'No sign of her then?'

'I'm afraid not. We did have a search around and called her name but couldn't find her. Mr Clements, the farmer, hadn't seen her either but said he'd keep a look out. I'm sorry.'

'Not your fault,' Russell said. 'I'm sure she'll turn up.'

~O~

After Lewis had gone the DI sat slumped in his chair for some time, his mind going round in circles. Eventually he sat up, shook his head and took a deep breath. This wouldn't do. Brooding wasn't going to help anyone. He needed to find out who had attacked Nettie. He was starting to jot down some notes when the phone rang. It was his friend, Merriman.

'Sonny. How are you?'

'Not great.'

'Oh, why's that?'

Russell told him the news he'd received from the hospital.

'Bloody hell! Who would do such a thing?'

'That's what I intend to find out.'

'Any ideas?'

'No, that's the problem. She'd obviously gone off on some quest of her own but I haven't a clue where.'

'And you haven't got Johnny Weeks to bounce ideas off either, have you.'

'No. I've got Clyde Barrow instead.'

'Bonnie Parker's sidekick?'

'The same.'

'Talking of whom, have you heard how he is?'

'Stable, as far as I'm aware, but I doubt he'll be coming back here any time soon – if ever.'

'That must be leaving you rather short-handed down there.'

'We would be, but Stout has drafted someone in from County.'

'Who's that?'

'DS Pollard.'

'No! Not PC Plod?'

'The same.'

'Ye gods, I remember him from years ago. Bet he's still as useless as he was then.'

'Probably, but he's not my problem. Apparently he's making progress with the body in Fountain's car.'

'Ah yes, about that. I went to see my contact, down in Elephant and Castle. I doubt you're bothered but I'm afraid what I found out won't be much help.'

'Why's that?'

'Apparently the two gangs – The Fireballs and The Blades – have made it up. They've joined forces to take on all comers.'

'So there's no turf war going on.'

'I don't think so. And as well as that, I don't think they've got anything to do with your body.'

'What makes you say that?'

There was a pause, then: 'We-ell. According to my snout, they don't have any interest in antiques; they're only interested in up-to-the-minute fashion. So it's highly unlikely there would be any connection with a dealer down in the sticks.'

'Ah well, another dead end.'

'I'm afraid so.'

'As I said, it's no longer my problem.'

'Fair enough.'

'Thanks anyway. I'll pass it on.'

~O~

When he'd put the phone down Russell made a few more notes but was still none the wiser about Nettie's exploits. Where on earth had she gone? And why? Was it an investigation of her own? Or was it connected with something they'd been working on together? He was struggling to fathom what could have taken her somewhere that ended in such a tragedy. The pad in front of him was soon covered with underlinings and crossings out and his mind was reeling. He was about to get up and go out to get some air when there was a hesitant knock.

'Come in,' he said, wearily. When the door opened he was surprised to see DC Barrow peering nervously in. 'What can I do for you?' Russell enquired.

Barrow crossed over the threshold and stood hesitantly just inside the room, clutching a road atlas to his chest. 'I think I might have found something out.'

'Sit down lad. Tell me what it is.'

The DC sat on the edge of the chair, held his balled fist in front of his mouth and coughed. 'It's about WPC Sharpe. I'm really sorry about what happened.'

Russell nodded. 'Me too.'

'But I think I might know where she'd been.'

'Really?'

'Yes, look.' He opened the atlas and turned it so Russell could see the area around Hurst Green. 'Weeks' car was found here.' He put his finger on the map.

'That's right.'

'But look.' A note of excitement entered his voice. He moved his finger to the east. 'Sowsden Manor, less than half a mile away, cross-country.'

Russell picked up his excitement. 'You're right.'

'What if she went back there last night?'

'To speak to David Peters?'

'Yes, and things got out of hand.'

'What, a fight do you mean?'

'I don't know. But if something happened and he drove the car and dumped it on that track, it would take him less than 20 minutes to get back, walking.'

'And no one would see him. Hmm. You could be on to something.' Russell suddenly stood up. 'Right. What are we waiting for? Get a car out of the pound. We're going to pay Mr Peters a visit.'

~o~

Russell felt he'd underestimated the DC. He'd always thought of Barrow as Parker's lapdog and yes-man – never having his own opinion, always kow-towing and agreeing with his bumbling boss. But now that Parker was in hospital and *hors de combat* – and likely to be for some time, if not indefinitely, perhaps Barrow was starting to blossom, out from under his shadow. Revising his ideas Russell turned to the DC in the driving seat.

'I feel I ought to refer to you as something other than Barrow. What's your Christian name, lad?'

'It's Clive.' He gripped the steering wheel tightly. 'And before you say anything, I know my nickname is Clyde and it's very similar, but there it is.'

Russell chuckled. 'Don't worry, I'll make sure I use the correct name.'

Barrow visibly relaxed and a slight grin spread across his face. 'That's okay. Thanks for taking me seriously.'

'Noticing that Peters' house was close by was something I'd missed. I'm just glad that you made the connection.'

Barrow changed down to negotiate a sharp bend. 'Do you really think he'd be capable of harming the WPC, sir?'

'On the face of it, I don't. He seemed so mild-mannered. The only time he became agitated was when I mentioned ownership of the business – that seemed to rattle him. But it didn't last long.'

'Maybe he feels inferior in some way.'

'Possibly. It seems everything is owned by Mrs Peters or comes from family money. Apart from that he seems rather benign.'

'It's often the quiet ones, sir.'

'True. But we'd best keep an open mind. Nothing worse than going in with prejudices.'

~O~

In half an hour Barrow was turning the car off the main road and motoring sedately down the gravel drive. As the house came into view he whistled. 'Wow! Some place.'

'You should see what it's like inside.' They pulled up by the fountain and Russell led the way to the front door. He mounted the steps and pressed the bellpush. As before he could hear a ringing somewhere deep inside the house. They waited for a minute while nothing happened. He pressed it again. There was a creaking of metal and they looked round to see a wrought-iron gate being opened in a wall running out from the house. A stooped figure wearing a floral pinafore and with a cotton scarf tied around hair appeared.

'Can I 'elp you?'

'You must be Mrs Floyd, the housekeeper.'

'I might be. Who wants to know?'

Russell walked across to her and offered his warrant card. 'I'm Inspector Russell and this is my colleague DC Barrow.'

'If it's about the madam she ain't 'ere.'

'So I understand. It's actually Mr Peters I'd like to see.'

''E ain't in the 'ouse.'

'Do you know where he is?'

'Out.'

'Yes, but out where?'

'I dunno.'

Russell tried to contain his exasperation. 'Is he in the nursery?'

'No. I said 'e was out.'

'You did. Perhaps you could tell us where?'

'In the grounds. Checkin' up on the estate.'

Russell sighed. 'Thank you. We'll go and look for him ourselves, if that's all right with you?'

'Suit yourselves.' With that the gate creaked closed and she was gone.

The two detectives looked at each other. Both grinned and Russell shook his head in disbelief.

'Eccentric or what?' Barrow wondered.

'Rather like her employer. Come on, let's see if we can track him down.'

They made their way back round the side of the house and along a wide gravel path.

'Must be a nightmare to keep these weed free,' Barrow said.

'Too true. I can't see Peters doing it himself.'

'He must have a gardener.'

'Perhaps more than one, judging by the size of this place.'

The path brought them to the lawned terrace with the parapet that Russell had seen from Peters' enormous bedroom. There was no sign of him so they continued along the façade with views out over the meadow.

'Look,' Barrow said pointing towards the distant woodland. That must be where Weeks' car was found.'

Russell stopped and looked too. 'I think you're right. It's not that far, is it? Let's see what Peters has to say.'

At the end of the terrace there was a flight of wide stone steps leading down to another gravel path, shorter this time, ending in a pair of tall green gates set between two substantial brick pillars. Russell pushed one of the gates open and they emerged into a large, walled kitchen garden. Along the north side were lean-to glasshouses and, down the centre, two long Victorian greenhouses filled with produce. Beyond were several beds, packed with vegetables in full growth.

'Definitely more than one gardener,' Russell observed.

A figure, pushing a heavy wooden wheelbarrow piled high with greenery, appeared from behind one of the greenhouses. The sleeves of his checked shirt were rolled up to the elbow and there were muddy patches on the knees of his chocolate-brown corduroy trousers.

'Can I 'elp you?' he asked.

'We're looking for Mr Peters.' Russell proffered his warrant card.

The man lowered the wheelbarrow, pushed his cap up, gave the card a cursory glance and said: ''E's in the peach case,' and pointed towards the lean-to glasshouses. He raised the wheelbarrow, and with a nod, continued on his way.

As they set off in the direction the man had indicated Barrow said: 'A peach case. That's a new one on me.'

'Same here. Let's see what he's up to.'

The structure was no more than five feet wide at the base tapering to nothing at the top of the wall, and perhaps 30 feet long. The door in the end was ajar and Russell opened it fully and they walked in. The rise in temperature was noticeable. They could see Peters bending down, halfway along, intent on something. It was so narrow they had to walk in single file. He didn't hear them approaching and as they drew near he looked up, startled.

'What the...!' As he straightened up his face registered surprise which changed to anger then softened. He forced a smile. 'Oh, it's you. Russell, isn't it? What brings you here?'

'We'd like to ask you a few questions, if we may.' The DI kept his tone even.

Peters held his arms wide. 'Of course. Fire away.'

'Could we go somewhere a little cooler?' Russell could feel sweat beading on his forehead and trickling down between his shoulder blades.

'Of course. It is rather warm in here. I don't notice when I'm busy.'

As they made their way out into the cooler air Russell was intrigued. 'What are you working on?'

'Oh, you know, tying the peaches in, checking for rotten fruit, that sort of thing.' There was a bench against the wall outside and Peters sat, stretching his arms out across the back, looking relaxed. The two policemen remained standing. Peters looked at Barrow and said: 'I see you've got a new companion. Where's that rather pretty policewoman who was with you last time?'

'That's what I wanted to talk to you about.'

'Oh?' His expression was blank, devoid of curiosity.

'I wondered if you'd seen her – whether she'd paid you a visit.'

Peters' expression turned to one of bafflement. He shook his head slowly. 'Not sure what you mean. The only time was when she came here with you.'

Russell noticed that the sleeve of his ginger jumper was torn, the wool unravelling, and that the man had a bandage round his hand. Although clean looking, fresh blood had seeped through the fabric, staining it. 'What have you done to your hand?'

'What this?' He held it up, as if noticing it for the first time. 'Oh, it's nothing. Caught it on some brambles. Should've been wearing gloves.'

'Nasty. Anyway, you're sure you haven't seen WPC Sharpe?'

'No, I'd say if I had. Why? Has something happened to her?'

'We believe she's been assaulted.'

Peters' eyebrows shot up and he gasped. 'No! What happened?'

'We don't know. That's why I wondered if she'd been here.'

Peters started rising from the bench. 'Now look here…' His voice took on a resentful tone. 'I said I hadn't seen her since you last came. Now if that's all…'

'That's all for now. By the way, I don't suppose you've heard from your wife?'

'Not a thing, I'm afraid.'

'Aren't you concerned about her?' Barrow asked.

Peters shrugged. 'Not really. She's a free agent – comes and goes as she pleases.'

'Will you let us know if you do hear anything? It'll save us trying to track her down,' Russell said.

Peters smiled, but there was no sincerity in it. 'You'll be the first to know, Inspector. If you'll excuse me, I must get on.'

'Fair enough. Do you mind if we take a look around?'

'I'd rather you didn't. This is private property you know. I'll get my gardener to escort you out. Dearborne!' he called. The man they'd spoken to earlier appeared.

'Yes boss?' His voice was sulky.

'Show these men the way to their car.' He gave them a cursory nod and went back into the peach case.

The gardener led them round to the front of the house by a different route, exiting the walled garden through another gate and passing an outdoor swimming pool. When they reached the car Russell asked: 'Has something upset your boss?'

'What do you mean?' the man grunted.

'Well, when I saw him last time he was very friendly – casual even. This time he seemed rather touchy.'

The man thought for a moment. ''E 'as been a bit off all day. When 'e's not in the peach case 'e's been criticisin' my work. *An'* there ain't nothin' wrong with it, I might add.'

'I'm sure there isn't. Can I ask, who else works here?'

'There's Mrs Floyd, the 'ousekeeper.'

'We saw her earlier,' Barrow said.

'And young Daniel, the undergardener. 'E's usually workin' 'ere but 'e ain't come in today.'

'No other staff?'

The man pushed his cap up and scratched his head. 'Let me think. There's the cleaning woman what comes in a couple of times a week – not sure which days.'

'Do you know where she's from?'

'Dunno. Don't 'ave much to do with 'er. Mrs Floyd might know.'

'Thanks, we'll ask her.' As the man turned to go Russell asked: 'Any idea what Mr Peters did to his hand? He told us he damaged it on some brambles. Seemed a lot of blood on the bandage just for that.'

The gardener snorted. 'Brambles? I'm the one what deals with those – none in this garden, I can assure you.' He pointed to his chest with his thumb and pulled himself up to his full height. 'Proud of the way I look after it, I am.'

'I'm sure you are. How do you think he did it?'

The man looked around, appearing to make sure no one overheard. He lowered his voice. 'I heard 'im cursin' earlier. Somethin' about a dog.'

Russell leaned forward, his eyes widening. 'A dog? What did he say?'

'That's all I 'eard. A load of cursin' then, "bloody dog!" Listen. Can't stand here talkin'. 'E'll be wonderin' where I've got to.' He turned and went back the way they'd come.

Barrow looked at the DI. 'Are you thinking what I'm thinking, sir?'

'Possibly… Aggie?'

'Well if Nettie was here then she probably had the terrier with her.'

'Yes, she could well have done.'

'So if it was him who attacked her then your dog might have bitten him in defence.'

'That's what I thought too. Trouble is he's denied seeing her, so we're no further forward.'

'Did you believe him, sir?'

'I'm not sure. He sounded plausible but he was definitely more on edge than when we saw him yesterday.'

'*And* the gardener said he was in a funny mood.'

As they were speaking the gate at the side of the house opened and the housekeeper appeared. 'You still 'ere?' she demanded.

Russell put on his best smile. 'Ah, Mrs Floyd. I'm glad we caught you. I wonder if you can help?'

'What with?' she asked suspiciously.

'The cleaner Mr Peters employs.'

'You mean the cleaner *Mrs* Peters employs. 'E'd let the place go to rack an' ruin, if it were up to 'im. What d'you want to know about 'er?'

'What's her name?'

'Edna Button.'

'Where does she come from?'

Mrs Floyd scowled. 'Somewhere in the village.'

Keeping up the charm offensive Russell said: 'I don't suppose you know her address?'

'Cor blimey! You don't want much, do you? It's Oak Cottage in Station Road.'

'Thank you. You've been most helpful.'

The gate clanged and she was gone again.

# Chapter 12

*The* ***dado*** *is the lower part of a wall, below the dado rail and above the skirting board. The word is from the Italian meaning "dice" or "cube", and refers to "die", an architectural term for the middle section of a pedestal or plinth.*

**DOUGLAS McDONALD** lay back in his tent, hands clasped behind his head and watched as the sun rose and the sky became lighter. He'd spent an uncomfortable night, confirming the notion that he wasn't cut out for camping; the ground was hard and lumpy and he'd managed to shut several biting insects in the tent with him. But… he was a free man. Free from debt, free from his nagging wife and away from that accursed house, at last. Things could only get better. He closed his eyes and at last drifted into a welcome, dreamless sleep.

Sometime later his slumbers were interrupted by the sound of voices close by which jolted him wide awake.

'Bloody stupid idea, the Super sending us out here,' a gruff voice said.

'I know. He could be anywhere – probably miles away by now,' came the reply.

McDonald lay still, rigid with fear. He didn't want to be found, not now, not ever. This was just too unfair.

'Only a bloody idiot would hide here.' It was the first voice again.

'And this bloke must be a bloody idiot. Why on earth does Stout want us to look for him?'

'Don't you know?'

'Nope.'

'Golf.'

'Eh?'

'He wants to join the golf club and thinks McDonald might propose him.'

'Bloody hell. And he's made us thrash about in this godforsaken place just for that? I've had enough. Come on, there's a café up the road from here. We can grab a cuppa and a bite. No one will be any the wiser.'

As the voices faded and the footsteps moved away, McDonald realised he'd been holding his breath for what seemed like minutes. His first reaction was to break camp as soon as they'd safely gone but then he had a rethink. If they'd been searching for him and had given up looking in that area he'd be safe for a while. Well for as long as his food supplies lasted at least. He decided to take stock of what he had.

He struggled out of his sleeping bag and pushed it to one side. Tipping out the contents of his rucksack he assessed the extent of his provisions: Several rashers of bacon wrapped in greaseproof paper, three eggs left in the box, a tin of sardines, another of Spam, one of garden peas and one of baked beans; a container half full of powdered milk, loose tea in a screw of paper and the end of a white loaf. There was a small frying pan, a saucepan and a set of cutlery. Hang on. Where was the tin opener? He shook the rucksack and rummaged around in the bottom. 'Blast!' he said out loud. How the hell was he going to open the tins? He sat back on his heels and thrust his hands into his pockets. His right hand closed round something solid. What was this? A big grin spread across his face as he withdrew the object. It was his trusty Swiss Army knife, complete with bottle opener and… tin opener! He breathed a sigh of relief. At least he could eat now. Then he had a thought: drink. His flask lay to one side. He shook it. Barely half full. He would need more water – he would have to find some, and soon. There had to be a stream nearby, surely? Breakfast first, he thought, then explore.

~O~

The news from the hospital was far from encouraging. Nettie had still not regained consciousness although the surgeons had done all they could for her. Russell was told it was a question of wait and see. There was still the possibility of a full recovery but they couldn't offer any other crumbs of comfort. He could only imagine what her parents were going through. As a colleague he felt bad enough, but to have a child in that situation must be devastating. It made him even more determined to find out who had done it to her.

His number one suspect was still Peters. In Russell's mind he was as guilty as hell – but how to prove it? There was scant evidence to prove that he had been involved with the attack on the WPC. True, his house was barely half a mile from where Weeks' car was found and he had an injury to his hand that *might* have been caused by the bite from a dog. As this notion crossed his mind he thought about Aggie. Hell! He was really missing the little terrier and couldn't imagine where she was or what had happened to her. His whole world seemed to be falling apart. He was missing his DC. Barrow was turning out to be surprisingly good, but he wasn't Johnny Weeks. Nettie had been a much better companion and now her life was in the balance and losing Aggie was the final straw. Perhaps he ought to share his thoughts with Isobel. He realised he was sinking into a maudlin depression. If he was a drinking man, he'd be turning to the bottle. This wouldn't do. He sat up and started jotting down what he'd found out so far.

**Rose Peters**

1. *The man's wife was missing but he was apparently unconcerned.*
2. *Rose Peters was known to go off without notice.*
3. *She usually returned, unaware of any fuss she might have caused.*
4. *The money for the house, business, and everything else came from her or her family.*
5. *Although he tried to conceal it, Peters appeared to resent this.*
6. *But he didn't seem the sort to do anything about it. He probably put up with being a 'kept man', enjoying the benefits it brought.*

***Conclusion***: Peters hadn't bumped his wife off.

**Nettie Sharpe**

1. *The WPC was inquisitive.*
2. *She tended to follow her own instincts.*

Russell stopped writing and sat thinking for a while. He wanted to blame himself for her actions but knew that the girl was quite capable of deciding what she wanted to do. He continued writing.

3. *Did she go back to Sowsden Manor that evening?*
4. *If she did, who attacked her? Peters? Or someone else?*

He needed to find out more about the man. Mrs Floyd had mentioned the cleaner, Edna Button. Time to pay her a visit. He was just rising from his chair when the telephone on his desk rang.

'I've got Isobel on the line,' Wickstead said.

Russell sat down again. 'Thanks, put her through.'

'Sonny,' she began. 'I've been worried.'

'No need, I'm okay – really.'

'No, not about you, silly. I know you can look after yourself. It's Duncan. He hasn't come back. I'm feeling really guilty for suggesting that he drove to the police station. I assumed he'd speak to you and it would all be sorted out.'

'Sadly I wasn't available.'

'So who did see him?' There was an edge to her voice.

'I'm afraid it was Bonnie Parker.'

'Oh God! That idiot.'

'I agree, but sadly, he's had a heart attack.'

'Oh. Sorry. Now I feel bad.'

'That's all right. I think he's okay.'

'So why is Duncan still there?' The anger returned.

'Someone else has taken over the case.'

'Not you?'

'No. I'm trying to find out what happened to Nettie Sharpe.' Russell explained about the attack on the WPC as succinctly as he could. When he'd finished Isobel spoke again, her anger dissolved, her tone conciliatory.

'Oh Sonny. I'm so sorry. I know how fond you are of her. I do hope she pulls through.'

'Me too. Listen. I'll find out what's happened to Duncan and let you know.'

~o~

Duncan Fountain had spent a miserable night in a cell at the police station. The day before he'd answered DS Pollard's inane questions until he was blue in the face and they'd got no further forward. The detective was convinced that *he'd* murdered the man but was obviously having the greatest difficulty proving it. It was almost a relief when they'd sent him down here. He lay back, wondering what the new day might bring. There was the rattle of keys and he heard the door being unlocked. He sat up on the hard bench, prepared for another round of fruitless questions. To his surprise, it was not the pasty face of DS Pollard or his lanky sidekick, DC Gordon, but the more welcome Sonny Russell.

'Hello Duncan,' he said. 'I won't ask if you spent a comfortable night as I'm sure you won't have done. If you'd like to come up to the front desk you can have your things back and you can go home.'

'I don't understand. I thought I was accused of murder?'

'I've had a word with Superintendent Stout. It seems all the evidence is circumstantial and until we've got anything more concrete you're free to go.'

Fountain blinked behind his large glasses. 'Well that's a pleasant surprise although I kept telling the other detective that it was nothing to do with me.'

'I know. I can only say that he was doing his job. Oh, one more thing. We'll have to hang on to your car – need to run more tests. I'll get one of the uniforms to run you home.'

~O~

After Fountain had gone, Russell returned to his office to get his coat and hat. Suddenly the door flew open and Pollard burst in, red-faced, his eyes blazing. 'Who the hell do you think you are? Interfering with *my* investigation!'

Russell had never liked the man. He'd had very little to do with him over the years but when their paths had crossed he'd found him not only incompetent but downright careless. He was sure that any number of people, who were one hundred per cent guilty, had walked free, mainly because of his clumsy handling of their cases. And also some of those innocent of crime had spent time behind bars owing to his mismanagement. If it had been anyone else he would have felt a twinge of guilt by going behind his back and speaking directly to Stout but in this case he had no such misgivings.

'And good morning to you too,' he said mildly.

'Don't you good morning me!' Pollard thundered. 'Fountain is as guilty as hell. You know he is.'

Russell let out a breath. 'I know no such thing. There's no evidence against him.'

Pollard's eyes bulged and his face grew redder. 'There's the bloody great knife with his dabs all over it!'

'Of course it's got his fingerprints on it. He admits it was his but it was stolen.'

'A likely tale…'

'Listen. Put yourself in his place. *If* he had killed the man, do you really think he would bring the body here?'

'I suppose not,' Pollard said sulkily.

'Have you identified the body?'

Pollard was wrong-footed by Russell's change of tack. 'I, er. No, not yet.'

'Well perhaps you should do that first.'

The DS's anger returned. 'How dare you tell me what to do!'

Russell had had enough. He leaned in close to the other man. 'Listen. You've been given a case that I should have had and so far you've made a complete hash of it.'

'Why you…!'

Russell leaned even closer so their faces were inches apart. He could smell Pollard's fetid breath. 'And don't forget, I outrank you. Now, if you'll excuse me, I need to get on.'

~O~

The head gardener at Sowsden Manor was concentrating so intently on the plants he was attending to that he didn't hear the door to the glasshouse open. He was suddenly aware that his boss was standing right beside him. He turned, surprised.

'Sir. I thought you was over at the nursery today.'

'I should be. I'm looking for young Daniel but I can't find him.'

'Daniel? 'E ain't turned up for work – again. That's why I'm in 'ere.' He pointed to the plants on the bench in front of him. ''E should 'ave bin doin' this – weedin' these pots.'

'Well where is he?' Peters sounded even tetchier than he had been the previous day.

Dearborne shrugged. 'Search me. You could ask 'is stepmother. She might know.'

'Hmm. I'll do that. I need to talk to him.' With that he stomped off, leaving the glasshouse door open.

Dearborne harrumphed. 'I'm not 'is bloody keeper,' he muttered. ''E's worse than useless anyway.'

~O~

Edna Button's home was grander than Russell had expected. At the end of a short drive there was a double-fronted Victorian property with white painted stucco, smart green window frames and a front door framed by a well-proportioned portico. A neatly-clipped Wisteria was trained across the front of the house; bush roses, underplanted with lavender, filled the beds surrounding a well-mown lawn. Button herself was a surprise, too. When she opened the door, Russell had expected an older lady, in a housecoat, with a turban round her hair, like Mrs Floyd. The woman, who asked: 'Can I help you?' was barely 40 years old, had a ready smile and was dressed stylishly in a pale pink floral dress. Her round, unlined face was framed by a dark bob, expertly cut.

Sonny felt the need for formality as he held out his warrant card. 'I'm Detective Inspector Russell and this is Detective Constable Barrow. We'd like to talk to you about Mr David Peters.'

'Oh. You'd better come in then.' She stood back and held the door open so they could enter the elegant hall. The floor was covered with encaustic tiles in terracotta, buff and blue. Below the dado rail the wood panelling on the walls was painted a soft blue with pale cream paintwork above. She ushered them into the light and airy drawing room. The furniture was simple, a cream coloured three piece suite; a large glass-fronted cabinet displaying a collection of china and a couple of occasional tables. 'Please, sit down,' she said. 'What would you like to know?'

The two policemen perched on the sofa while she sat decorously in one of the armchairs. 'I understand you clean at Sowsden Manor,' Russell began.

She smiled. 'That's right.'

'Forgive me for saying so, but you don't look like a cleaner.'

She gave a laugh. 'I suppose I don't. But then I'm not really a cleaner.'

Russell looked puzzled. 'I don't understand. You said you clean at the house.'

Again the laugh. 'I *do* clean at Sowsden, but nowhere else.'

'I see... I think.'

'Inspector, you look so baffled, let me put you out of your misery. I'm friends with Rosey Peters – we knew each other at school. I do it as a favour. Believe it or not, I love cleaning and it's such a beautiful house. Anyway, you wanted to ask about Davey.'

'That's right. Did you know that his wife has been missing for nearly a week?'

'Rosey? Yes, I know she's away, but I wouldn't worry about it. She's always going off on little jaunts. She'll come back, she always does.'

'Isn't it strange that no one has seen her, not even her friends?'

'Not really.'

'Felicity Valiant said she stayed there at the end of last week.'

'Flick?' Edna actually put her head back and gave a full-throated laugh this time. 'I doubt that *very* much.'

'Why do you say that?'

She lowered her voice. 'I shouldn't really say this but Davey and Flick were – you know…'

'Having an affair?'

Her hand flew to her mouth. 'How do you know?'

'That's what Joanna Stone said.'

'Huh! She can talk.'

'What do you mean?'

'Look, I don't like to gossip – he's a nice man – and as I said, Rosey and I are old friends.'

'Go on.'

'I suppose it won't do any harm if I tell you. It's bound to come out anyway, if you're investigating him. Let me explain.' She settled herself in her chair. 'They've been married for years. They rub along pretty well but, for a long time, they've lived more or less separate lives.' Russell recalled the cavernous bedroom with single beds set yards apart. 'As long as he was discreet it seemed to work for them. Rosey was very happy for Davey to look after the running of the nursery, which he seemed to enjoy. She could then pursue her own activities.'

'Which were?'

'Oh you know, the occasional round of golf, lunch with girlfriends, weekends away, that sort of thing.'

'What about affairs?'

Edna looked startled. 'Rosey? No. She was faithful to a fault.'

'But Mr Peters wasn't?'

'I'm afraid not. It was common knowledge among their close friends but rarely mentioned.'

'Mrs Peters didn't mind?'

She frowned and seemed to consider. 'Put it this way. As long as he didn't interfere with what she wanted to do she was prepared to turn a blind eye.'

'It seems like several of their friends have been involved with him. At the risk of sounding indelicate,' Russell said, 'have you had an affair with him?'

She laughed. 'Me? Good gracious, no. I was married and divorced years ago. Haven't been interested in men since – and he knew it.'

Russell nodded sagely. 'I understand.' He seemed to consider for a few moments, then asked: 'Do you know Douglas McDonald?'

'Doughy McD? That little squirt? He tried it on with Rosey once. She let him know in no uncertain terms that she wasn't interested.'

'So there's no chance they would have gone off together?'

'None at all. Why do you ask?'

'Oh, he happens to be missing too.'

Edna leaned forward. 'Listen. The chances of Rosey going off with Doughy are about as likely as hell freezing over.'

'Fair enough. There's something else I wanted to ask. How do you get on with Mrs Floyd, the housekeeper?'

'Flossy? We rub along pretty well. She gets on with the day-to-day running of the Manor but is happy for me to do the cleaning. Rosey likes her because she runs the place pretty efficiently. But as for that son of hers...'

Russell cocked his head to one side. 'Oh?'

'Well, stepson, really.'

'Who's that?'

'Daniel. He works in the garden. Well, I say works. As far as I can make out he does as little as possible. I think they only keep him on because of Flossy.' She frowned. 'It's funny though.'

'What is, madam?' Barrow spoke for the first time.

'Davey treats him a bit like a son – the son he never had. Seems to forgive him however lazy or rude he is – most of the time.'

'What do you mean, "Most of the time"?'

She gave a little laugh. 'Sometimes he's furious and wants nothing to do with him.'

'What about Mrs Davies? How does she get on with Daniel?'

Edna's pretty face darkened. 'Get on with him? She doesn't get on with him – she loathes him.'

'That's a bit strong, isn't it?'

'I wouldn't say so. She only tolerates him because Davey likes him – and he knows it.'

'I see. We haven't actually met Daniel yet. Apparently he hasn't been in to work for a couple of days.'

'No surprise there. He seems to come and go as he pleases.'

'Do you know where he lives?'

'With Flossy, his step-mother.'

'Where is that?'

'There's a gatehouse at the entrance to the Manor.'

Barrow looked up from his notebook. 'We passed it on our way in, didn't we, sir?'

'Yes, you would have done. That's where you'll probably find him – *if* he's at home.'

~O~

They drove back towards the Manor. The gatehouse was at the top of the long gravel drive, set at right-angles to the road and tucked behind some mature trees. As they turned into the courtyard they could see the Land Rover parked and Peters standing at the door.

'Hello. What's he doing here?' Russell wondered.

'He doesn't look very happy,' Barrow added.

The horticulturist certainly looked agitated. His face, above the beard, was slightly red and he was nursing his bandaged hand with the other. Russell got out of the car and approached him.

'Hello, Mr Peters. What are you doing here?'

'Hmm? I'm looking for that lazy, good-for-nothing Daniel. He's supposed to be at work.'

'We'd like to speak to him, too.'

Peters looked slightly alarmed. 'Why? What for?'

'Just routine,' Russell said.

'Looks like we're both out of luck. Doesn't appear to be anyone at home.'

'What about his step-mother?'

'Mrs Floyd? She's working at the Manor.' He nodded in the direction of the main house. 'I spoke to her earlier. She doesn't know where he is either.'

Barrow noticed a slight movement of the curtain in the window by the door. 'Look, sir! There's someone in there.'

Peters crouched down and pushed open the flap of the letter box. 'Daniel?' he called. 'We know you're in there.'

There was a noise from behind the house. 'Sir!' Barrow cried. 'Sounds like the back door.'

'Quick lad. Get round there. See if you can catch him.'

The DC took off like a rocket, vaulted the gate at the side of the house and disappeared round the back. Russell reacted at a slightly more sedate pace, throwing open the gate, and following him. Behind the house was a square of lawn, surrounded on three sides by narrow flower beds and a picket fence. On the right was a wooden gate leading into a steeply sloping meadow. The gate was swinging open and Russell could see Barrow running down across the grass in pursuit of another man, a dozen yards ahead of him. Russell followed, somewhat slower. The field ended in dense woodland and he could see the two figures growing smaller as they disappeared into the trees. When he reached the wood, he stopped, breathing heavily, and listened. He could hear crashing as the two men ran through the thick undergrowth. After a few minutes the figure of Barrow reappeared – alone. He held his arms out, palms upwards, in an "I don't know" gesture. He stopped in front of the DI, leaning over and putting his hands on his knees while he caught his breath.

'Sorry,' he panted. 'I tried my best but he lost me. Disappeared out of sight – I didn't stand a chance.'

'I expect he knows these woods like the back of his hand,' Russell said.

'It seems like it. He took off like a hare. I had no chance of catching him.'

'Makes you wonder why he didn't want to be seen by us.'

'Do you think it's got something to do with Nettie, sir?'

Russell pondered. 'I don't know, but I think we need to talk to him. Come on. No point in staying here. Let's get back to the house. Then we can ask his mother some questions.' He was just turning to go when Barrow said:

'Wait! I think I heard something.' The two men stood stock still listening. 'There!'

The DI could hear a rustling sound and whimpering, then a short, sharp bark. Russell's heart leapt. 'It's a dog!' The sound had come from within the wood, over to the left. They pushed through the bracken and undergrowth. About thirty feet in they were stopped by an impenetrable patch of brambles. There was another bark, fainter this time. 'Aggie?' The bark was repeated. 'She's in there!' he said.

'We'll never get through this,' Barrow said.

'Let's see if there's a way round the back.' They skirted the briars, which were thick and inpenetrable, and pushed their way round behind them. All the time they could hear the dog giving the occasional woof, each time growing fainter. At the back of the tangle of brambles it was as thick as it was at the front. 'It's no good,' Russell said, miserably. 'We need something to cut a path through it.'

'I don't think we should delay, sir. The dog doesn't sound great.' Indeed, the whimpering had become almost pathetic. Barrow made up his mind. 'I'm going in.'

'Take these.' Russell pulled a pair of leather gloves from out of his coat pocket.

Barrow put them on. 'Thanks, sir.' He started tearing at the briars, making slow but steady progress. Russell followed close behind. In the centre of the thicket was a big old, fallen tree. Short stubs of branches stuck out from the trunk. Barrow forced his way towards it. They paused and could hear the dog thrashing about in the undergrowth, whimpering, with the occasional faint bark. With a final almighty heave, Barrow reached the tree. On the far side was a bundle of brown and white fur, jerking up and down. 'She's caught!' The brambles were more open here and he swung his leg over the trunk and dropped down on to the other side, disappearing from view. Russell waited, holding his breath. In a few moments, Barrow reappeared, holding the dog and passed it across to the DI

'It is Aggie!' Russell was overjoyed and held her close, scratching her ears, while she covered his face with frantic licks. Screwing up his eyes and pulling a face, for once he allowed her to carry on.

Barrow started climbing across the tree. 'Her collar was caught on a branch. She'd got herself in a real state.'

'Poor little thing. She looks so thin. I wonder how on earth she ended up here?'

~O~

Two hours after the police had gone off to find their breakfast McDonald decided to risk setting off in search of water. He couldn't recall seeing anywhere where a stream might have been on his way along the beach. So he set out, heading roughly west, pushing through more gorse and gaining more scratches. As he progressed the ground became boggy, then suddenly he was sinking into mud. Quickly stepping back on to firm ground he smiled. He'd found it. Moving cautiously upwards, towards the sound of running water he came into a clearing. There was a shallow pool surrounded by rocks and ferns. At the back was a vertical mossy face with several small streams cascading down the surface and splashing into the pool. He crouched and scooped up a handful and took a sip. It was cool and fresh and tasted good. He filled his flask, tipped it up and drank deeply. Then he refilled it to the brim, and descending carefully, returned to his camp.

# Chapter 13

*A **tattoo** is a form of body modification where a design is made by inserting ink, dyes and pigments, either indelible or temporary, into the dermis layer of the skin to create a pattern or motif.*

**INSPECTOR PETER** Pollard and DC Murray Gordon were sitting in DI Parker's borrowed office. The stench of stale tobacco was overwhelming. They had both tried to force the window open, to let in some air, but it wouldn't budge.

'No wonder he had a heart attack,' Pollard had stated. 'Bonnie's arteries must be almost solid with tar. The quicker we get this wrapped up so we can return to County the better. How are you getting on with going through the missing persons lists?'

Gordon, sitting on the other side of the desk, looked up. 'Nothing so far, sir. They're either older, younger, or female.' The detective constable showed his Scottish origins in his red hair and pale skin. But his accent was pure southern English with a slight Sussex burr. 'How about you, sir?'

'Much the same.'

'Perhaps we should widen our search.'

'Good idea. Go and look for the files for missing persons outside the county. Have a word with Sergeant Wickstead, he'll know where to find them. Oh and leave the door open, I'm going to have another go at this window – I can't stand the stench any longer.'

While Gordon was gone Pollard started going through the desk drawers to see if he could find anything that might help in getting the window open. Most were stuffed with old cigarette packets and screwed up paper but the one at the bottom looked more promising. Under a dusty file was a wicked looking sheath knife. The blade was rusty with age but it looked sturdy enough. He walked over to the window, lifted the latch and unhooked the stay. Forcing the blade between the frame and the bottom rail he pressed down on the handle of the knife. He kept pushing, gradually exerting more pressure until, with a tearing sound of wood on wood, the window flew open and the knife fell to the floor. He leaned on the sill and breathed the fresh air into his lungs.

Gordon reappeared. 'Here we are, sir. They were surprisingly easy to find, with Wickstead's help. They cover Surrey, Kent and South London.'

For the next hour they sifted through the papers, comparing notes. They'd been working from a description that had been given to them by the pathologist:

*The victim is five feet ten inches in height, of medium build with dark hair, a pale complexion and hazel eyes. He is clean shaven. He is between 18 and 25 years of age. Distinguishing mark is a tattoo reading "ELVIS FOREVER" and a badly drawn face with an elaborate hairstyle on his left upper arm. He has an old scar running down his right leg, from his knee to his ankle. He has all his own teeth, although they are in poor condition.*

Suddenly Gordon sat up. 'Sir! I think I might have found him. "Sidney Barrett, aged 22. Last known address, Wateringbury in Kent, five foot ten, brown hair, hazel eyes and he's got the tattoo mentioned.'

'Well done. How long has he been missing?'

There was a pause while Gordon read further down the entry. 'It says his girlfriend reported him missing a few days ago. He hasn't been seen since.'

'It could well be our man then. Progress at last.' He looked at his watch. 'We need to go to Wateringbury. It'll take us the best part of an hour to get there and time's getting on. It's too late to start out today. We'll go first thing. I'm sure we can find enough to occupy us till knocking-off time.'

~O~

The little terrier was as delighted to be back with her master as he was to have her back. She'd obviously been caught on the branch for more than a day and her neck had bare, sore patches where she'd been trying to wrench herself free. She was also weak and in desperate need of a drink. When they got back to the house, Russell remedied this by filling a bowl he found with water, and the dog drank for long minutes until she was sated. Her spark seemed to return and when Russell gave her a couple of small Bonios he'd found in his coat pocket she wolfed them down and wagged her tail furiously. Satisfied that no lasting harm had been done he turned to Barrow. 'Right, let's go and find Mrs Floyd. She needs to answer some questions. The Land Rover has gone so I expect Peters has gone back to the Manor. If he has, we need to speak to him too.'

~O~

This time they went straight to the wrought-iron gate at the side of the house. The entrance led to a much less grand doorway. There was no bellpush, just a large, ornate knocker. Russell knocked and they waited. After a few moments the door opened and Mrs

Floyd stood there, wiping her hands on a tea-towel, a scowl on her face.

'It's you again. What do you want this time?'

'We'd like to have a word about Daniel.'

'Oh God. What's 'e done now? You'd better come in.' They were ushered into the cavernous kitchen but no tea was offered.

Russell explained about the chase into the woods and how Daniel had disappeared. 'Have you any idea why he would run off like that?'

'I'm not surprised. 'E's not a fan of you lot.'

'Has he been in trouble before, Mrs Floyd?' Barrow asked.

Alarm crossed her face. 'A bit, but nothin' serious.'

'What do you call "nothing serious"?' Russell said.

'Oh you know, petty pilferin'. 'E's not a bad lad. Just lacks a bit of discipline. Trouble is, I can't control 'im on me own.'

'What about his father?'

'His father? Huh! He buggered off a few years ago.'

'I'm sorry.'

'Don't apologise. 'E were a waste of space. It were a blessin' really.' She scowled again. 'Except for leavin' me with that good for nothing.'

'Daniel?'

'Yeah.' She shrugged her shoulders. 'I suppose 'e's all right.'

'How long were you married to his father?'

'Too long! Five years.'

'How come Daniel didn't go with him?'

'You're jokin'. He couldn't wait to dump 'im – glad to be shot of the lad.'

'I'm sorry to hear that.'

'That's okay.' She looked sad. 'I miss my own lad, though.'

'Your lad?'

'Yes, my *own* son. We was 'appy then.'

'Were you married before?'

'I was.' Her face took on a dreamy look. 'Now *he* was a lovely man.'

'What happened?'

Mrs Floyd produced a handkerchief from a pocket in her housecoat and dabbed her eyes. 'I lost 'im.'

Russell wasn't sure how to respond so he remained quiet and waited for her to continue.

She finished wiping her eyes then blew her nose before putting the handkerchief back in her pocket. 'It was the war – 'e was in the Army, part of the First Airborne.'

'Was he at Arnhem?' Barrow asked.

'That's right. He was one of the unlucky ones. We'd been so 'appy till then. We 'ad such plans. Then I end up 'ere.'

'It's not so bad, is it?' Russell asked gently.

'I s'pose not. Just as well Mr Peters' 'as taken Daniel under 'is wing.'

'Yes, I'd heard that they got along.'

'They certainly do. 'E spends nearly all 'is time with the guvnor – in the garden 'ere or over at the nursery.'

Russell frowned. 'That's what baffles me. Why would Daniel stay away for two days?'

She shook her head. 'No idea. You'll 'ave to ask 'im.'

'We would if we could find him.'

'I expect 'e'll be back. I ain't seen 'im for a few days, neither.'

Russell was puzzled. 'I thought he lived with you in the gatehouse.'

''E does, but 'e's been shut away in 'is room – wouldn't let me in.'

'Is that usual?'

'Yes, it is, really. 'E's very private. Keeps 'is door locked when 'e goes out.'

'Don't you clean his room?'

She gave a snort. 'Not likely! Does it 'iself.'

'What about food? He must have to eat.' Barrow said.

'I leave a tray outside the door. 'E puts' it back when 'e's finished with it.'

'I see. Perhaps you'll let us know if you do see him.'

'I suppose so.'

Do you know if Mr Peters is around?'

''E's not in the 'ouse. If 'is Land Rover's ain't on the drive then 'e ain't in the garden neither.'

'Right. Thanks, you've been most helpful.' Russell was just about to leave when he had a thought. 'Where is *your* son, Mrs Floyd?'

She looked crestfallen. 'I ain't got a clue.'

'Really? Why not?'

She took a deep breath. 'After Daniel's father buggered off, things was much better. The boys got along really well. They did everything together – thick as thieves, they was. They looked so alike people thought they was real brothers. They 'elped me – life was the best it 'ad been for a long time. But then something changed.'

'What was it?' Russell asked gently.

'I dunno. One minute they was as 'appy as sandboys, the next they was at each other's throats. It got so bad I couldn't stand bein' near them.'

'What happened then?'

'I tried to reason with them – get them to see sense and stop fighting – but it were no use, they just wouldn't stop. It got to a stage where I thought one of them would get seriously hurt. Then my own son just upped and left. No idea where 'e is now.'

When they got outside, the Land Rover was conspicuous by its absence. 'What a sad tale,' Russell said.

'It didn't get us very far though, did it, sir?' Barrow observed, as they sat in the police car.

Russell rubbed his chin. 'I don't know. We've found out that Daniel has been in trouble with the police.'

'And that he's got a step-brother.'

'Yes. I wonder what really happened. Surprising that Mrs Floyd's son would go off like that. Whatever happened sounds serious.'

'You'd think it would have been the stepson that would have gone off.'

'Possibly. But without knowing them better, it's difficult to tell.' Russell breathed out noisily. 'Anyway, we'd better see if we can catch up with Peters at the nursery.' He noticed Barrow glance at his watch. 'Have you got somewhere to be this evening, lad?'

'It's all right, sir. Nothing that can't wait.'

'Let's get going then.'

~O~

The drive took the best part of forty minutes. Finally they were turning into the gravelled entrance to Chambers' Nurseries. Greenhouses seemed to stretch for acres, the sun glinting off the glass. There were a couple of cars and several bicycles but no sign of the Land Rover. 'Looks like Mrs Floyd got it wrong. It could be a wasted journey,' Russell said.

There was no one around so they walked through the open door into the nearest greenhouse. Inside the air was warm and humid. The smell of damp compost was strong. Wooden staging, running the length of the building, was topped with terracotta flower pots in neat rows. Each contained a healthy looking plant.

Metal pipes were suspended above the staging with sprinklers fixed at regular intervals. Water sprayed from these, wetting the plants below.

'Can I help you?' Russell had been so engrossed admiring the professional-looking set-up that he hadn't noticed the figure approaching. The man was in his early thirties, with a full beard and an elaborate moustache with upswept curlicues. He was wearing a pair of tan dungarees and the sleeves of his checked shirt were rolled up to the elbow.

Russell introduced them. 'We're looking for Mr Peters,' he said.

'I'm afraid he's not here. He wasn't due in today.' His voice was soft and light.

'I see. And you are?'

'Godfrey Heartenoak. I'm the manager.'

'How long have you been here?'

'I started straight from school –worked for old Mr Chambers, before he died.'

'Oh, when was that?'

'Let me see.' The man stroked his beard, his brow furrowed as he tried to recall the date. 'I started here in '39. We grew food crops throughout the war and started on ornamental plants in the late '40s. He had a knack for knowing what the customers wanted – that's why he was so successful. He was pretty fit right up to the end – actually died right here in the nursery. We'd just started supplying Woolworths so it must have been around '51 or '52. That's when his son-in-law took over. Russell noticed Heartenoak's faced darken slightly.

'Do you get on with Mr Peters?' he asked.

'We rub along,' he said, his voice non-committal. 'He generally leaves the day-to-day running of the nursery to me. He deals with the big contracts.'

'Do you know Daniel Floyd?'

Heartenoak reacted as if an electric current had been passed through his body. 'That little so-and-so!'

'You're not a fan then?' Barrow asked.

'Far from it. Mr Peters wanted him to work here – with me. I put up with him for a few weeks. Then I'd had enough.'

'What happened?'

'I said I'd leave unless he was removed.'

'Why, what was wrong with him?'

His voice took on an edge. 'Where do I start? Not only was he a lazy sod and skived off most of the time but, when he was here, he tried to tell me how to do my job. And that's not to mention the thieving.'

'Oh?'

'Tools started disappearing first – I could put up with that, but then money went missing from bags and coats in the staff cloakroom. I couldn't prove anything but I knew it must be him – it only started when he arrived. Of course, Mr Peters wouldn't hear a word against Floyd when I first told him. But he didn't want to lose me, so Floyd was given a job at Sowsden Manor.'

'What about the stolen money?'

'Huh! It miraculously reappeared and the staff were paid back. Between you and me I think it came out of Mr Peters' own pocket.' He seemed suddenly to make a decision. 'Anyway, I think I've said enough. If that's all, I need to get on.'

# Chapter 14

***Anti-fouling paint** is a specialised category of coatings applied to the hull of a ship or boat below the waterline. It is used to slow the growth of subaquatic organisms that attach themselves and to improve the flow of water past the hull.*

**THE NEXT** morning Pollard and Gordon set off up the A229 for Wateringbury in a police Wolseley, with the PC concentrating on driving and his boss dozing in the passenger seat. They passed through Staplehurst and turned left onto the B2163 after Linton. The road went over the River Medway just below Teston lock, on an impressive mediaeval bridge constructed of local ragstone. Neither detective noticed it however. After crossing the main Maidstone to Paddock Wood railway line, Gordon had to stop to let traffic pass before turning on to the A26. In a few minutes they were at the crossroads in the centre of the village. He brought the car to a halt. He shook the DS's sleeve.

'Sir. Where to now?' he asked.

Pollard rubbed his eyes and took a few moments to come to. 'Where are we?'

'Wateringbury. What's the address we're looking for?'

Pollard put his hand in his jacket pocket and pulled out a crumpled piece of paper. He smoothed it out. 'It's a houseboat apparently. At somewhere called Bow Bridge – near the station.'

Gordon pointed. 'That's Bow Road and there's a sign for the station.'

'Well let's go down there then, shall we?'

Ignoring the sarcasm in Pollard's voice he set off again. After half a mile the bulk of a brick-built goods shed came into sight on the left. 'That's the station,' he said.

'Turn down there then. It's got to be close.'

Just before they reached a bridge that re-crossed the river there was an unmade road with a hand-painted sign proclaiming BOW BRIDGE BOATYARD. At the end of the short track stood a two-storey building surrounded by the paraphernalia associated with a boatyard: a couple of upturned dinghies, numerous coiled ropes, rusty chains, lengths of timber, a stack of old fenders. A smart looking motor cruiser was supported on half-a-dozen rusty oil drums. A man wearing paint-spattered blue overalls was using a broad brush to put a coat of anti-fouling below the waterline on the hull. The detectives walked up to him.

'We're making enquiries about Sidney Barrett.' Pollard held out a photo. 'Is this him?'

The man stopped painting and balanced the brush on top of a paint pot standing on one of the oil drums. He took a pair of half-moon spectacles out of a top pocket and perched them on the bridge of his nose. Peering at the picture he said: 'Yes, that's him.'

'We understand he has a houseboat here. When did you last see him?'

'Not for a couple of weeks – he owes me a month's rent.'

'So he doesn't own the boat?'

'Huh! No. I do. He just rents it.'

'I'm sorry to bring bad news but you won't be getting your money.'

'I'm surprised. I thought he was a nice lad.' He sighed. 'I

suppose he's done a runner then.'

'No, he's dead.'

The man's manner changed immediately from one of casual annoyance to outright shock. 'Oh my God! What happened?'

'I'm afraid we can't divulge that at present. I can only tell you that we think a body we have found to be that of Mr Barrett.'

'I can't believe it. He was actually very pleasant, quiet and helpful.' The man rubbed his hand over his head, leaving a smear of red paint in his blond hair.

'We'd like to have a look at the boat,' Pollard said.

The man frowned. 'I suppose I ought to ask to see some sort of identification.'

Pollard showed him his warrant card.

'Right. In that case, follow me.'

He led them past the building, which housed the office and store, and along the river bank. They passed a row of moored boats before the man stopped by a solid looking craft moored to some wooden staging. It had a white-painted hull with varnished topsides. A sign on the bow proclaimed the name ***LIZA.***

'Can we go on board?' Pollard asked.

'I suppose so. If it's locked I might have a spare key.'

The two detectives climbed into the cockpit. Gordon tried the cabin door – it opened. Inside it was very tidy – spartan even. Along one side was a two-ring cooker, a sink and wooden worktops. On the other a small table with benches either side. Forward was a bulkhead. Gordon opened the door. In the next compartment were two bunks, one either side, with a rolled sleeping bag on one. 'What are we looking for, sir?' he asked.

Pollard scratched his head. 'I don't really know. I rather hoped the place would be a mess. Thought it might be where he was done in.'

'Wonder what's in here?' At the aft end of the main cabin were two doors, facing one another. Gordon opened the one to port. Inside was an Elsan toilet and a strong smell of disinfectant. He quickly closed the door. Opening the facing door they could see it was a hanging locker, filled with clothes.'

'No one hiding in there then,' Pollard observed drily. 'Seems like we've had a wasted journey.' He tutted.

'What about the girlfriend – the one who reported him missing?'

Pollard let out an exasperated breath. 'I suppose we could try to find her while we're here. Probably be more wasted time, I expect.'

~o~

Russell was sitting in his office, leaning back in his chair, hands clasped behind his head. Normally he'd be whistling a tune – something from the hit parade or perhaps a piece of light classical music. Today there were too many thoughts swirling round his head – too many different avenues to pursue. Aggie was lying beneath the desk, her head resting on his shoe. The DI was still debating which task to tackle first when the telephone rang.

'Sonny!' Even through the tinny sounding appliance the pathologist's voice boomed out.

'John. You're up bright and early. What can I do for you?'

'Any chance you can pop over and see me? I've got something to tell you that might be of interest. Rather do it face to face.'

'Certainly. I was planning on visiting the hospital sometime – to see how Nettie is. I'll come over straight away.' Now that he had a definite purpose he was galvanised into action. He grabbed his raincoat and trilby from the coat stand and set off.

When he arrived at the forbidding red-brick building he went straight to the mortuary. Crooks was waiting for him in the anteroom. Without preliminaries he started. 'A funny thing happened yesterday afternoon, Sonny.'

'What was that?'

'I had a visit from David Peters.'

'The *horticulturalist*?'

'Yes, that's right.'

Russell nodded sagely and said quietly, almost to himself: 'That's why he wasn't at the nursery.' Then more loudly: 'Do carry on.'

Crooks gave him a quizzical look. 'I only know him as a passing acquaintance, from functions etcetera. So I was rather surprised to see him turn up here.'

'What did he want?'

'Well that's the odd thing. He wanted to talk to me about a medical matter.'

'That is odd. Why didn't he go to his doctor?'

Crooks smooth brow creased into a frown. 'I asked him that. He said, and I quote: "I don't trust quacks".'

'Strange.'

'That's what I thought. Anyway, I explained that my job was dealing with the dead – not the living. He said he knew that but I must have a wealth of medical knowledge and I was someone he could trust.'

'So what was "the medical matter"?'

'His hand.'

'His hand?' Now Russell was baffled.

'Yes, he said he'd injured it and wanted me to take a look.'

Realisation dawned. 'Oh. I see. He told me he'd caught it on some brambles.'

'Pah! Brambles, my arse. It was a dog bite.'

Russell gave a wry smile. 'That's what his gardener said. Did he say how it happened?'

'No, he was a bit cagey about that. The wound was starting to look a bit nasty. If he'd left it much longer, infection would have set in. Stupid man should have had it seen to immediately.'

'Were you able to do anything for him?'

'Well I cleaned it up, dressed it and gave him a tetanus shot. Told him to see his GP in a couple of days.'

'And did he agree?'

'Reluctantly. At first he was adamant that he would only see me but I persuaded him otherwise. Went off muttering.'

'John,' Russell said slowly. 'I think I know how he got the bite.'

'Oh really?' Do tell.'

Russell explained about the visits to Sowsden Manor and the gatehouse; Floyd running off and finding Aggie caught in the woods. 'I'm trying to make sense of it,' he said. 'Apparently Peters has been acting strangely over the last couple of days and I was becoming convinced that he had something to do with the attack on Nettie. Now I wonder if I've been barking up the wrong tree and it's Daniel Floyd who I should be looking into.'

The pathologist rubbed his chin. 'Perhaps it's both of them.'

Russell was quiet for a moment. 'You could be right, John. It's seems that Peters is very fond of the lad – treats him like a son.'

'Maybe he's covering up for him then.'

With a head full of new thoughts Russell made his way to the main hospital. The receptionist with the fancy glasses told him which ward Nettie was on. He walked down a long, echoing corridor and pushed open the swing door at the end. Further progress was barred by a formidable female figure in a starched blue uniform.

'Can I help you?' she asked, sternly.

'I've come to see how Nettie Sharpe is.'

'And you are?'

Russell pulled himself up to his full five foot eight. 'I'm Detective Inspector Russell.'

'I see. Well I'm the matron on this ward and I decide which patients can have visitors.'

'But…' Russell got no further.

The matron held her hand up. 'Miss Sharpe is very poorly and only close relatives are allowed to see her.'

'But I'm her senior officer,' he protested.

'You could be the Chief Constable, but it wouldn't make any difference. It's still only family.'

'*And* it was me who found her.'

The matron exhaled loudly. 'I'm sure she'll be very grateful to you, *when* she recovers, but you still cannot see her.'

Russell knew that he was beaten. He held his arms out – palms upwards. 'Fair enough. Can you at least tell me how she is?'

The woman folded her arms across her ample bosom and took her time to reply. She seemed to be weighing up how much to tell the detective. Finally she said: 'As I mentioned, she is very poorly. I understand that the operation to relieve the pressure on her brain was successful. Now she needs to rest. The next 24 hours will be critical to her recovery.' She looked at him quizzically. 'If that's all?'

'Yes, thank you,' he muttered.

Without another word she turned on her heel and walked back down the ward, her rubber soles squeaking on the polished floor.

Russell stood, completely dumbfounded by the encounter. After several moments he shook his head and wondered what had just happened. He was used to his position giving him authority in most circumstances and this reversal was a new experience for him. Even when his boss, Superintendent Vic Stout, hauled him across the carpet – something that happened all too often – he generally managed to get the upper hand – eventually. This time he knew he was bested. Slowly turning he made his way back to the receptionist.

She looked up and smiled when he approached. 'Did you find the patient you were looking for?'

'I'm afraid not. I was thwarted by your matron.'

The woman's smile widened. 'Oh, that must be Josephine Jacques. She is rather intimidating.'

'You can say that again.' He breathed out noisily. 'Anyway, hopefully I won't have the same problem seeing another patient.'

'Who's that?'

'Another policeman, DI Parker.'

'Ah. You should have more luck there. He's in ward nine.

Indeed, Russell was able to walk straight into the ward. A nurse smiled when he asked where the detective was and showed him to a private room. As he pushed the door open his nostrils were assailed by the stink of tobacco smoke. Parker was sitting up in bed, his hands beneath the table set across the bedclothes and a guilty look on his face.

'Oh, it's you,' he said. 'I thought it was the nurse coming back.' He withdrew his hand and took a deep drag on one of his foul Capstan Full Strength cigarettes.

Russell looked at him, rather surprised. 'I thought you weren't allowed to smoke in here.'

'I'm not,' he grunted. 'But I'm getting bored.'

'You must be feeling better then.'

'Much the same – don't know what all the fuss was about.'

Russell frowned. 'Didn't you have a heart attack?'

'So they said.'

'What do you mean?'

'We-ell,' he drawled. 'It was that blasted antique dealer – Fountain.'

'Sorry?'

'When he attacked me.'

Russell was astonished. 'But he didn't!'

Parker's eyebrows lowered and he frowned. 'That's not what I understood.'

Russell decided to put him straight. 'Listen. I came in just after it happened. Duncan Fountain was trying to help you. Barrow got the wrong end of the stick and *thought* he was attacking you. Nothing could be further from the truth. If it wasn't for Fountain you might not be here now.'

'Hmm.' Parker's expression was sour enough to turn milk.

'What have the doctors told you?'

'*They* said it was just a mild heart attack. I can go home in a few days.'

'What about work?'

'I dunno. I've got to rest up for a while. Not sure when I'll be back.' He took one final drag on his cigarette, ground the stub out on a saucer, opened the drawer of his bedside locker and dropped it in. 'I hear you let the antique dealer go.'

'Blimey! News travels fast. Yes, there was no firm evidence to hold him on. Don't worry, I got it okay'd by Stout.'

Parker sneered. 'I bet PC Plod wasn't best pleased.'

'No, *Pollard* was rather put out. But at least he found out who the victim was.'

'Did he? Who is it?'

'Some lad who's been living in a houseboat on the Medway, apparently. They've gone up there to see what else they can find out.'

'That's something, I suppose.'

'Anyway. Is there anything you need? Anything I can get for you?'

'Thanks for the offer,' Parker said grudgingly. 'The missus is coming later. I expect she'll bring me something.'

'Right. I'll bid you farewell. I'll open the window first. Get rid of the evidence. Don't want the nurses confiscating your fags.'

'Not too wide,' Parker protested. 'I don't want to get a chill.'

Russell rolled his eyes and opened the window a crack.

'Hang on,' Parker said. 'What's happened about the lass – the wopsie?'

'Do you mean WPC Sharpe?'

'Yes, that's her. I understand she's in here.'

Russell decided he might as well stay a bit longer, pulled up a chair and sat down. 'Someone bashed her over the head. She's in rather a bad way, I'm afraid.'

'Sorry to hear that,' Parker grunted. 'Any idea who it was?'

Russell detailed his suspicions about Peters but as soon as he mentioned Daniel Floyd, Parker, who had been slumped against the pillows, struggled to sit up straight in bed. 'That little tyke. I wouldn't trust him as far as I could throw the slimey bugger.'

'Sounds like you know him well.'

'I do. I've had more than one run in with the sod.'

'Has he done anything serious?'

'No, not really. Just petty pilfering.'

'That's what his stepmother said.'

'I feel sorry for her. She does her best but he's a wily little git – runs circles round her. She's tried to be the mother he should have had, but it's a struggle. He ought to appreciate her like her own son did.'

'Oh yes, she mentioned him – went off, didn't he? Any idea why.'

Parker snorted. 'Bloody Daniel Floyd – that's why.'

'What happened?'

'They got on okay at first, then they began to fight. As far as I know her own son was a decent kid. Wouldn't hurt a fly – the complete opposite of Daniel. *He* was like a cuckoo in the nest – couldn't wait until he'd pushed his stepbrother out.'

'Any idea where he went?'

Parker shook his head. 'None. As I understand it he just packed a bag and skedaddled. Left poor Flossy to get on with it.'

'When did he leave?'

'Not that long ago – less than a year, I think.'

Russell considered this new information as he walked back down the corridor. He was more than surprised that Parker had opened up and told him so much. They'd never exchanged more than cross words in the past – perhaps the heart attack had mellowed him. He was so deep in thought that he almost collided with a man when he turned into the entrance foyer.

'I'm do apologise,' he said, then looked up and saw the white dog collar. 'Oh, I'm sorry – Reverend.'

The vicar smiled. 'That's all right.' Then he looked a little closer. 'It's Inspector Russell, isn't it?'

'That's right.' The DI was perplexed. 'I'm sure I know you.'

'Yes, you do. I'm Nettie's father.'

'Of course. I'm so sorry about what has happened.'

The man gave a sad smile. 'Yes, it's a tragedy.'

Russell was trying to think of something to say when Sharpe spoke.

'Listen, My wife is with our daughter at the moment. Is there somewhere we could get a cup of tea?'

'I know just the place. Miss Smollett's. It's not far.'

Russell had been introduced to the tearooms by Isobel. Her shop and workshop was next door. He noticed that Isobel's establishment was closed. He assumed she was visiting clients. In Miss Smollett's they sat at a table in the corner and made small talk until the tea arrived.

'Nettie always speaks very highly of you,' the clergyman began.

'I think a lot of her, too,' Russell replied. As he poured tea for them he said: 'I'm not sure what to call you – your reverend?'

Sharpe chuckled. 'No need to stand on ceremony – it's Richard. And can I call you Sonny?'

'Of course.' He looked serious. 'How is Nettie? The rather fierce matron wouldn't let me see her.'

'Josephine Jacques. She certainly runs a tight ship, but the ward is all the better for that.' He paused and took a breath. 'I'm afraid my daughter is not that good. They've done all they can for her, we've just got be patient and wait.'

Russell took a sip from his cup. 'Can I ask what they have done?'

'Well,' Sharpe began, 'as a result of the blow on her head she suffered something called a subdural haematoma.'

'So I understand.'

'Apparently her injury was classed as chronic. If it had been acute her chance of survival would have been slim, to say the least. Also, her youth is in her favour. However, they had to cut a hole in her skull…'

'Trepanning.'

'That's right, although they prefer to refer to it as craniotomy nowadays. They did this in order to relieve the pressure on the brain.'

'It sounds awful.'

'Yes, awful but necessary. I had a talk with the surgeon who operated on her and he's quietly confident that she will recover.'

'That's good news.'

Sharpe held up his hand. 'But, it's possible there will be long-term side effects.'

'Such as?'

'Mood changes, memory problems, even fits.'

'I'm so, so sorry.'

'The doctors have done all they can, she's in the hands of the Lord now.'

After this statement there was an uneasy silence between the two men. Russell's leaning towards Buddhism meant he couldn't agree with the clergyman's blind faith. He had long ago come to the conclusion that there was no God; that each individual needed to be responsible for his own actions. No superior being was going to come and rescue him from peril. However, his compassion held him back from contradicting the other man. Instead, he poured more tea. Sharpe thanked him and said:

'What I don't understand is where she was and what she was doing when she was attacked.'

'I'm not completely sure either, but I've got a good idea.' Russell took a drink and looked round the tearooms, making sure he wasn't being overheard. 'What I'm about to tell you has to be in the strictest confidence. It must go no further.'

'I understand.'

Russell told Sharpe about his suspicions concerning David Peters; about the dog bite he tried to cover up. Then he went to explain that his attention had turned towards Daniel Floyd and how the boy had run away, making him appear even more guilty.

'I wouldn't be surprised if he was involved,' Sharpe said.

'Oh. Do you know him?'

'I did.'

'How was that?' Russell asked.

'He used to come to my church. He was in the Boy's Brigade – with his brother.'

'You say "brother". Do you mean stepbrother?'

'Oh yes, that's right. I forgot. They looked so alike they could have been twins. At first, all was well. The lads seemed to enjoy the discipline and the exercises but after a few months things changed.'

'Oh?'

'The one lad – Daniel – became restless. He was argumentative, which upset some of the other boys, whereas his brother settled in really well. I could see him progressing to take on more responsibility. But it just seemed to make Daniel even more difficult. Also, things started going missing and, although nothing could be proven, I had my suspicions that he was responsible. I, and the other leaders, had to take him aside on more than one occasion and have a quiet word, but it made no difference. Eventually I had to issue an ultimatum – either he needed to shape up and stop being disruptive or we'd have to let him go. He just stormed off and I didn't see him again.'

'What about the brother?'

'Sadly, he wasn't the same after Daniel left. He started missing parades and when he did turn up he was moody and difficult. Not long after his brother went he too left. It made me sad as he had such potential. I did call round to the house they were living in then but he didn't want to talk to me.'

'So you lost touch with him?'

'I'm afraid so. I heard that Daniel's father had left the boy's mother and she'd taken a job as housekeeper at Sowsden Manor. As far as I'm aware she's not a churchgoer so I don't know any more details.'

'Apparently the boys fell out at home and her son left.'

'I'm really sorry to hear that. He was a nice lad. Where did he go?'

'No one seems to know – not even his mother.'

# Chapter 15

*The Boys' Brigade was founded in Glasgow by Sir William Alexander Smith on 4 October 1883 to develop Christian manliness by the use of a semi-military discipline and order; gymnastics, summer camps and religious services and classes.*

**DECIDING THERE** was no point in searching the boat further, Pollard had asked the owner of the boatyard where he could find Sidney's girlfriend.

'Nellie Gwynne? She's a barmaid at the Railway Inn. Very popular with the locals.'

'Where is it?' Pollard asked.

'I saw it at the end of the road, when we turned down here,' Gordon said.

'That's right,' the man said. 'You can't miss it.'

They thanked him and returned to the police car. The DC did a neat, three-point turn and headed back to the village. He parked the car and they went into the pub. The room had a low, beamed ceiling and a plain wooden floor. An unadorned timber bar ran the length of the wall opposite the entrance. A pretty, round-faced girl, who looked about twenty, buxom with red hair, stood on the other side, talking to the only other occupant, a man sitting on a bar stool with a pint mug in front of him. An early drinker. She looked up, smiled, then said something that made the man laugh.

She addressed the policemen. 'What can I get you gentlemen?'

'We haven't come for a drink.' The DS held out his ID card. 'Miss Gwynne? Could we have a quiet word?'

The girl's smile vanished and was replaced by a worried frown. 'I suppose so. Come into the back bar.'

They went through a door at the side. 'I think you'd better sit down,' Pollard said. 'I understand that you reported your boyfriend missing a few days ago?'

'Sid? Yes. Have you found him?'

'We think we have.'

'Where is he? Is he in trouble?'

'No, he's not in trouble.'

She let out a big breath. 'That's a relief.'

'I'm afraid he's dead,' Pollard said baldly.

Her hand flew to her mouth. '*NO!* What happened?'

'Looks like he might have been in a fight and he got stabbed.'

'Oh, that's awful. I can't believe it.' She gave a great sob and fat tears started rolling down her cheeks. She made no attempt to dry them and sat crying freely. Eventually she pulled a hanky from out of her sleeve and dabbed at her face then blew her nose.

'I'm sorry miss. I didn't mean to upset you.'

'Well if you didn't mean to you've got a funny way of doing it. How did you think I'd react?'

'Well it wasn't as if you were married or anything,' Gordon said.

Pollard gave the DC a stern look. Then turned towards the girl and said gently: 'You must have been fond of him.'

'We were engaged.' She started crying again. 'We were going to get married next year,' she said between sobs. 'Once he'd got a proper job.'

'What work was he doing?'

'Just odd jobs – helping in the boatyard – a bit of gardening, that sort of thing.'

'Do you know if he had any family?'

'No, I don't think so.'

'No one?'

'He told me he was an only child. He said his parents were killed in the war. I think a bomb fell on their house.'

'How long had he lived here – in the boat?'

'About six months, I think.'

'Where was he before that?'

'I don't know. He said he been travelling.'

'I don't suppose you know where he grew up?' Gordon asked.

'Somewhere down in Sussex, he said. Didn't talk much about it. I can't believe he's dead.' The tears fell again.

Pollard swallowed. 'I don't like to ask, but would you be prepared to identify the body?'

She actually wailed. '*Nooo!* I couldn't.'

'Only it appears there's no one else.'

She sniffed several times loudly and dabbed at her face. She seemed to consider. 'I suppose so then. When? I can't come now.'

Pollard was relieved. The thought of the journey back with a distraught girl was more than he could contemplate. He patted her arm. 'That's all right. We'll send a car for you. Tomorrow?'

'I suppose so.' Her voice was muffled through the handkerchief.

'Is there anywhere you can go – anyone who can look after you?'

'I live with my mum.'

'Can you go there?'

'I'll have to tell Bert – he's the landlord.'

'I'm sure he'll understand.' Before there was another bout of tears Pollard decided it was time to go.

'Perhaps you could give us your mum's address,' Gordon said, stalling him. There was a pause while she recited it, between sobs, and he jotted it down. Then they left.

~O~

When the two detectives were back in the car Gordon said: 'Blimey. She was in a right state. I thought we were going to have her weeping all the way back to Collinghurst. Mind you, did you see the chest on her?'

Pollard rolled his eyes. 'I noticed you couldn't stop looking at her cleavage.'

'Well. It was a bit obvious.'

'That's as maybe. Just hope she covers up before she comes down to identify the body.'

'Anyway. I'm glad *we* haven't got to take her back.'

'That's why I said we'd send someone for her tomorrow.'

~O~

'Tell me what you reckon, lad – your thoughts on the case,' Russell said.

He and DC Barrow were sitting in his office, Aggie safe, snoozing beneath the desk. The DI had summarised his discussion with the Reverend Sharpe and his observations on Daniel Floyd. How he and his brother had been in the Boys' Brigade but Daniel had been disruptive and dishonest. Then he explained what DI Parker had told him.

'I'll be honest with you. I've never made a secret of the fact that we don't get on, but I was impressed with the way he opened up to me. It sounds like Daniel is a bad lot. But it seems strange that he's gone from petty crime to assault – *and* on a police officer. What do you think?'

Barrow scratched the back of his head and pursed his lips. 'Well, the more I think about it, the more certain I am that it was Daniel who hit WPC Sharpe.'

'Not David Peters?'

Barrow shook his head. 'No, I just don't see it.'

'Nor do I,' Russell agreed. 'But by all accounts he's been acting a little strangely recently.'

That *could be* because his wife is missing, sir.'

'Possibly. But from what he's told us he's used to her going off on a whim, then blithely returning, as if nothing has happened.'

'Perhaps he knows something about Daniel – is covering up for him.'

'Now that's a thought.' Russell paused, eyes downcast, brow furrowed, as he considered. 'I think we need to go and have a look in young Daniel's room – see if we can find any clues.'

'Won't we need a search warrant, sir?'

'Hopefully not. I think his stepmother will be anxious to help. If not, I'll have to talk to the Super about getting one. Let's pay Mrs Floyd a visit.'

~O~

There was no one at the gatehouse when Barrow knocked on the door so they continued down the drive to the Manor. The housekeeper appeared at the side entrance, her face dark with suspicion. 'Yes?'

Russell gave her his most charming smile. 'We're a bit concerned about Daniel, Mrs Floyd.'

'Why's that?'

'Well, as he's gone missing we're concerned he may be in some sort of trouble.'

She rolled her eyes, clicked her tongue and folded her arms across her chest. 'Typical. I thought things had been peaceful for too long.'

Russell pressed on. 'I wondered if we could take a look in his room – see if we can find any clues to his whereabouts there.'

Flossie sighed loudly. 'I suppose so.' She looked alarmed. 'I can't come with you though.'

'That's all right. I think we can manage.'

'If you're sure?' Russell nodded. 'Wait there while I get the key.'

When she'd scuttled back into the house Barrow said: 'That went more easily than I'd expected, sir.'

Russell grinned. 'Must be my dazzling charm.'

After a few moments Mrs Floyd reappeared. She held out a very large, ornate key. 'You ain't gonna touch nothin' else are you?' she asked.

'Of course not, we will be very careful. Can you tell me where we'll find Daniels' bedroom?'

'Top of the stairs on the right.'

In a few minutes they were back at the door of the gatehouse and Russell was fitting the key into the lock. The hall was small but spotless. A staircase led up to the first floor. The carpet was narrow and slightly threadbare, with polished brass rods holding it in place. Either side the wood was dark and dust free. They made their way up. At the top was a small landing with three doors. Russell turned the handle of the one on the right and they entered Daniel's bedroom. He'd expected it to be a complete contrast to what they had seen of the rest of the house – scruffy and uncared for – but was surprised to find that it was just as tidy. Two single beds – one neatly made up, the other with tangled bedclothes – were against one wall with a large, dark wood wardrobe between them. Beneath a leaded glass window opposite the door was a small chest of drawers. The top was bare apart from a little mirror on a stand, a comb and a pot of Brylcreem.

'Well, this is a surprise. I was expecting far more mess.'

'Me too, sir. Doesn't look like we're going to find much here, does it?'

'So it would seem. Let's have a look anyway.'

The wardrobe held several jackets including one tweed, one blazer, with elbow patches and an electric blue drape jacket, all on hangers. There were a number of pairs of trousers, several with a narrow leg, equally neatly hung up and a single hanger with ties. Several were conventional striped ties and two were bootlace, one with a buffalo skull slide, the other with a silver star. Russell opened the drawer beneath. It contained several pairs of boots and shoes, mostly conventional foot-wear.

Russell pointed to one pair with thick crepe soles and a leopard skin panel on the vamp. 'Look at these. Seems that our lad was into Teddy Boy gear in a big way.'

'You can say that again, sir,' Barrow said, holding up several pairs of neon socks, in luminous pink, orange and green he'd found in the chest of drawers. 'Nothing else here out of the ordinary though – just the usual shirts and underwear.'

'Seems like we've drawn a blank. Better put everything back as we've found it and be on our way.'

Barrow carefully put the socks back and closed the drawer. As he turned to leave he looked down and stopped. 'Sir, this doesn't look right.' He pointed to the rug on the floor. Although slightly frayed at the ends, it looked too luxurious for this austere room. It had an elaborate repeat pattern in red, blue and cream with a rich and deep texture.

Russell crouched and lifted a corner. 'It looks hand-knotted – maybe Persian or Kashmiri. Certainly expensive.'

'What's Floyd doing with it?'

'That's an interesting question. Parker suggested that he was a petty crook but this looks like an antique. We'll have to ask him – when we find him.' Russell stood up again, took a pace forward, then stopped. 'Did you hear that?' he stepped back again and there was a definite creak from the floor. Crouching again he rolled back the rug. 'Hello, what's this?'

One of the wooden floorboards had two neat cuts across it, about a foot apart. Taking a penknife out of his pocket he opened the blade. He inserted it into one of the cuts and gently levered upwards. The cut board came up easily, leaving a dark space between the floor joists.

'Have you got a torch, lad?'

Reaching into his pocket Barrow produced a slim pencil light and handed it to Russell. 'Here you are, sir.'

'Well done.' He clicked it on and shone the beam into the exposed cavity. 'Well I'll be...' The DC looked over Russell's shoulder and could see a tin box in the torchlight. Russell reached into the hollow and lifted it out. He opened the lid and tipped out the contents. Barrow gave a gasp. Inside were a couple of pocket watches, a gold bracelet, a pearl necklace and three or four rings. 'Looks like our man indulged in a bit more than just petty pilfering. This lot must be worth a bob or two. Let's see if there's anything else.' He shone the torch into the cavity again. This time *he* gasped. 'I don't believe it.' He took a handkerchief out of his pocket and reached down and carefully lifted something out. 'Look.'

'It's a knuckleduster! Hadn't the body that was found in Fountain's car been hit with one of those?'

'So John Crooks said. I bet we'd find a bicycle chain in a shed if we looked.'

'What are we going to do with this lot – should we put it back and tell Mrs Floyd?' Barrow asked.

'No fear. I doubt she knows about it, and, I'm sure, would be horrified if she did. Best keep it from her for now.'

'What should we do with it then?'

Russell put the items back in the box and started getting to his feet again.'I don't know much about antiques, but I know a man who does,' he said. 'We'll take this – and the rug. I doubt his stepmother knows about that either. Let's go to Nottery Quay.'

They locked up the house and returned the key to Mrs Floyd. 'Find anything?' she asked.

'Not really,' Russell said noncommittally.

'That's a relief then.'

# Chapter 16

*Newton, Chambers & Co. manufactured* ***Izal****,*
*one of the best know toilet papers in Britain. It was hard,*
*and 'medicated' with disinfectant and had 'Now wash*
*your hands' printed on every sheet.*

**NOTTERY QUAY** was known by the locals as *Nottery*. Down towards the Strand, where the timber boats unloaded, was a broad, cobbled thoroughfare called Rope Walk. Towering on either side were tall, black-painted weatherboarded warehouses. At one time they would all have been used to store goods – preserved fish in barrels, sacks of grain, chandlery and all sorts of rope, chain and the paraphernalia associated with ships and the sea. Nowadays, fewer were used for this purpose, the majority being taken over by those dealing with the sale and restoration of antiques. At the far end was one building in dire need of repair. The weatherboard was rotten in places and it was a long time since any of the timber had seen a new coat of tar. Russell pulled the sagging door open, the bottom scraping across the cobbles, and stepped inside. The interior was so gloomy that he thought at first the place was unoccupied. He was just about to turn and leave when a voice, a cross between that of a pterodactyl and a cormorant, called out.

'Well? What do you want?'

'Septimus, you *are* at home.'

'Detective Inspector Sonny Russell, as I live and breathe. Please come in,' the man cackled.

'Any chance of some light in here? The DI asked. 'I've got something to show you.'

'Don't want much, do you? Wait a minute.' There was some fumbling, a match was struck and, in a few moments, a yellow light appeared from an oil lamp, making shadows dance around the room.

'That's better, old chap.'

The face that was illuminated by the lamp had a look that matched the voice – a hooked nose, sunken hooded eyes and a wispy beard.

The DI had known Septimus Pike for a long time. Despite his Dickensian looks and lair, Russell knew that he was one of the most honest dealers around and that he could trust him, and his judgment. But he could still be intimidating to those who didn't know him.

Pike looked up from the battered wing chair he was sitting in. 'Who's this you've brought with you?' he croaked. 'It's not your usual sidekick. Has he grown tired of you?'

Russell chuckled. 'No, Johnny Weeks is studying for his sergeant's exam. This is DC Barrow.'

Pike stroked his straggly beard. 'Come closer. Let me look at you.' Barrow took a couple of faltering steps. Pike's arm shot out, gripped the DC's with his bony fingers, and pulled him forward. 'That's better. Now I can see what I'm up against.' He examined Barrow's face in the lamplight for a few moments then, satisfied, pushed him away. 'Looks harmless enough.' He turned to Russell. 'Now, tell me what it is you want. Because you wouldn't be here if you didn't want something.'

The DI put the tin box down on the table at the side of the chair. Pike reached out and flipped the lid open with a talon-like fingernail. 'Ah, *trinkets*,' he breathed. He looked up, his black eyes glinting in the light. 'Where did you find these?'

'That's not important at the moment, Septimus. There's this, too.' He held out the rug.

'Mmm. That's a nice bit of schmutter.'

'Have you seen them before?'

Pike caressed his beard again. 'Maybe I have and maybe I haven't. I'd still like to know where you got them from.'

'Let's just say that I believe they're stolen property.'

Pike gave a throaty chuckle. 'That'll do. I thought as much. Otherwise you wouldn't ask.'

'Have you seen them before?'

'As a matter of fact, I think I have.'

'When was that?'

'Let me think.' There was a pause. 'Two or three weeks ago. Someone brought them in.'

'To sell?'

'Of course. Why else would they bring them to me?'

'And you didn't want to buy them?'

'Not likely,' he snapped. 'I know stolen goods when I see them. These were definitely nicked.' He slammed the lid of the box closed and pushed it away.

'Can you remember who brought them in?' Barrow asked.

'Ah! It speaks,' Pike cackled. 'Of course I can. I never forget a face.'

'Who was it?'

'Some skinny youth.'

'That's not much of a description,' Russell said.

'I suppose you want more?'

'A *bit* more would help.'

Pike sighed. 'Very well then. He was around twenty. But it was his look that got me.'

'And that was?'

'Teddy Boy.'

The two detectives exchanged a glance. 'Can you remember exactly what he was wearing?' Russell asked.

'Maybe I can and maybe I can't.'

'Come on, Septimus. Spill the beans. I know you've got a photographic memory.'

'Don't try to flatter me, it won't work.' He breathed out noisily. 'The youth was wearing one of those long, drape jackets – bright blue it was. I thought it strange because of the socks.'

'Why's that?'

They were luminous pink.' Again the cackle. 'And he was wearing those thick-soled shoes.'

'Brothel creepers.'

'If you say so. Oh, and they had some sort of animal print on the uppers.'

'Leopard skin?'

'It may well have been.'

'I don't suppose you remember what he looked like – his face?

'Pale. He had a pale face.'

'Hair?'

'Never satisfied, are you?'

'Come on, Septimus, it's not a lot to ask, is it?'

'I suppose not.' Russell detected mock resentment in his voice but knew that Pike would answer in his own time. Finally: 'It was dark, combed up into one of those elaborate quiffs that Teds like so much.'

'I suppose you sent him away with a flea in his ear.'

'I certainly did. As you know, I'm an honest dealer.'

Russell grinned. 'You may say that but I couldn't possibly comment.'

'Cheeky. Now if that's all, I've got business to attend to.'

~O~

Back in the police car Barrow spoke. 'Doesn't seem to be any doubt that it was Floyd who tried to flog that stuff, does it, sir?'

'No, there doesn't,' Russell agreed. 'Just one problem.'

'What's that, sir?'

'We don't know where he is. Still, we now know that he's done more than just petty pilfering. And that means that he might be capable of even more – violence perhaps.'

~O~

Nellie Gwynne sat on her bed, her eyes puffy, her nose sore. By her side a wastepaper basket overflowed with damp tissues. She'd emptied a box of Kleenex and had started on a roll of Izal toilet paper, which was rough and no substitute. She couldn't believe that Sid was dead. He'd seemed so full of life when she'd last seen him. He was excited about finding a proper job, moving into a flat or a little house and planning their wedding. They'd had a few words but she was convinced it was only a lovers' tiff and they'd soon make it up. Then he'd gone before they could, saying he was going to look for work further afield. She was dreading the next day, when she'd have to identify the body. Thinking about it brought a renewed bout of sobbing. Her chest heaved but no tears came. She'd shed them all.

She tried remembering the good times they'd had together. She'd loved visiting him on *LIZA*. It allowed her to play house, cooking him simple meals and keeping the boat tidy. Not that it needed much cleaning. Sid prided himself on keeping it shipshape. He was also surprisingly honourable. They had indulged in what her mother would have called *heavy petting* but he'd never pushed her to go *all the way*, although she'd been tempted and they had come close on more than one occasion. He said he respected her wish to wait until they were married. She couldn't wait to be wed but as she was still a few months short of her twenty-first birthday she knew she would have to be patient.

She wondered what job he had been going to look for. He'd been very secretive about it – said he'd be away for a few days. She actually found the prospect exciting as normally he was very straightforward and conventional in his attitudes. Not boring though – oh no.

He was a very good photographer. He had a decent Kodak camera which was his pride and joy. Although it was second-hand he'd saved up for it for ages. He'd taken some lovely photos: swans and geese on the river, boats, several beautiful shots of sunsets and lots of the surrounding countryside. As her mind roamed through the pictures she had a sudden thought. 'Oh God!' she said out loud. *Those* photographs.

They'd gone down the river for a picnic. It was a lovely sunny day and they'd walked for half an hour until they found a quiet spot, beneath some willow trees. Sid had packed a bag with sandwiches, bags of Smith's crisps, apples and a bar of Cadbury Dairy Milk. He'd spread a blanket on the ground and they'd settled down to enjoy the picnic. She'd sneaked a couple of bottles of cider out of the pub – not just any old cider but the local brew made by Bob Luck from Kentish apples. She was used to drinking Babycham – the locals in the Railway would sometimes treat her to a glass – but this was quite different, strong and heady. They drank it straight from the bottle and in no time she was feeling warm and woozy. She lay back on the blanket, enjoying the warmth of the sun on her face and hardly noticed when Sid took out his camera. He took a couple of snaps of her then asked if she'd take her top off. As she was so relaxed she didn't see the harm in it and duly obliged. Within a few minutes she was down to her bra and knickers and started posing for him. She'd seen the way models posed in copies of Reveille magazine that had been left in the pub, and tried copying them. After a few more mouthfuls of cider she was happily posing topless while he snapped away. Later, they'd lain under the trees kissing but, when his hand strayed too far, she slapped it away, pushed him off her and put her clothes back on. He'd seemed rather embarrassed and nothing more was said about it at the time.

But, a couple of weeks later, when they were on the boat, he'd shown her some prints he'd had done by a friend. Some were general views along the river but half a dozen were from that day. Secretly she was flattered, as she thought she looked rather good in them. But she was also alarmed in case anyone else saw them – especially her mum – but Sid assured her that he'd keep them safely hidden. But now he was dead, wouldn't the police search the boat? They'd be bound to find them, then her mum would know and there would be hell to pay. There was nothing for it. Tears forgotten she would have to find them before the police did.

~O~

'There's no doubt. It's the same one that caused the bruising on the victim's head.' Lewis had worked quickly and efficiently, subjecting the knuckleduster they'd found under the floorboards to rigorous tests. 'There were flakes of skin, traces of blood and one or two hairs adhering to it. All matched the samples from the man's body. Unfortunately, no fingerprints.'

'Even so, it looks like Daniel Floyd killed him.'

'Well, it seems he was certainly involved.'

'Presumably that's why he ran off,' Barrow observed.

'Most probably.'

'But what about Nettie?' Russell asked. 'Can we link him to her attack?'

'I'm afraid we can't. Not until we find whatever was used to deliver the blow that caused her injury.'

'That's a pity. I was hoping it would get us a bit further forward.'

'Sorry, Sonny. I wish I could be more helpful.'

'Not your fault. I know you've done your best.'

'There is one thing though.'

'What's that?'

'The other items you found – the rug and the jewellery. They were on the list of goods that Fountain said had been stolen.'

Russell grinned. 'Septimus Pike was right with his description.' Lewis nodded his agreement and left the room.

'It fitted Floyd to a T, didn't it, sir?' Barrow said.

'It certainly did. The sooner we find him the better.'

'Perhaps it's time you had a chat with PC Plod, sir.'

'Sergeant *Pollard* to you lad. But yes, you're right. I'll see if he's around now – strike while the iron's hot. Keep an eye on Aggie will you? I don't think he likes dogs.'

~o~

DS Pollard visibly bristled when Russell walked into his borrowed office. He stood up and, his mouth set in a thin line, folded his arms tightly across his chest. Russell held up his hands. 'It's all right, I haven't come here for a row. Some new evidence had come to light which should help with your case.'

'Oh?' Pollard said, suspiciously.

'Can I sit down?' Russell asked.

Pollard unfolded one of his arms and held it out. 'Be my guest.' Then, shrugging, he made himself comfortable on one side of the desk. Russell took a seat opposite. 'So what's this evidence?' the DS asked.

'I think we've found out who killed Barrett.'

'I'm listening.' There was a note of sarcasm in his voice which the DI noted.

'Don't come it,' he said. 'I'm prepared to help you, even though this should be my case.'

'Fair enough.'

'I know you've made little progress – apart from finding out who the victim was.'

'Well…' Pollard began.

'Come on, admit it. That's all you've got.'

'We're following several lines of enquiry.'

Russell gave a short laugh. 'Which will lead precisely where?'

'I thought you came in to help me.'

'Yes, I did. And it looks like you really need that help.'

Pollard sighed. 'Okay, maybe I do. To be honest, the case has stalled.'

'Right, now that you've admitted that, I *might* tell you what we've found out.' Russell was aware that he was being uncharacteristically difficult but he just couldn't help it. The DS was a worm and for two pins he'd let him wriggle in his ineptitude until Stout saw through him and chucked him off the case. But he was a compassionate man and had, reluctantly, decided to help him.

'We believe the killer is called Daniel Floyd. He lives with his stepmother in the gatehouse at Sowsden Manor and works for David Peters, the horticulturalist.'

Pollard, who had been slumped in his chair, sat up straight. 'Really? Are you sure?'

'All the evidence points towards him.'

'So I should arrest him.'

'You should, but there's a problem.'

'What's that?' Pollard looked nervous.

'He's run off. DC Barrow tried to catch him but he obviously knows the woods around the area and gave him the slip. But I doubt he'll get far. All the patrols have been alerted to keep a lookout for him.'

Pollard relaxed. 'That's okay then.'

Russell held up a warning hand. 'We may have *some* evidence, but you'll need more, if you're going to make this stick.'

'What else do I need? We've got the murder weapon.'

'Yes, but do you know where the killing took place?'

'Well no.'

'Where have you looked?'

'Er. We haven't, actually. Been a bit busy finding out who the victim is.'

Russell breathed out noisily. 'Now that you know who it is *and* the probable perpetrator, I suggest you find out.'

'Can I ask where you *suggest* we look?'

'Use your initiative! Where was the body found?'

'I'm not sure – the antique dealer, Fountain, brought it in – in his car.'

'And where was his car when he found the body?'

'In a bombed out warehouse – I think. Locked away apparently.'

'But someone must have been able to access it, mustn't they?'

'I suppose so – if Fountain *isn't* guilty.'

'For heaven's sake, we've been through that. There's so little evidence against him, it has to be someone else – and I've given you a name. Now, you need to discover where the deed was done.

I think you'd better find out where it was – and quickly.' With that Russell decided he'd had enough. He rose from his chair and left the office without another word.

Pollard sat in his chair, a thin film of sweat beading his forehead. A feeling of dread was spreading through his body. He knew he was out of his depth. He'd been acquainted with Vic Stout since he'd joined the force and had jumped at the chance to take on the case when it had been offered to him. It had seemed so straightforward at first. The antique dealer was quite obviously the murderer: his prints were all over the weapon; he'd admitted that the scimitar had belonged to him plus the body had been found in *his* car. Then that bloody DI Russell had demolished the case. If he'd kept his nose out of it Pollard was convinced that Stout would have backed him and Fountain would now be facing a long prison term – if not the hangman's noose. Instead, he was going to have to start searching for the killer all over again. This meant extra leg work, which he'd never enjoyed. He supposed he was going to have to take Russell's advice and find out where the killing took place, which meant more work *and* he'd have to talk to the antique dealer again.

He knew he'd struggle to be civil. He'd disliked the man from the start; thought he was a jumped-up, toffee-nosed twit. Was convinced he'd looked down on him – just because he was only a detective sergeant. He should have stayed at County – dealing with petty thefts and stolen cars, things he understood and could cope with. Now he was really regretting taking on this case. Stout should have given it to Russell. He shook his head. As it was he would just have to muddle through. He couldn't afford to cock it up – with retirement so close. At first he'd had a whimsical notion that, if he cracked this case, he could go out in a blaze of glory. But if he didn't he'd be leaving with his tail between his legs. And that outcome was looking increasingly likely. Then he had a shocking thought. If it did go belly up would it affect his pension? He mopped his brow as the sweat was starting to trickle into his eyes. There was nothing for it, he would just have to talk to Fountain –*and* try to keep his temper. He felt a little better, now he'd made this decision. He got up out of his chair and went to look for DC Gordon.

~O~

Russell had called DC Barrow into his office. 'I think we should go and talk to Duncan Fountain – confirm that the items of jewellery we found under the floorboards in Floyd's bedroom were indeed stolen from his shop.'

'Is that really necessary, sir?' Barrow was perplexed. 'Surely Lewis confirmed it was the same as the stuff on the list.'

'Very probably. But I expect that Sergeant Pollard will be paying the antique dealer a visit and if we happen to be there at the same time…' He grinned and gave Barrow a wink.

~O~

'Murray, how do you feel about doing the interview?' Pollard asked when they were in the car.

The DC was so surprised to be addressed by his Christian name that he was speechless for a moment.

'You know, ask Fountain where he keeps his car, and so on.' Pollard continued, encouragingly.

'I suppose so, sir. I thought you'd want to do it.'

'No, that's all right. It'll be good experience for you.'

'If you say so.' Gordon concentrated on driving out of the police station car park before speaking again. 'What do you want me to ask him?'

Pollard rubbed his chin. 'Essentially, where he parks his car, in case that's where the stabbing took place. That's what DI Russell thinks anyway.'

'I suppose he could be right.'

'Mmm. I'm not so sure. I still favour that blasted antique dealer for doing it.'

'Perhaps that's because you don't like him,' Gordon ventured.

The DS exhaled noisily. 'That's got nothing to do with it. The evidence all points to him. Just because he's a mate of Russell's squeeze, Isobel whatsername, doesn't mean that he's not guilty.'

'I think that's a bit unfair, sir.'

'*You* might think it's unfair, but just wait until I'm proved right.' With that he folded his arms tightly across his chest and set his mouth in a thin line.

~O~

'Can you show me where you parked your car, Mr Fountain?' DC Gordon asked.

'Of course. It's where I always park it when I'm here. Follow me.' He led the way out of his shop on to the pavement, carefully locking the door behind them. He glanced at the police car which was parked across the street, but didn't ask why DS Pollard was still slumped in the passenger seat. He was glad not to have to confront the man. Walking round the corner they entered an unmade road, its surface rutted, pockmarked with rainwater-filled potholes. Along one side was a row of dilapidated warehouses. They had caught the worst of a German bomber, limping home after a raid on London. The pilot had dumped the last of his load, which landed on this row of buildings, rendering them roofless and derelict. There had been talk of restoring them, but lack of cash –or lack of will – meant they were still in a tumbledown state more than ten years after the end of the war. Half-hearted attempts had been made to close them off but they still made great playgrounds for the local lads. Fountain walked up to one of the sturdier looking buildings, closed off with a pair of doors. A padlock on a chain held them shut. Undoing the lock, Fountain slipped the chain off, and with an effort swung one of the doors open.

'This is where I park my car.'

The interior was empty apart from rubble and pieces of timber lying about. The floor was concrete, virtually intact, surround by four wooden walls, but no roof.

Gordon, looking upwards, was puzzled. 'Why do you bother to lock it up?'

'Stops anyone pinching my car – it's my pride and joy.'

'So no one can get in here?'

'I didn't say that. They might be able to get in, but they can't get my car out.'

'I see. I think.'

Fountain took pity on the DC. 'Look. There is a door at the rear – leads onto some waste land. I *suppose* someone might be able to get in there.'

'Shall we take a look, sir?'

'If you want to.' Fountain led him to the back of the warehouse where there was indeed a door. He gave it a half-hearted tug. 'Doesn't look like it's been opened in a long while.'

'Can I see?' Gordon asked.

Fountain stood aside. 'Be my guest.'

The DC took a small flashlight out of his pocket, clicked it on and crouched in front of the door. 'I think you're wrong. I reckoned it's been opened – and recently. Look.' He played the beam of the torch across the floor. There were a series of concentric arcs where the bottom of the door must have scraped through the dust. In the light, footprints showed up clearly and there were some dark stains tracking across the floor. He stood up and stepped back. 'I think we need to get forensics in here. Please make your way back carefully to the entrance. This is a crime scene.'

As they stepped out into the road another police car came bumping over the potholes. It drew to a halt beside them, the passenger door opened and a smiling DI Russell climbed out.

He nodded a greeting at the DC and said to Fountain: 'Just the man I wanted to see. I need to talk to you about some goods you reported stolen.'

Pollard had been slouching in the other car but had sat up straight when he saw Russell arrive. Moving surprisingly fast he'd got out and crossed the road before the DI had finished speaking. 'I think we've got more important things to worry about than a few stolen knick-knacks,' he said. 'This is a murder enquiry.'

'So, have you found anything?' Russell asked.

Pollard turned to the other detective. 'DC Gordon?'

'I've found a rear entrance that has been used recently. And what look like bloodstains.'

Russell smiled. 'So you'll be getting Lewis and his team in then. You'd better ring the station and get them to send him over.'

~O~

The two detective constables stood around making small talk, Pollard went back to the car while Russell spoke to Fountain.

'You're sure these are the things that were stolen from your shop?' He was holding the tin box that they'd found under the floorboards.

Light glinted off the lenses of Fountain's oversize spectacles. 'Absolutely. I'm astonished. I never thought I'd see them again.' He held his hand out to Russell. 'Can I have them back now?'

'I'm afraid not. They may be needed for evidence. You can have them when we've finished with them.'

Fountain shrugged. 'Ah well. I suppose at least they'll be in safe hands.'

They had only to wait for a few more minutes until the bottle green Morris J-type van turned into the rutted track. It rocked and dipped as if it was on a fairground ride, finally coming to a halt and settling on its springs. The engine was switched off, the door opened and Lewis climbed elegantly out of the driver's seat. As usual he was immaculately turned out: green checked shirt, tan moleskin trousers and well-polished brown brogues. He walked up to Russell.

'Hello Sonny. What have you got for me?'

'Ahem. It's not me you want to speak to, it's DS Pollard. It's his case.'

Lewis nodded. 'Right.' He looked around. 'Where is he then?'

Russell dipped his head towards the police car, parked on the other side of the road. 'He's over there. Surprised he didn't rush over when you arrived.'

Lewis narrowed his eyes and squinted at the police car. 'Looks like he's having forty winks.'

Russell grinned. 'That's how excited he is about the case.'

'But he *is* in charge?'

'That's right.'

'I'd better let him know I'm here then.' He was just turning to go, then stopped. 'Oh, I've found something out. I don't know whether you knew, but when Nettie was taken to the hospital she only had one shoe on – the other was missing.'

'No, I didn't.'

'We had a good search around the area where Weeks' car was dumped but we didn't find anything – sorry.'

'So, it could still be somewhere out there?'

'It could, but I think finding it would be like looking for the proverbial needle in haystack.'

Sighing, Russell said: 'I suppose so. Thanks for letting me know. Anyway, you'd better go and speak to the detective sergeant.'

Lewis nodded his agreement, strode across to the police car and tapped lightly on the partly open window. Pollard jerked in his seat his head shaking rapidly from side to side.

'W-what?' His eyes blinked open and he focused on Lewis's face, peering at him. 'I w-wasn't asleep,' he stammered.

'Of course you weren't,' the fingerprints man said, trying to keep amusement out of his voice.

Pollard grunted, opened the door and clambered out of the car, his ungainly exit in complete contrast to Lewis's suave manoeuvre. 'Come on,' he grunted. 'It's over here.' He led the way to the warehouse. 'This is where he...' he pointed his thumb at Fountain. 'Where he *claims* he parked his car.'

'But it's true!' Fountain protested.

Pollard gave him a withering look. 'We'll find out about that, won't we?'

'Has anyone been in here?' Lewis asked.

'We had a look at the back door,' DC Gordon said. '*I* saw that it had been opened. And there are dark patches on the ground. Could be blood.'

'Right. Leave it to me. I'll see what I can find.' Lewis fetched a large case out of the back of the Morris and stepped just inside the front door of the warehouse.

Russell turned to Barrow. 'Right. I think we've finished here. Lewis doesn't need our help and I'm sure the DS would rather we weren't around.' Pollard scowled. Russell chose to ignore him. 'We'll push off. I've got an idea.'

As they drove away Barrow turned to him and said: 'What's this idea, sir? Where are we heading?'

'It's a bit mad – the fool's errand that Lewis suggests, but I think it's worth a try. Head for Pashley Road.'

'You're going to look for the shoe, aren't you?'

'That's the idea. But not where the car was found. We're going to trace the route on foot back to Sowsden Manor.'

'I don't understand. It's certain that Nettie was driven there in the boot of Weeks' car.'

'Yes, that's right.'

Barrow was baffled. 'So it's highly unlikely that her shoe will be anywhere in the woods.'

'Highly unlikely. But I've got a feeling, and however mad it sounds, I have to follow my instincts. Yes, we may find nothing, but I know I won't settle until we've looked.'

~O~

They arrived at the farm track where the Ford Popular had been found. Barrow switched off the engine and the two men sat quietly for a few moments, the metal tinkling as it cooled. 'Is there any point in looking round here again, sir?' he asked.

'I don't think so. Lewis would have been particularly thorough. He's as concerned about Nettie as I am.'

'So what's the plan?'

'Let's have a look and see if there's any obvious path from here to Sowsden.' They got out of the car and started walking along the track towards the farm. Russell called Aggie to heel and clipped the lead on her collar. 'Don't want to upset the farmer if there's any stock about.' There was no sign of a break in the hedgerows on each side and no one challenged them as they continued past the buildings and through the deserted farmyard. At the far end a fence cut off the end of the yard with a five-bar gate leading into a small meadow surrounded by trees. The summer grass was long but there appeared to be a path running through the middle.

'Do you think this is it, sir?' Barrow asked.

'It could well be. I reckon it's heading in the right direction. Let's see where it goes.' They crossed the field, the terrier, free of her lead, scampering ahead, and at the far side was another fence with a stile leading into the trees. 'I had a look on a map earlier and I think this is probably Sowsden Wood.'

They climbed over the stile, Aggie squeezed through a gap beneath the lower step, and entered the wood, following a definite path between the trees. Apart from the occasional oak the trees were predominately chestnut. At some time, not so long ago, they had been coppiced and slender young trunks grew from gnarled stumps. The ground underfoot was soft and spongy with a thick carpet of leaves in varying stages of decay. The branches closed in, cathedral-like, overhead while the sun broke spasmodically through openings in the canopy creating dappled patterns, breaking and reforming as the trees swayed in the gentle breeze. The atmosphere was hushed, the only sound the officers' muffled footsteps and laboured breathing as the pathway wound ever upwards. Surprisingly there were very few birds, just the occasional cooing of a wood pigeon. Every now and again there was a burst of rustling as Aggie danced through the undergrowth in pursuit of unseen creatures; the sudden clattering of wings and alarm call of a pheasant as it exploded through the trees. Then silence. They'd been going for ten minutes when Russell stopped, panting, and leaned forward, his hands on his thighs.

'Give me a minute,' he puffed.

The younger man, who had barely broken sweat, smiled. 'Take your time, sir. There's no rush.' Walking a dozen yards forward, he peered at the trees along the path. He stopped, walked back a few paces and leaned towards the nearest trunk. 'What's this…?'

By now Russell had regained his breath and caught up with him. 'What have you found, lad?'

'Look!' Barrow plucked something from a stubby branch sticking out from the tree.

'It's wool,' Russell said.

'Yes, and look at the colour.'

'Ginger.'

'That's the colour of Peters' tatty old jumper, isn't it?'

'It is.'

'So could this be from the torn sleeve?'

'Very possibly. Let's see if he's at home.'

They continued along the path which suddenly emerged on the edge of an area of pasture. After the gloom of the woodland the light was almost blinding.

Barrow held his hand over his forehead and shielded his eyes. 'Look, sir,' he said pointing. 'Isn't that the house?'

The far side of the sloping meadow was bordered by a tall, stone wall. Rising majestically behind it was the elegant façade of Sowsden Manor.

'Yes, you're right, but I'd quite like to arrive unannounced,' Russell said. The wood continued along the left side of the field. 'Let's stay in the trees for as long as we can.' He whistled for the dog, which came bounding back. 'Sorry Aggie,' he said, clipping her lead on again. 'We need the element of surprise.'

This path was much less well defined so they made slower progress, stepping over fallen branches and pushing past Rhododendrons which had started appearing among the trees. The chestnuts had thinned out and were replaced with a wider variety of species: ash, sycamore and hornbeam. After a few minutes of stumbling along their way was suddenly blocked by a tall, mellow brick wall.

'Do you think this is the side of the walled garden?' Barrow asked.

'Most probably. Let's see if we can find a way in.'

They turned left and skirted the brickwork until they came to the corner. Just round the back was a green-painted door. It didn't look as if it had been opened for some time. Cobwebs garlanded the wooden frame and there was red rust on the latch.

'Give it a try, lad. You never know...'

Barrow squeezed the latch. It was stiff and didn't budge. He applied more pressure, using both hands. Reluctantly, and with a grating sound, it moved. The DC looked round at Russell and grinned. Putting his shoulder against the door he shoved. Slowly, it opened, the bottom grating across a build-up of dirt and detritus on the other side. He stopped pushing when there was a gap just wide enough for them to edge through, he with ease and the slightly more rotund Russell with an effort. They stood inside the doorway. There was no sign of Peters or Dearborne, the head gardener.

'Where do we start, sir?' Barrow was whispering.

Russell stood, assessing the situation, one hand on his hip the other holding tight to the lead. Aggie was raring to go. Her tail wagged and her ears were pricked. She sensed that something was afoot. 'We're unlikely to find anything in the greenhouses, but it's probably best to have a look anyway,' Russell said. 'Let's split up and see what we can uncover. You go to the left and I'll go to the right. Make sure you look underneath the staging.'

They set off on their search. Although Russell kept Aggie on the lead she was keen to investigate and darted back and forth, tail wagging. There was very little to see – just the occasional broken terracotta pot, a discarded fertiliser sack, a worn-out glove. Eventually Russell exited the door at the end and met with the Barrow again.

'Anything?' he asked.

'Sorry, sir. Nothing. You?'

Russell shook his head. 'Perhaps we'd have more luck in an outhouse or a shed?' He looked around. They'd come in through the door in the north wall where the peach case was situated. The east and west walls were devoid of any structures but along the south side, where the main entrance was situated, a shed was attached to the wall. Russell pointed. 'Let's have a look over there.'

They made their way between the neat vegetable beds. 'Plenty of home produce here, sir,' Barrow observed.

'Yes, they look pretty healthy too.' However, as they reached the last bed Russell stopped. He looked puzzled. 'That's strange,' he said. 'Those don't look so good.' The leeks had begun to flop over and the carrot tops looked pale and flaccid. 'I wonder what's wrong with them?'

'Dunno, sir. Afraid I don't know anything about veg – only how to eat it.'

'They definitely look unhealthy. I'm surprised Peters hasn't done something about it.' He shook his head and carried on walking. They reached the shed and Russell tried the door. 'Damn, it's locked.'

Barrow peered through the window next to the door. 'It's too dark. Can't see a thing.'

Russell joined him and rubbed on the glass. 'Hmm. That's no better, must be grimy on the inside.'

'I suppose we could try forcing the lock,' Barrow suggested.

'We could,' Russell said slowly. But we don't know if we're likely to find anything in there.' He stepped back to the door and rattled the handle. It was locked fast.

'*What the hell do you think you're doing?*'

Startled, the policemen turned in unison. Dearborne was standing a few feet away holding a shotgun, the barrels pointing directly at them. He had appeared from nowhere.

Russell held his hand up – palm outwards. 'I'm sorry. We just wanted to have a look around.' When the man didn't respond he said: 'I'd rather you didn't point that thing at us.'

Dearborne lowered the gun slightly. 'You're trespassing. You might be the police but you have no right to be here without Mr Peters' permission. I think you'd better leave. If you want to look around you'd better make an appointment with him,' he growled. 'Or better still, get a warrant. Now clear off.'

Russell was quietly furious although he knew that he was on shaky ground. He lowered his hand. 'Right, we will go, but don't worry, we'll be back. And I hope, for your sake, that we don't find anything.'

~O~

Barrow had driven Russell back to the police station at Collinghurst. The DI was smarting from his treatment by Dearborne. He knew that he shouldn't have been searching the walled garden without official permission but was certain that if he'd had time he may well have uncovered some crucial evidence. He was determined to go back. He'd need to talk to Stout.

~O~

'You want to do what?' The Superintendent was aghast.

'I'd like you to authorise a search warrant.'

'On what grounds?'

'I'm certain that we'll find evidence to link the place to the attack on WPC Sharpe.'

'Yes, but – I repeat – on what grounds?'

'I just have a feeling that there's a strong connection.'

Stout shook his head in disbelief. 'You and your feelings again. Listen. There is no way that I am prepared to issue a warrant. David Peters is not only an upstanding pillar of society but also a very good friend. And, don't forget, he's someone whose wife is missing. Which reminds me. Have you made any progress with finding out where she is?'

'Not as yet. I spoke to a good friend of hers, Edna Button, who also happens to be the cleaner at Sowsden.'

'The cleaner? I thought Mrs Floyd looked after the Manor.'

'Apparently she looks after the day-to-day running of the house but Mrs Button does the cleaning – loves it apparently.'

Stout averted his eyes and shook his head disbelievingly. 'Strange, that anyone would enjoy cleaning.' He looked up. 'You said you'd spoken to her – and…?'

'She was of the opinion that Rose Peters is a free spirit and often goes off on a whim. She's convinced she'll be back as if nothing has happened.'

There was a pause while Stout shuffled some papers on his desk. Russell waited. The Super looked up again, his brow lowered. 'You say she's a *free spirit*. Would you care to elaborate?'

Russell disliked discussing someone's private affairs based on hearsay but it did seem that the Peters' open relationship was fairly common knowledge – at least among their close friends. He took a deep breath and exhaled slowly. 'I know that you say David Peters is a good friend of yours, sir. But I'm afraid he's not all he seems.'

The brow remained low and his eyes narrowed. 'What do you mean, *not all he seems*?'

'Not to put to finer point on it, he's a bit of a lady's man – plays the field, as it were.'

'Preposterous! They're one of the happiest married couples I know – rock solid.'

'On the surface, maybe.'

Stout's colour started to darken. 'And you have evidence for this?'

'Not as such. But her friends say...'

'Tittle-tattle!' the Super cut in. 'I didn't expect that you would listen to gossip.'

Russell chose not to rise to the bait and said nothing.

Stout took his silence as acceptance. 'Anyway. I'm sure you've got plenty of work to get on with – I know I have. So if that's all?'

~O~

As Russell was making his way back to his own office Wickstead called out to him. 'Sonny, a member of staff from the hospital phoned just now.'

The DI stopped in his tracks. 'About Nettie?'

'Yes. Apparently she gained consciousness briefly.'

Russell crossed the floor and leaned on the counter, his eyes sparkling. 'Has she said anything?'

'I've written it down here.' The desk sergeant turned a notepad round so Russell could read it.

*Miss Sharpe said to tell Inspector Russell*
*look for the manner of sick plants.*

'Is that all? Are you sure that's what they said?'

'That's all. Apparently Nettie is heavily sedated and she was only conscious for a few minutes before drifting back to sleep.'

'And how is she?'

'They said she had turned the corner and was making better progress than they'd hoped for.'

'Thank God. Do you know who it was that rang?'

'Yes, it was the matron.'

Russell grinned. Josephine Jacques. Perhaps she wasn't such a dragon after all. He took the piece of paper and continued on to his office, his heart lighter than it had been for some time. He leaned back in his chair, linked his fingers behind his head and whistled: *The Surrey with the Fringe on Top*, from the musical, *Oklahoma*. He was lost in the music for some minutes, briefly forgetting all the problems that had been weighing down on him. Inevitably though, his improved mood was destined not to last.

The door burst open and Stout stormed in, his face red from the sparse roots of his hair to his bulging collar. In a single pace he had crossed the room, curled his fingers into fists and rested his knuckles on the desk. He leaned so far forward, his florid complexion was inches away from Russell's own face. Beneath the desk Aggie gave a low, throaty growl but stayed where she was.

'*How dare you!*' Stout spat through gritted teeth.

Russell sat back as far as the chair would allow. 'How dare I what?'

'I've just had David Peters on the phone. He's furious!'

The DI groaned inwardly. He knew what was coming.

'You had the temerity to ask me for a search warrant when you've already been sniffing round Peters' garden! What the hell got into you?'

'I thought I'd find some evidence,' he said meekly.

'For crying out loud! How many times do I have warn you about your thoughts? Not only have you not followed my instructions but you've also managed to deeply upset one of my friends.'

'It wasn't my intention to upset him.'

'It may not have been, but you certainly have. And it's going to take a lot for him to trust the police again. You'd better just hope that you're right about his wife and that she's going to come back soon!' With that, he turned on his heel and marched out of the room.

Russell sat for some time, dazed by the encounter. He'd crossed swords with the superintendent on more than one occasion in the past and it never got any easier. Stout rarely agreed with him when the initial evidence wasn't substantial enough, even though, more often than not, Russell was proved right in the final analysis. He was growing ever more certain that Sowsden Manor was at the heart of the case involving the attack on poor Nettie. It was bad enough that Peters was a tricky character but now that he'd angered Stout it was becoming increasingly difficult to see how he could move the case forward. He knew he needed something concrete – but how to get it?

~O~

He was sitting pondering his options when there was tap at the door. 'Come in,' he said. Lewis entered. 'Ah, what a pleasant surprise, please do take a seat. What can I do for you?'

Lewis reached down and ruffled the hair on Aggie's head. The little terrier wagged her tail, pleased to see him too. 'I know it's DS Pollard's case, but I thought you'd be interested to know what I've found out,' he said.

'Thanks, I appreciate that. Do go on.'

'The search of the warehouse where Fountain parked his car proved most interesting.'

'Oh yes?'

'I think we can be sure that's where our victim was killed. The pattern of blood splatters and the disturbances in the dust and dirt on the floor suggest some sort of fight or tussle. It looks like only one other person was involved and they were very careful to cover their tracks. Except for one thing.'

'What's that?'

'We found a pair of thin leather gloves.'

'I suppose whoever did it was being careful not to leave prints.'

'Agreed. But that's the strange thing.'

'Oh?'

'Pollard said that Daniel Floyd was the number one suspect.'

'That's right.'

'And by rights, any evidence should point towards him.'

'By rights.'

'Well, we were able to get some partial prints from inside the gloves.'

'That's something at least.'

'It might have been.'

'I'm sensing a *"but"*.' Russell had a sinking feeling. He had an idea this wasn't going in the right direction.

'But they don't match his prints.'

'You are joking.'

'That's what Pollard said.'

'I bet he did. Did he also say it was me who told him that Floyd was guilty?'

'He did, and was overjoyed when he thought you'd got it wrong, and he'd got it right. Mind you, I quickly burst his bubble.'

'How did you do that?'

'He was convinced that he knew along that it was Duncan Fountain.'

Russell smiled. 'Don't tell me, the prints weren't his either.'

'No, they weren't.' A frown clouded Lewis's normally crease-free brow. 'That's the odd thing. They don't match anyone we have on record.'

'That is strange. I suppose we're back to square one.'

'Well, *Pollard* is. You're not supposed to be involved, are you?'

'I guess not,' Russell said wearily. 'I'm still trying to find out what happened to Nettie.'

'Oh yes. How is she? Have you heard?'

Russell brightened. 'It seems she's a lot better.'

'I suppose youth is on her side. Fingers crossed that she makes a full recovery.'

'I agree. Now we'll just have to wait.'

They sat in companionable silence for a while before Lewis spoke again. 'Are you any further forward with finding out what happened to her?'

Russell went over his journey through the woods and visit to the kitchen garden at Sowsden Manor. He told him about the piece of wool that DC Barrow had found snagged on a twig.

'You think it matches Peters' jumper?'

'I can't be certain, but if I'm right that he was involved then it probably does.'

'It sounds like you need to have a good look round – especially in that shed,' Lewis said.

'That's right. But Stout has put the kibosh on that idea.'

'How annoying.'

'He's more worried about upsetting someone with influence than finding out who bashed poor Nettie over the head. Doesn't want to spoil his chances of getting into the golf club.'

'So it seems.' Lewis paused. 'What are you planning on doing now?'

'I really don't know. As you said, I need to have a good look round.'

~O~

Waiting until the daylight had started to fade from the sky Nellie made her way down the road to the boatyard. She'd crept out of the house and closed the front door as quietly as she could, not wanting her parents to know. They'd been very sympathetic about Sid but she knew they wouldn't approve of her going to the boat. However, she felt she just had to find those photos. It was just too embarrassing to think that anyone might look at them. She was glad to see that the office was in darkness when she arrived at the boatyard. She knew that Jim, the owner, often worked late doing paperwork but it seemed he was having the evening off. Probably in the Railway. She picked her way carefully past the piles of junk and along the riverbank until she reached *LIZA*. Climbing over the gunwale she stepped into the cockpit and stood still, listening. The boat rocked gently on the river. She could hear the leaves in the trees gently ruffled by the breeze. A coot squawked nearby and an owl hooted in the distance. Tentatively she tried the door to the cabin. It opened easily. She switched on the torch she'd brought with her and shone it inside. Then she screamed and dropped it and clutched the door frame for support.

'Shh! Keep it down for God's sake.' he said. 'Come inside and close the door.' He struck a match and lit a candle.

She stood, rooted to the spot, staring at his face, ghostly in the candlelight. She couldn't believe her eyes. 'What are you doing here? I don't understand.'

'I can explain.' He pulled her towards him and went to hug her but she pulled back and began to pummel his chest.

'You bastard! I hate you, I hate you…'

He gripped her wrists and held her until her anger had subsided. 'Come in and sit down. I've got a lot to tell you.'

~O~

Russell returned to his railway carriage and changed out of his work suit. He pulled on a pair of dark serge trousers and slipped a navy-blue rollneck over his head. He put his feet into a pair of old, but sturdy brogues. The terrier danced around, convinced they were going on an adventure.

'Sorry, Ag,' he said, patting her head. 'I'm going to have to leave you here to guard the house. I need to go out on my own.' Picking up on his tone of voice she slunk off and flopped down in her basket, resting her chin on her paws. Her brown eyes stared up sorrowfully at her master, as if she'd been betrayed. 'Don't look like that,' he chuckled. 'We'll have a long walk tomorrow – I promise.'

He'd booked out an unmarked Wolseley from the police compound. Normally he would have relied on one of his junior officers to drive him – DC Weeks or WPC Sharpe. The former was still on leave, studying for his sergeant's exam, and Nettie, well, poor girl, it would be a while before she was back at work. DC Barrow had already gone home so there was no surprise or raised eyebrows that he'd chosen to drive himself. However, there would have been astonishment or, in the case of Superintendent Stout, raw anger, if they'd known where he was going.

Russell left his home, the car bumping along the stony track until it reached the smooth asphalt of the road. There was little traffic and he was soon speeding up the A21 towards Hurst Green, the headlamps forming two pools of white light ahead of him. He'd travelled this way many times and knew that there was another gateway, a little further along the road from the gatehouse and main entrance to Sowsden Manor. He'd calculated that this was probably the access to the walled garden, used for bringing in compost, plants, and so on. He hoped he was right. Once through the village, past the Pashley turn and the main entrance, he slowed and looked out for the gateway. Sure enough, a pair of tall wooden gates appeared in the lamplight. He pulled off the road, killed the engine and sat for some minutes, letting his eyes acclimatise to the dark. Getting out of the car he closed the door quietly. When headlights appeared from the north he panicked slightly and crouched down by the side of the Wolseley. He could feel sweat prickling on his skin as the lights grew brighter. It was a false alarm – the car carried on past without slowing, its engine note fading as it disappeared. He relaxed and stood up straight again.

The next task was to get through the gate. There was a large metal ring on the latch. He lifted and twisted it. Much to his surprise it turned easily, there was a metallic click and the door swung inwards. He allowed it to open far enough so he could he slip through, then closed it carefully behind him. Although there was a gibbous moon there was also intermittent cloud cover so he switched on the small, but powerful torch he had brought with him, keeping the beam low. Knowing he had entered on the east side of the garden he turned and followed the wall, being careful where he put his feet. He reached the lean-to shed. Feeling in his pocket, his hands close round a bunch of keys. Not just any old keys but a particularly special set he'd confiscated from a cat burglar some years before and had failed to hand in. Now he was glad he'd hung on to them. Gripping the torch between his teeth he tried several of the keys in the lock until, with a satisfying *click* it opened. Quickly he entered the shed and pulled the door closed behind him.

He stood still for some moments, listening.

Nothing – not a sound.

Realising he'd been holding his breath he exhaled then breathed normally. He shone the torch round the room. It was obvious that he was in a potting shed. A waist-high bench stretched the length of the front side. In the centre was a large shallow box filled with compost. To one side were several dozen terracotta pots, lying on their sides, nested together. On the other side were brown seed packets, with contents hand-written in blue ink. Turning the torch toward the opposite wall he could see a number of different shaped trowels hanging from hooks in a neat row. Below were spades, forks and other long-handled tools, the polished woodwork of the shafts gleaming and the metalwork shining in the torchlight. He could see several pairs of leather boots and rubber wellingtons lined up under the bench. Crouching he pulled out a pair and shone the torch into the space beneath. There was more dust here, crumpled newspaper and some shards of broken pots. He put the boots back in their place. Standing upright he shone the beam round again.

On the far end wall hung a calendar. Russell recognised the picture as a reproduction of one of Rowland Hilder's paintings, showing a bucolic landscape of gently rolling countryside and distant oast houses. Then his eye was attracted to an untidy pile of hessian sacks on the floor below. He walked the length of the shed and knelt down. With a feeling of anticipation he crouched and started pulling them aside. He wouldn't have been able to explain it to anyone but he had a sense that he was about to make a discovery. Superintendent Stout would dismiss it as one of his *feelings* but he hoped, as had often happened in the past, that it would prove to be more than that. His optimism was rewarded when he pulled the last sack aside and a woman's black lace-up shoe was revealed. He grinned. He just knew that it belonged to Nettie and its discovery connected it unequivocally to Sowsden. However, his euphoric bubble slowly deflated as he realised the truth. He wasn't supposed to be there. In fact, he was breaking the law. He sat back on his heels and heaved a sigh. What to do? If he took the shoe back to the station he would have to explain how he came to find it. When he did it would be certain that he'd be hauled over the coals. But worse than that, the discovery would be deemed as inadmissible evidence in court. Reluctantly, he pushed the shoe back and carefully rearranged the sacks as he'd found them. Standing up again, he brushed dust off his trousers. Somehow he was going to have to find a way to return – legally.

# Chapter 17

*Chanel No. 5* *was the first perfume launched by French couturier Gabrielle "Coco" Chanel in 1921. It was chosen as a scent that would appeal to the flapper and celebrate the liberated feminine spirit of the 1920s.*

**THE FOLLOWING** morning a police car arrived outside Nellie's house. She had dressed carefully, choosing a navy, knee-length skirt and a coat to match. Her red hair was tied back with a velvet bow and she wore no makeup. PC Beaumont, the driver assigned to collect her, asked if she would like to sit in the front with him. She declined, saying she would rather sit in the back, and the journey passed with barely a word between them. When they arrived at Collinghurst General, he escorted her along the corridor to the anteroom and handed her over to John Crooks.

'Thank you for coming, my dear,' the pathologist said. 'I appreciate this must be hard for you.'

Nellie sniffed and dabbed at her eyes with a white handkerchief. 'That's all right,' she mumbled. 'It's the least I can do for poor Sid.' This brought on another bout of crying.

Crooks waited until her sobs had died down. Gently he took her hand and led her into the mortuary. When they reached the slab he reverently peeled back the sheet, revealing the young man's face. Looking earnestly at her he asked: 'Is that Sidney?'

'Oh God! Yes, that's him.' And the tears flowed again.

The pathologist quickly folded the sheet back and led her out of the room. Beaumont had been replaced by PC Lees for the return journey and he escorted her to the car. Again she elected to sit silently in the back. When he dropped her outside her house she gave him a whispered 'Thanks.' He didn't see the sly smile creep across her face as she made her way up the garden path.

~O~

Russell was true to his word. He was up with the lark to take Aggie for the promised walk. But his motive wasn't totally selfless. He'd woken, after a night of restless, broken sleep, feeling just as confused as when he'd reluctantly left Sowsden Manor empty-handed the evening before. A brisk walk was just what he needed to clear his muzzy head. He set off across the coarse grass of the neighbouring meadow. The terrier dashed ahead, scattering surprised rabbits that scuttled into the safety of their underground burrows, and they were soon clambering up the steep bank that buttressed the sea wall.

Once over the top it was a slip and a slide down the shingle on the other side and out on to the flat sand, exposed by the outgoing tide. The small dog loved it – running in huge circles and making a dash for the seabirds lined up where the sea met the beach. A curlew, more nervous than the rest, took off long before she got anywhere near. It flew in an arrow-straight line, with fast, strong wingbeats and a mournful cry, the rising glissando so typical of the bird. Oystercatchers, piping as they flew, were close behind. Just the herring gulls left it until the last moment, lifting into the air, almost casually, and curving round in an arc then touching down further along the beach.

Russell strode out, heading east. In the distance he could see the breakwater that protected the entrance to the estuary that led to Compass Point. The tide was turning and the waves started to creep across the beach forcing him to move closer to the shingle bank. He could see a fishing boat, battling out against the incoming tide. It reminded him of the curious case from a couple of years before that revolved around two German brothers. The old boy in The Smuggler had mentioned earlier that he'd been a deckhand on *Moonshine*, the boat the brothers had owned. He smiled to himself when he realised that the boat he could see was close to the position where they had overcome *Moonshine* and Wolfgang was finally captured.

For once, Stout had not interfered in the case and the little German was taken into custody and later convicted and sent to prison. There was no doubt that he had aided his much larger and stronger brother, Wolfgang, in the killing of ex-Nazis but Russell couldn't help feeling a little sorry for him. Not only was he quite severely disabled, he had also suffered the cruel loss of a beloved brother during the war. But, when all was said and done, he was still involved in murder and, if it were not for a trick of fate, he would have added Russell's loyal DC, Johnny Weeks, to the three men he'd helped to kill.

Thoughts of the Superintendent brought him back to his current dilemma. Namely, how to return to the walled garden at Sowsden and legitimately find the shoe he'd left hidden there. How could he persuade Stout to agree to it? He stopped and watched the boat as it rose and fell on the swell. A flock of gulls rose and fell in time, anxious to scavenge any fish scraps that might be jettisoned. After a few moments of observing it he slid back his cuff and peered at his watch. Gosh! He'd lost all track of time and if he didn't hurry he wouldn't get any breakfast before heading for the station. The tide had now crept swiftly to the bottom of the shingle bank, forcing him to clamber up the stones and set off back home, walking along the top of the ridge.

As he walked he turned over various options in his mind. Stout had flatly refused to agree to issuing a search warrant – most likely because he didn't want to upset David Peters. But, perhaps he could try a different approach – one that the Super might approve. Now what was Stout's biggest concern? Getting into the horticulturalist's good books, mostly. And how could Russell help him do that? By finding his wife. That would be a good move. The trouble was, judging by what her friends had told him, he was almost certain that she'd gone off on a jaunt and would reappear in her own sweet time. But – Stout wasn't convinced. So if Russell was to double his efforts to find her, that would please him. And if Russell suggested they look for clues round the grounds of Sowsden Manor, he would be bound to agree that it was a good idea, wouldn't he? With that thought, he increased his stride, eager to get back, have breakfast, then put the suggestion to his boss.

~O~

No one was more surprised than Douglas McDonald himself to realise that he had lasted another night under canvas. His mattress was thin and the ground was hard but he'd slept better than he had for as long as he could remember. He'd had plenty of time to think and had come to the conclusion it was because, for the first time in months – if not years – he was free from worry. Worry about work, which he'd grown to loathe; worry about money; worry about his marriage, which had grown sour; worry about trying to maintain a position in polite society. He grinned to himself as he realised how happy he was, living this simple life. But, as much as he was enjoying it, he knew he would have to make a decision about the future – and soon.

Not only had his food almost run out but the small amount of cash he'd managed to hang on to wasn't going to last very long.

Something had to be done – he couldn't survive much longer here, however relaxed he felt. It was time for action. He sighed. He supposed he would have to get a job. Not as an accountant, oh no. He was done with that world. Perhaps something menial, something that came with accommodation. As much as he enjoyed his current freedom he couldn't live in a tent for ever. Perhaps a position in a hotel? That would at least give him bed and board, wouldn't it? And if he was prepared to take a lowly post, surely no questions would be asked? Questions about where he'd come from, what he'd done before. Well, he thought, there was no time like the present. So, with that intention, he started collecting his few belongings and prepared to strike camp.

~o~

Pollard sat disconsolately in his borrowed office. DC Gordon sat on the opposite side of the desk, not sure what to say. He'd listened to the DS rave on, for what seemed like hours, about how it was so unfair. How he'd been convinced that the blasted antique dealer was guilty of killing Barrett and was just about to nail him for the crime. Then that blasted Russell had demolished his case and given him the name of the probable killer. Fat lot of use that was though. Blasted Daniel Floyd had absconded and no one knew where he was. And now, it turns out it might not even have been him. Unless he could come up with some new clues the case was dead in the water – and so were his chances of retiring with a feather in his cap *and* a decent pension.

'So if it wasn't Fountain and the prints found inside the gloves didn't belong to Floyd, who are we looking for?' Gordon ventured tentatively.

Pollard rubbed his head violently with both hands and when he took them away, what little hair he had was standing up in all directions. 'How the hell should I know?!' he screeched. 'Haven't you listened to a word I've said?'

'Of course, sir.' The violence that the DS had directed at him made him sit back in his chair and squirm. 'I was just asking…'

The wind seemed to go out of Pollard's sails. 'Sorry. I know it's not your fault, I'm just finding it so bloody frustrating.'

~o~

In contrast, Russell was feeling happier than he had earlier. When he'd tentatively suggested to Stout that it might be an idea to search for clues as to the disappearance of Rose Peters the Super had jumped at the idea. Russell was doubly surprised as he knew it was a paper-thin excuse.

'Good man,' the Super said, beaming. I'll get on to Peters straight away.' With that he picked up the telephone. 'Get me David Peters, please,' he said to the telephonist. Russell found the grin on his face rather unnerving. In a few moments Stout spoke again.

'Ah, David. How are you?' A pause. 'Yes, I'm sorry about that. I've hauled him over the coals. He understands that he was out of order.' He winked at Russell, which was even more disturbing than the Cheshire cat-like grin. There was another pause while the Super listened to the other man, then: 'Look, old chap, to make up for his earlier gaffe, Russell has agreed to come over to the Manor and see if there are any clues relating to your wife's disappearance.' Stout frowned. 'No, no. It would just be him and a detective constable. Of course. I'll make damn sure that he uses a softly, softly approach. The last thing I want to do is upset you.' Stout listened for a while. 'So that's all right? Fine. I'll send them over this morning.' He put the phone down.

'He agreed then?' Russell enquired.

'He did. Good plan of yours. But for heaven's sake don't muck it up. I can't afford for you to upset him again.'

'You can rely on me to be discreet, sir.'

'I bloody well hope so. Now get going before I change my mind.'

~O~

Russell couldn't help grinning as he left Stout's office – his ruse had worked. Now they'd be able to search legitimately and if anything turned up connected with the attack on Nettie… He put his head round the door of the constables' office.

'Barrow? Get a car out of the pool. We're off to Sowsden Manor.'

~O~

On the way over Russell filled the DC in on what had happened the evening before.

'A bit risky, wasn't it, sir? Going in at night like that.'

'I suppose so.'

'But you think the shoe you found belonged to WPC Sharpe?' Barrow asked as they drove though Hurst Green.

'I'm certain. I'll leave you to "discover" it. It'll look more natural like that.'

'How come only two of us are going? It's a big place to search.'

'Superintendent Stout is concerned about upsetting Mr Peters. I'd rather have gone in mob-handed, but the two of us should suffice as I know what we're looking for.'

'Where are we going to search?'

'I've thought about that. There's little point looking in the Manor itself. It's unlikely there will be any evidence there and I don't think Peters would thank us for tramping all over his house. But, we'll definitely make a thorough search of that potting shed.'

'What about any other outbuildings?'

'I don't recall seeing any others within the walled garden. Do you?'

'No, I don't think so.'

'I don't know about elsewhere in the grounds. We'll ask and see what comes up.'

~O~

The tyres of the Wolseley crunched on the gravel as they travelled slowly down the drive. Barrow brought the car to a halt outside the Manor. There was no sign of the Land Rover so Russell went straight to the back door and knocked. After a brief wait Mrs Floyd appeared. Her face was drawn and her skin looked sallow.

''Ave you found him?' she asked. 'Daniel.'

'I'm afraid not, Mrs Floyd.'

'Why are you 'ere then? Why ain't you looking for 'im?'

Russell gave her his most sympathetic smile. 'There are any number of officers out there at the moment. Stations have been alerted and rest assured we'll find him very soon.' He paused and waited for her to speak. When she folded her arms and set her mouth in a thin line he continued. 'However, we're here to try to see if we can find some clues to your mistress's disappearance.'

'Well you won't find any in the 'ouse.'

'That's all right. We weren't planning on coming in. We want to look in any outhouses. I rather hoped Mr Peters would be here to show us round.'

''E's gone out. Said 'e 'ad business to attend to.'

'That's a shame.'

'Dearborne is 'ere though.'

'Ah.'

''E's probably in the kitchen garden. You know your way. If that's all?' Without waiting for a reply she turned and closed the door.

The head gardener was indeed in the walled garden. His sour expression told them he was far from pleased to see the two detectives. 'Oh, it's you,' he growled. 'The boss said you might turn up. Whadderyer want?'

'We'd like to take a look in the outhouses – see if we can find any clues to the disappearance of Mrs Peters,' Russell said, his voice mild and non-committal.

Dearborne grunted. 'You can look, but you won't find nothin'.'

'All the same…'

There's only one shed 'ere.' He nodded towards the lean-to. 'It's unlocked.' With that he turned on his heel and disappeared into the glasshouse.

They made their way to the building and Russell pushed the door open. Although light came in through the windows it was diffused and weak so they both switched on torches.

'Over there,' Russell said quietly, nodding towards the far end of the shed. Barrow made his way and crouched down, carefully lifting the sacks. He seemed to be taking longer than Russell expected. He was starting to get a feeling of dread. 'What is it lad?'

'It's not here, sir.'

'It must be. It was there last night.'

I'm sorry, but it's not. Come and look.'

Russell joined him in shaking out the sacks. 'You're right. Bugger! Someone must have moved it.' There was anger in his voice. 'How the hell did they know it was there?'

'We can't ask, can we?'

'Annoyingly, we can't.'

'What do we do now?'

'Well, we can't let Dearborne know. Better show willing and find out if there are any other outbuildings.'

'There's just the tennis pavilion,' he said when Russell asked. 'Go out of the gate and turn left. Doubt you'll find anything though.'

The pavilion was an elegant single-storey structure with weatherboard sides and a pegtiled roof. Along the front was a raised veranda overlooking an asphalted tennis court with a high mesh fence around it. The court was obviously well-maintained, with a smooth, dark green surface and crisp white lines. They climbed up the broad steps to the pavilion and walked into the main building. Along the back was a low wooden bench with a row of coat hooks above it. From one hung a towel, from another a cream-coloured jumper. Several pair of tennis shoes were pushed untidily under the bench.

'What's through there, sir?' Barrow asked, pointing to a door.

'Let's find out, shall we?'

The door opened into a cloakroom. There were two washbasins with mirrors above, a lavatory and a tiled shower cubicle with a curtain, half pulled across. Another towel was bundled up in the corner, but apart from that there was nothing else.

'Looks like it's been a wasted journey,' Barrow suggested.

'I reckon you're right, lad. It's rather frustrating.' They were just about to leave the building when something caught Russell's eye and he stopped. 'Hold on, what's that?' He knelt down by the bench and pulled the tennis shoes aside. 'Well I'll be…' By moving the shoes he'd revealed a small burgundy valise. 'If I'm not mistaken this is a piece of luggage that was missing from Mrs Peters' walk-in wardrobe. I wonder what it's doing here.'

He undid the clasps and opened the lid. Inside was a notebook and gold pen; a pair of spectacles in a case; a neatly folded and pressed handkerchief; a packet of extra strong mints. There was also a matching make-up bag. Russell opened it. 'This *is* strange,' he said.

'Why's that sir?' Barrow asked.

Emptying the contents out he spread them on the bench. Among the items was a lipstick, a powder compact, a mascara wand and a small bottle of Chanel No 5 perfume. 'I find it hard to believe that any lady, especially one of Mrs Peters' standing, would go anywhere without these. It just doesn't make sense.'

'Perhaps she has an identical set in another make-up bag,' Barrow suggested.

'It's possible, I suppose. But in my experience women only tend to use one set of everything and, I think, this is the clincher.' He held up the pale gold cylinder. 'Lipstick is very personal to the user. I can't see her going anywhere without this.' He pulled off the cap to reveal the vivid scarlet tip. 'Just her colour I would imagine, if her car is anything to go by.'

'Oh?' The DC's brow wrinkled.

Russell smiled at his confusion. 'Apparently she drives an MGA sports car – bright red.'

'I see.'

Russell stood for some time, not looking at the objects but just staring into the distance. Barrow waited patiently, aware the DI was turning things over in his mind. Finally he spoke. 'You know what this means.'

'What's that, sir?'

'I think I've been wrong all along.'

'About what?'

'About her disappearance being innocent.'

'You don't think that she's gone off on a jaunt?'

'I don't. I'm starting to get a sinking feeling that something has happened to her – something unpleasant.' He linked his hands behind his back and began pacing the length of the changing room, turning at the end and walking slowly back. 'I think Nettie must have discovered some crucial detail about Mrs Peters' disappearance. I'm convinced she was here, at the Manor, found out something she shouldn't have and was stopped before she could go any further.'

Barrow had sat down on the bench, his chin in his hand. 'That's why she was bashed over the head?'

'Yes.'

'But why did they bundle her into the boot of Weeks' car and then dump it? Why not finish her off?'

Russell shuddered. 'That would have been a step too far. The thought of the gallows would put anyone off. I suppose whoever did it hoped a connection between the place where the car was found and the Manor wouldn't be made.' He let out a big sigh. 'The trouble is, without any evidence the link *can't* be made. If only we'd found that shoe...'

'But we didn't. I wonder who did move it?'

'If Daniel Floyd was still on the scene I would have put money on him but as he's disappeared it can only be Peters himself – or Dearborne.' Russell stopped pacing and started putting the items back into the make-up bag. 'Somehow we've got to find something more – some sort of connection. Anyway, I think we're finished here. Let's return to the station.' He put the bag back in the valise and tucked it under his arm. 'We'll take this with us,' he said, as he descended the steps. As they turned the corner of the pavilion Barrow stopped.

'Hello, what's this?' he said. Surrounded by trees and shrubs there was another building attached to the back of the pavilion. 'Looks like a garage, sir.'

'It certainly does.'

Across the front were three wide wooden doors, linked together. They were suspended from a metal rail and sitting in a channel at the bottom. The end door was secured with a heavy steel padlock. Russell gave it a shake but it was firmly locked. Along the top of the doors was a row of narrow windows. Barrow, being the taller, tried to peer through but they were just too high. He looked around. Crouching he pulled a thick tree stump out from under a laurel bush, placed it in front of a door and carefully climbed on top. Putting his hand either side of his eyes he peered through the glass.

'What can you see lad?'

'Not much – it's bit gloomy. Here. You have a look.'

Russell took his place on the stump. Inside he could make out a couple of vague shapes covered with dark tarpaulins. He rubbed at the dirt on the window pane with his hand, but it made little difference. He was just about to climb down when he stopped. 'Wait a minute!' he said excitedly. 'Have another look. Tell me if you see anything strange.' He made way and Barrow got back up.

'Well they're obviously cars. One big one, probably a saloon of some kind. The other is much smaller. A sports car? Hold on!' Excitement had crept into his voice too. There's a hole in the cover. I can see part of the wing.'

'What colour is it?'

'I think it's red. Yes, bright red.'

'The colour of Mrs Peters' lipstick?'

'Yes. So could that be her car?'

'If it is then Peters has been lying to us all along. Come on, let's get Dearborne to open up for us.'

They found the gardener in the glasshouse potting up plants. But when Russell asked if he could unlock the garage he looked decidedly shifty. 'There's only one key and Mr Peters keeps it on 'im,' he said.

Russell frowned. Why? What's so special about it?'

'Oh, er, 'e stores 'is 1930s Bentley in there – doesn't want anyone touching it.'

'And is that the only car in there?'

Dearborne was lost for words for a moment but quickly recovered. 'I think 'e might be lookin' after a car for a friend.'

'I don't suppose you know what sort of car?'

'Dunno. I ain't seen it.'

'I see. And when will Mr Peters be back?'

The man shrugged his shoulders. 'Can't say. 'E comes and goes as 'e pleases. I ain't 'is keeper.' Dearborne's voice had turned surly.

'Well let him know we'd like to see inside the garage when he returns.'

Dearborne nodded and turned back his work.

'I reckon he was lying about the key,' Barrow said.

'I'm convinced of it,' Russell agreed.

'He knows what's in there, doesn't he, sir?'

'As sure as eggs is eggs. I'm going to have to take this to the Super.'

'What will you tell him?'

'I'll have to confess to coming here last night and tell him about the shoe. He'll blow up at first, but with this…' he'd picked up the valise. 'And with the car, I reckon I can convince him to change his mind about a warrant. Then we can search this place properly.'

# Chapter 18

*A **rail motor** has a locomotive at one end of the train, connected by some form of remote command to a driving trailer, equipped with a control cab, at the other end of the train.*

**DOUGLAS McDONALD** finished packing up his gear, sat down on his haversack and unfolded the Ordnance Survey map he'd brought with him. He remained firm in his decision to find a job, the lowlier the better, but where? He was close to Hastings but finding employment there could prove risky. Although he didn't think his old employer, Thomas Staggs, would bother to pursue him for the piddling amount he'd fiddled from the books, the police might be looking for him closer to home. So, it was prudent go further afield. What about Eastbourne? Hastings was close enough that he could walk there but Eastbourne... He traced the distance on the map with his finger. Wow! He'd be lucky if he made it in a day – and that would be without the pack on his back. No, there was no question that he could walk that far. Plus, he reasoned, there would be a much greater chance of being spotted on foot, so for that reason alone, it was out of the question. What about the train? Hmm. It would be far too risky to march into the station at Hastings and buy a ticket. If they were still looking for him there was bound to be a police presence. But how about a minor station? He looked more closely at the map. Following the line from Nottery Quay to Hastings his finger stopped at Three Oaks. That had to be a small station. May not even be staffed. And it was only about three miles cross country. He could make that comfortably in an hour or so. Right. He folded the map so that his route was clear, stood up and shouldered his pack.

The first part of his journey was such hard toil he almost chucked his knapsack away in frustration. He had to clamber up steep inclines over loose rocks and soil, several times almost losing his balance as the weight of his knapsack overwhelmed him and he ended up on his knees. Each time he got to his feet, he cursed the load, but wisdom prevailed. He might need his equipment if he failed to find a roof for the night, so he struggled on. Once at the top he breathed a sigh of relief, sat down again on his pack and took a deep draught of water. Below, the English Channel was azure blue, reflecting the sky. Consulting the map he saw that he would have to head just west of north. He looked at the little brass compass he had brought with him, then over the road and could see a waypost marking a footpath on the other side. He scuttled quickly across Fairlight Road and dropped down into the path. The going was much easier as it descended gently between trees and undergrowth. He was feeling quite positive and even managed to hum a little tune as he walked.

When he'd been walking for half an hour he could see that there were houses ahead and as he didn't want to risk being spotted he pushed through some woodland on the right, climbed over a fence and into a fallow field. Keeping to the edge, he walked along its length, climbed over another fence and found himself close to the edge of a road. He looked at the map and was pleased to see that he was still headed in the right direction. Waiting until a car had passed, he crossed quickly, over yet another fence, and strode out across a field of waving grass and into a dense wood.

After battling through the trees, stumbling over roots and brambles he'd lost his sense of direction but pressed on, vaguely heading northwest. Another half an hour and he was convinced that he was walking in circles and was completely lost. Frustrated he sat down again. He wasn't cut out for this Boy Scout lark. Why didn't he just give himself up and accept the consequences? The worst they could do was bung him in prison for a few months. At least he'd get a roof over his head and three square meals a day. Then he thought about Heather, and shuddered. Oh God, no. He'd have to face her wrath and that was the last thing he wanted. Misery started to descend. He put his head in his hands and felt like weeping. Then he heard a distant sound that changed his mood in an instant.

A train whistle! And close by.

Getting up he grabbed his pack and started running in the direction the sound had come from. The trees thinned and he found himself standing on a low embankment. The noise of a train approaching grew louder, the wheels pounding on the metal rails and smoke streaming from the chimney as it passed and slowed. He watched as it drew to a stop, just beyond an overbridge. A single door slammed, a whistle was blown and with a short 'toot', the train was off again. He'd found the station. Clambering down the bank he walked along by the side of the track, stumbling over the uneven ballast but feeling quite jubilant. When he reached the platform he climbed up the steep ramp and stood, grinning. The train he'd seen was obviously travelling north. Which meant, hopefully, that another would soon appear heading south. There was a bench on the platform so he settled down to wait. He didn't have to wait long. After ten minutes he heard a distant "toot" and stood up in anticipation. As the train came into view he was baffled. He'd expected to see the smokebox of a locomotive, instead the flat front of a railway carriage came towards him. As it drew closer and slowed he could see a large, round brass bell and beneath, a figure wearing a peaked cap, staring through the screen. The engine appeared to be at the other end of the train, facing in the opposite direction. As the train stopped the head of a uniformed man appeared from an open window in one of the carriages.

'Do you want to get on?' he asked.

'Please,' McDonald replied.

'Well hurry up then. We're running late.'

Stirred into action, he pulled one of the doors open, climbed aboard and with a judder, the train set off again. McDonald sank down gratefully onto the moquette seat. Almost immediately the uniformed guard was standing beside him.

'Where to?' he asked.

'Er, Eastbourne?'

'You'll be lucky! This train only goes as far as Hastings – you'll have to change.'

Panic started rising in McDonald's throat. He didn't want to go anywhere near a mainline station. That was the whole reason he'd gone across country. 'Isn't there a stop before Hastings?' he asked, trying to keep his voice steady.

The man sighed. 'Next stop is Ore. You can get a connection there – if you must.'

'Right. A single to Eastbourne then please.'

There was another sigh, more heartfelt, as the carriage swayed and the man swayed with it, like the captain on the bridge of a ship at sea. He found the relevant ticket. 'Three and tenpence.' McDonald gave him two florins and waited while the man fished around in his leather bag for the change.

After he'd been handed the coins he said: 'Can I ask a

question?'

'I suppose so.'

'Why's there a carriage at the front and the engine at the back?'

The man snorted. 'It's a rail motor. Now you'd better hurry and get off. This is your stop.' McDonald stood again as the train came to a halt. Only a few minutes had passed and he was alighting already. He stood on the platform looking round. A porter came towards him, pushing a sack barrow with a large wicker basket balanced on it.

'Can you tell me how long I've got to wait for the Eastbourne train, please?' McDonald asked.

The porter lowered the barrow, pulled a fob watch out of his pocket and consulted the dial. 'Twenty minutes.' He nodded his head, put the watch back in his pocket and carried on with the barrow.

There were a handful of passengers spread along the platform but none took any notice of him. He found an unoccupied bench and sat down to wait.

When the train arrived this time, there was no locomotive, it was all electric. He climbed up into an empty compartment, lifted his pack on to the luggage rack, made himself comfortable on the seat below and settled done for the journey. In a few minutes the train was pulling into Hastings. He sunk his chin on his chest and half-closed his eyes, hoping people would assume he was asleep and not disturb him. But he was aware of the door opening, someone struggling to get in and the door finally closing again. As the train pulled away he risked a sneaky glance through his eyelashes at the passenger who had invaded his privacy. He could make out the form of a buxom young woman, surrounded by shopping bags. She made quite a performance of settling herself at the other end of the opposite seat, making sure her purchases were safely tucked around her legs. He observed all this through half-closed eyes. He could see that, although she was a little rounded, she had a pleasant, open face, with a slight blush to her cheeks, which might have been as a result of her efforts. The train got under way and after a few minutes she gave a little cough, apparently trying to attract his attention.

'Excuse me.' Her voice was light with a musical lilt.

He made the pretence of waking. He gave her a weak smile and answered slowly. 'Yes?'

'Don't suppose you've got a light?' She had a cigarette in the crook of her finger and held it out towards him.

'Of course. Just a minute.' He fumbled in his jacket pocket and brought out a box of matches. Taking one from the box he struck it and held out the burning end towards her. She put the cigarette between her lips and leaned forwards. He couldn't help but notice her deep cleavage revealed by a low-cut top. She drew hard on the cigarette, leaned back, took out it of her mouth and exhaled a long plume of grey smoke.

'Cor! I needed that!' she exclaimed.

'Had a bad day?' he asked.

She giggled; a pretty bubbling sound. 'No, not really. Just my sister's kids.'

'Oh?' Despite himself, McDonald was intrigued by this pretty woman. He'd thought at first that she was just a girl but could see that she was older, not far off his age.

She drew on her cigarette then laughed again. 'That's where I've been – to visit my sister.'

'In Hastings?'

'That's right.'

'So you don't live there?'

'God no!' she exclaimed. 'Wouldn't be seen dead in that dump. Can't wait to get home.'

'So where's home.'

'Eastbourne,' she said, sitting a little more upright. 'Well, I say home, I'm actually living in a hotel.'

At this McDonald's ears pricked up, but determined not to show his interest he replied coolly: 'Oh, really? What do you do?'

Another giggle. 'A bit of everything, really. It's only a small place – family run really. I suppose I'm a chamber maid but I do other things.'

'Like what?'

'Oh, Sometimes I'm on reception. I like that – I can get dressed up, put on a bit of lippy. Now and again I help in the kitchen. I like that too, 'cause I can sample the food. I like my food.' She arched her eyebrows and grinned. 'What about you? What's your job?'

He thought quickly. 'Me? Oh, I'm between jobs. That's why I'm going to Eastbourne – looking for work.'

She took one final drag, dropped the butt and ground it out with the toe of her shoe. 'What sort of work are you after?'

He shrugged. 'I'm not really fussed. I thought about something in a hotel.'

'Really?' She leaned towards him, displaying her cleavage again. 'Anything in particular?'

'Something simple – just to get my hand in like.'

Her smile widened into a broad grin that showed a set of even white teeth. 'I might be able to help you there.'

His heart was thumping, and not just because he found her particularly attractive. He tried to sound nonchalant. 'How's that?'

Without being asked she changed sides and sat down next to him. 'You're in luck. Danny's just left.'

She was so close he could smell her perfume and the faint scent of cigarette smoke. 'Danny?'

'Yes, he is, or rather was, the odd-job man – did a bit of everything: washing up, shopping, taking the laundry, repairs around the hotel.'

McDonald frowned. 'What's happened to Danny – has he died?'

'Oh you!' she punched him playfully on the arm. 'Course not – he's only young. He was called up. Got to do his National Service. Didn't want to go but had no choice.'

'And you reckon there might be a job going?'

'I'm certain of it. They won't be able to do without someone for long. It's been busy this season. You interested?'

'I could be. Is it live-in?'

'Oh yes. Danny had a pleasant little room at the top of the house.' She paused and looked earnestly at him. 'You seem like a nice man. I could put a word in for you. If you like.'

'That would be wonderful, thank you.' He smiled to himself. It looked like he had fallen on his feet. 'Listen, I don't even know your name.'

'It's Mary.'

He held his hand out. 'Pleased to meet you, Mary. I'm David.'

~o~

When Russell got back to the station he was frustrated to find that the Super was in a meeting and he would have to wait before he could ask for the search warrant. So he sent Barrow off to do some paperwork while he sat in his office, thinking. He leaned back, linked his fingers behind his head and turned the new information over in his mind. If it was indeed Rose Peters' vehicle in the garage then it was most unlikely that she had gone on a jaunt. She was an independent woman and would hardly have set off without her beloved sports car. So where was she? He had to admit that he'd been barking up the wrong tree all along. How could he have been so badly mistaken? It was times like this when he really missed having Johnny Weeks around. The lad would frequently offer an insight into the case that brought a fresh approach and often paid dividends.

The more he thought about it the more he realised that Peters was just too good to be true. In retrospect, Russell was now sure that the horticulturalist's vague manner and woolly answers had been far too contrived. It seemed the man probably wasn't such a bumbling duffer after all, but a skilled actor.

Unless it was Dearborne? Russell hadn't warmed to him from the moment he met him but just thought that he was a grumpy boor and hadn't considered that he could be in any way connected with the woman's disappearance. The discovery of the valise and the sighting of the car in the garage put a different spin on things. And Nettie. Had she discovered something about Rose Peters – something that she shouldn't have seen? It all started slotting into place. The trouble was, there was no way of finding out exactly what had happened but also, at present, no way of proving it, if he did.

But he mustn't forget the other, much more likely suspect – Daniel Floyd. Could it have been him all along – not just stabbing Sidney Barrett, thumping Nettie, but being responsible for the disappearance of Rose Peters as well? The trouble was, Russell just couldn't imagine him doing it all on his own. If it was indeed Floyd, he had to have an accomplice. But who? Peters? Judging by what he had been told about their relationship, it wasn't beyond the bounds of possibility for the horticulturalist to support the lad. But in the killing of Barrett? That seemed quite a stretch. Or was it Dearborne? His manner suggested that he didn't have time for Floyd, but that could have been a bluff.

He needed more evidence so he could question them properly, not at Sowsden, where they were on familiar ground, but here at the station, where he could get them on the back foot. Russell realised that he was going to have to put a convincing proposition to Stout in order to get him to agree. He sat up in his chair, unscrewed the cap of his fountain pen and began jotting down notes. After half an hour he'd roughed out what he wanted to say and hoped it would be sufficiently convincing. There was a light tap and Lewis put his head round the door.

'Can I have a word, Sonny?'

Russell smiled. 'Sure. Come in and sit down.'

'This is a bit awkward.' The fingerprint man squirmed in his seat. He looked more discomfited than the DI had ever seen him.

'What's the problem?'

'Fingerprints.'

'Well, that is your speciality,' Russell observed wryly, grinning at him.

'I know. That's what makes it so embarrassing.'

'Come on, you can tell me. I won't hold it against you.'

'It's not funny, Sonny. It's serious.'

The DI's smile faded. You'd better tell me then. A problem shared, etc.'

'That's why I've come to you first.'

Russell nodded. 'I appreciate that. So what is it you want to share?'

'I've made a monumental blunder.'

'That's certainly not like you.'

'It isn't. I pride myself on being meticulous. I don't know how I missed it.' Lewis took a deep breath then exhaled slowly before he spoke again. 'You know we found traces of fingerprints in the gloves that were discovered in the warehouse in Nottery?'

'That's right – but they didn't match Floyd's.'

'No. And there's a good reason for that.'

'Oh?'

Lewis took another deep breath. 'I can only think the confusion has come about because of the change in personnel – DI Parker starting with the case and having a heart attack – then DS Pollard taking over…'

'…And not very well.'

'True. But it's something *I* should have spotted.'

Russell was wondering where this was going. 'You're obviously embarrassed by this but I am your friend you know.'

'More than embarrassed – mortified.'

'Come on, tell me the worst.'

'The body Fountain found isn't that of Sidney Barrett.'

Russell's eyes widened and he started. Even Aggie, asleep under the desk, sat up and gave a gruff little bark. 'What! Whose is it then?'

'Daniel Floyd.'

'Say that again.'

'Daniel Floyd,' Lewis repeated, miserably. 'Flossie Floyd's stepson.'

'How can it be? The description fitted Barrett perfectly.'

'Not all of it.'

'How so?'

'The details of the description *did* fit, except for one fundamental thing.'

'What was that?'

Lewis opened the folder that he'd brought with him and laid it on the desk. He took out a sheet of paper and handed it to Russell. 'Read this.'

*"The victim is five feet ten inches in height, of medium build with dark hair, a pale complexion and hazel eyes. He is clean shaven. He is between 18 and 25 years of age. Distinguishing mark is a tattoo reading "ELVIS FOREVER" and a badly drawn face with an elaborate hairstyle on his left upper arm. He has an old scar running down his right leg, from his knee to his ankle. He has all his own teeth, although they are in poor condition."*

After reading it carefully Russell looked up. 'I'm baffled. It certainly seemed to fit Barrett.'

'Except for one thing.'

'Which is?'

Lewis took the paper back and ran his finger down the page. 'Here. "*He has an old scar running down his right leg, from his knee to his ankle.*" But he hasn't.'

'Are you sure?'

'I've just been over to the mortuary to see John Crooks and we examined the corpse.'

Russell leaned back, digesting this startling new information. 'Yes, but what makes you think the body belongs to Daniel Floyd?'

'His fingerprints. We had them on file from when he got arrested for stealing. Somehow no one bothered to check. Pollard and Gordon were convinced that it was Barrett, they convinced us too, and we all went blissfully along with them.'

'But his girlfriend, Nellie Gwynne, identified the body.'

Lewis shook his head. 'She must have been lying.'

'But why?'

'Who knows?'

'We need to talk to her. She's guilty of perverting the course of justice.'

'Sonny,' Lewis said patiently, 'We've been here before. It's not your case. I only came to you as a friend. I've got to take this to

Pollard – and to the Super now. Heaven knows how *he's* going to react.'

'I'm waiting to see him too. I suspect he's going to be in an even worse mood than usual after I tell him what I've found out.'

'Sounds ominous. What's happened?'

Russell detailed his visits to Sowsden Manor, both the clandestine and the legitimate one. How he'd found the shoe, that almost certainly belonged to Nettie, and how it had disappeared overnight; the discovery of the valise with the make-up bag in it; the car in the locked garage, covered with a tarpaulin but showing a flash of red. He told him about his suspicions, that Peters, Dearborne or Floyd were involved in the disappearance of the horticulturalist's wife.

'Who do you favour for it?' Lewis asked.

Russell shook his head and took a sharp in breath. 'I'm really not sure. Could be any one of them. But there's definitely a cover-up going on so I'd be surprised if they weren't all involved in some way.'

'What's your next move?'

He tapped the page in his notebook. 'I'm going to present my findings to Stout and hope there's enough to persuade him to raise a search warrant. With any luck we'll find enough so we can haul Peters and Dearborne in for questioning – away from familiar territory.'

'But this still begs the question, if Floyd is the victim, who killed him?'

'That is a puzzle. And how does Sidney Barrett fit into it?'

Lewis frowned. 'There's got to be a connection – two people with the same tattoo is just too much of a coincidence.'

'I know. This case is getting more puzzling by the hour.' Russell pulled his sleeve back and looked at his wristwatch. 'Stout should be out of his meeting by now,' he said.

'Right. I'll go and break the news to Pollard, you see the Super first. Do try not to upset him though. I've still got to have an audience with him.'

~O~

The Superintendent sat stony-faced while Russell gave his rehearsed report. When the DI had finished, Stout remained immobile for some minutes. He didn't speak at first but reached for his tin of cheroots and made a performance of selecting one then lighting it with his Zippo. He inhaled deeply then blew a thick column of blue smoke towards the ceiling. He stared at Russell with his beady eyes for a long moment.

'So you're telling me you made a mistake about the disappearance of Rose Peters all along?

'I'm afraid so, sir.'

Stout shook his head sadly. 'How could you have got it so wrong?'

'I don't know. It just seemed so obvious that she'd gone off on a trip and would return as if nothing had happened.'

'And you think this ties in with what happened to the WPC?'

'Nettie Sharpe? Yes. I think she made a discovery but, before she could report it, someone found her and tried to silence her.'

'But you have no evidence that she was actually there,' the Super stated.

'At the moment, no. She's still heavily sedated.'

'Then she hasn't said anything.'

'She briefly came round and spoke to one of the nurses.'

Stout leaned forward, an eager look on his face. 'What did she say?'

Russell frowned. 'It didn't make a lot of sense. Here.' He took the piece of paper Wickstead had given him out of his pocket and passed it to the Super.

*Miss Sharpe said to tell Inspector Russell*
*look for the manner of sick plants.*

Stout studied it for some moments, his brow furrowed and his lips moving silently. 'No, it doesn't make a lot of sense.' He looked up. 'Are you sure this is exactly what she said?'

'That's what the matron told Wickstead.'

'But what if it got garbled in translation – like Chinese whispers?'

'What do you mean, sir?'

'The WPC spoke to a nurse who passed it on to the matron. She rang the station, and telephone lines aren't always that clear, are they?'

'True. So what are you suggesting?'

Stout concentrated hard. 'Well... instead of saying, "*look for the manner of sick plants*", what if she said, "*look **at the Manor** for sick plants*"?

Russell actually struck himself on the forehead with the palm of his hand. 'Ye gods! Why didn't I think of that? Of course!'

'*Of course*, what?'

'The plants. I thought there was something odd.'

'Explain.'

'When Barrow and I went to look round we passed the vegetable beds. As you'd expect, the crops were very healthy, but in the middle of one bed the leeks and carrots looked decidedly sickly. I didn't think much about it at the time as I had other things on my mind, but looking back it was more than strange. By all accounts Peters not only has green fingers but is known for the wonderful plants he grows. I just can't see him allowing something like that to remain.'

'Perhaps they'd been sprayed by mistake?'

'Possibly, but I would have thought he'd have had them straight out and replaced with healthy plants.'

'So you think that's what Sharpe saw?'

'I'm convinced of it now.'

'The trouble is, finding some sickly plants proves nothing on its own.'

'But the car in the garage…'

'*If* it does belong to Rose Peters.'

'I'm certain of it. That's why I need the search warrant.'

Stout took a drag on his cigar. 'I'm not happy about this. If you've got it wrong…'

'I haven't, sir. You can rely on me.'

'Just don't let me down.' He ground out the cheroot in the heavy glass ashtray. 'If you do, we'll be having words. Serious words.'

~O~

Meanwhile, Lewis was having a difficult conversation with Pollard. The DS was sitting behind the desk while his DC leaned against the wall to one side, arms folded.

The detective sergeant slouched back in his chair. 'How come you didn't spot the fingerprints?' he drawled.

'I really don't know. I can't explain how I missed them.'

Pollard was enjoying making the forensics man squirm. 'But it's your job to keep on top of these things, isn't it?'

'Mostly.'

'I would say totally.'

The normally unflappable Lewis was starting to get annoyed. 'I think you'll find that the police must take some of the blame for the error,' he said, his voice low and measured.

Either the DS didn't notice the subtle change in Lewis's manner – or didn't care, and pressed on, sitting up and saying:

'Oh no, you can't shift your guilt on to us as easily as that. Admit it – you're in the wrong.'

Lewis had heard enough. He rose from his chair, rested his knuckles on the desk and leaned so far forward he was only a few inches from Pollard's face. His voice was barely above a whisper. 'If you hadn't insisted that you'd found the murderer then perhaps it wouldn't have been missed.' He leaned even closer. 'Think about that,' he hissed. He stood upright, turned on his heel and marched out, leaving the door swinging on its hinges.

~o~

The confrontation with the Superintendent was no more harmonious.

'How the hell did you miss it?' he thundered.

'I can't explain, I'm afraid. But I wasn't the only one.'

'What do you mean?' Stout's brow was lowered, like an angry bull. 'It's *your* job to notice.'

'I know, but in my defence, DS Pollard convinced everyone, including me, that the body was Barrett's.'

Stout gave a short, sharp snort. 'Don't worry, I'll be having words with the detective sergeant.' His anger seemed to dissipate a little. 'So let me get it right. This leaves us with a victim that everyone – including you – thought was the murderer.'

'That's how it seems.'

'And a murderer who has disappeared without trace.'

'I'm afraid so.'

Stout shook his head sadly. 'What do we do now?'

'I think that's for you to sort out with Pollard – sir.'

'And I think you're right.' His mood softened further. 'Listen. I understand your dilemma and thank you for bringing this to me. You're rarely wrong, and never careless, but this is one monumental cock-up. You'd better tell Pollard to come in now.'

~O~

It took a few minutes before the DS knocked tentatively on the door. By now Stout was really fired up. When Pollard answered the summons to enter the office, thick smoke hit the back of his throat and reduced him to a fit of coughing. Tears sprang from his eyes and his nose ran.

'What's the matter with you?' the Super demanded.

'Sorry, sir,' he spluttered. 'It'll go in a moment.' He blew his nose and dabbed at his eyes.

He was just pulling the visitor's chair out when Stout thundered: 'I didn't ask you to sit! Remain standing!'

'Sir,' Pollard said, quivering. He couldn't have looked more miserable if he'd tried.

Stout rapped on the desk with his knuckles. 'Listen. I called you in on this case as a favour – for old time's sake. It would have been a real accolade for you – before you're put out to grass – if you'd got it right. How the hell could you have got it so wrong?' Pollard was about to speak but Stout held his hand up to silence him. 'Quiet! That's what's called a rhetorical question. Not only have you got the murderer wrong but you couldn't even identify the victim correctly. Someone's got to go and tell Mrs Floyd that not only is her stepson *not* the suspect but that he's actually dead.'

'I can do that, sir.'

'Oh no you can't. I want someone with sensitivity to do that – and it's not you. I want you to go and interview that girl who wrongly identified the body.'

'But it's in Wateringbury, nearly all the way to Maidstone. Can't the local boys do it?'

'*No they bloody well can't!*' Stout yelled. 'If you want to come out of this with any honour you better start doing what you're paid for.'

'What's that, sir?' Pollard said miserably.

'*DETECTING!* Now clear off, find DC Gordon and get your arse up into Kent and find out why that girl lied.'

# Chapter 19

*The parish church of St Mary the Virgin in* **Nettlestead** *has links with William the Conqueror's half-brother, Odo. An Agincourt veteran, Reynald Pympe, who lived in neighbouring Nettlestead place, was so impressed with the stained glass in the church that he installed further magnificent windows.*

**THE ONLY** car left in the pool was the Ford Pilot. DC Gordon had as much trouble with it as Johnny Weeks and regularly crunched the gears.

'For Christ's sake!' Pollard snarled. 'What's the matter with you?'

'Sorry, Sarge. I'm trying to get the hang of this column change.'

'Well bloody well hurry up. You're getting on my nerves.' He slumped back in his seat and stared out of the window. The weather had changed and there was drizzle in the air, blurring the glass and rendering the passing landscape dull and featureless. The wipers slapped from side to side but the rubbers needed replacing leaving the windscreen smeary so Gordon had to lean forward to make out the road ahead. The rest of the journey was long and tedious with a sulky silence maintained throughout. As they approached Wateringbury Gordon spoke.

'Where are we going first – sir?'

'To her bloody house, where do you think?'

'I just thought…' The DC's voice trailed off.

'Well don't – just drive.'

They pulled up outside Nellie's house. Gordon switched off the engine and opened the car door. 'Listen,' Pollard said, menace in his voice. 'Let me do the talking. I don't want you interrupting.' Gordon just nodded and got out of the car. There was still a fine drizzle in the air which beaded their clothes as they walked up to the house. Pollard knocked on the door and they waited. It was only a few moments before it opened and a big-busted, rotund woman stood there, staring suspiciously at them, nervously turning her hands one over the other.

'Yes?' she said.

Pollard held his warrant card out. 'Are you Mrs Gwynne?'

'Ye-es,' she said slowly. 'Is this about Sidney?'

'It is. We'd like to speak to your daughter.'

'She's not here.'

'Do you know where she is?'

'Staying with a friend – at least that's what she said.'

Pollard let out a long sigh. He'd felt this wouldn't go well from the outset. 'Who is this friend?'

'Janice.'

'And where does Janice live?'

'Other side of the village. Near Nettlestead.'

'Could we possibly have the address?' Pollard didn't bother to keep the exasperation out of his voice.

'I suppose so.' She turned and disappeared back along the passageway. They waited, Pollard tutting impatiently, until she returned. 'Here you are. Gibbs Hill.' She held out a scrap of paper.

Pollard took it from her and, with an effort, managed to grunt: 'Thanks.' Then, turning to his DC: 'Come on. I suppose we'd better see if we can find this place.'

Back in the car, they set off along the Maidstone road towards Nettlestead. They hadn't travelled far when the DS called out: 'Stop! There it is.' He pointed to the right. Gordon stood on the brakes and peered back over his shoulder. Sure enough there was a small sign, *GIBBS HILL*. He crunched the gears once more, put the car in reverse then turned up the side road. They drove along it for half a mile, with an unkempt hedge along one side and open fields on the other, until they reached a pair of cottages. The construction was curious: red brick with parallel stripes of a lighter colour across the front. Perhaps it was a builder's idea of stylish decoration, but it just looked odd. Pollard wasn't bothered either way as he spoke. 'That must be it. I only hope this isn't going to be a waste of time, like the rest of our visit.'

The rain was falling more heavily as they stood, waiting for the knock on the door to be answered. Pollard's mood darkened as the rain soaked into his clothes. It took some minutes, and several more raps with the knocker before finally the door opened to reveal a small child, peering up at them.

'Yeth?' The child appeared to be a little boy with a lisp.

'Is your mummy at home?' Pollard asked.

The boy shook his head. 'No.'

'Your dad?'

'He's athleep.'

What about Janice?'

'She'th not here.'

The DS let out an exasperated sigh. 'Can you wake your dad up?'

'He won't be pleathed.'

'Why's that?'

'Nighth.'

'Sorry?'

'He works nighth.'

'Look, sonny. This is important. Tell him the police want to speak to him.'

The boy stood his ground. 'He'll be croth.'

Pollard was struggling to keep his temper. 'I don't care if he is cross,' he said through gritted teeth. 'Go and wake him up – now.'

The boy looked blankly at them, turned and went back into the house.

'Do you think it would be all right to step inside – get out of the rain, Sarge?' Gordon said.

'I suppose so.' They shuffled just inside the door, dripping water onto the doormat and stood for several more minutes until they heard someone clumping down the staircase. The figure of a man appeared. He was wearing a nightshirt, untidily tucked into a pair of trousers, the braces hanging down. His feet were bare.

'Who are you? What the hell is this about?' He stared accusingly at them.

Pollard held his warrant card out. 'Sorry to disturb you – sir. We're looking for Nellie Gwynne.'

'Who?'

'Nellie Gwynne. She's the barmaid at The Railway.'

'Why the hell would I know where she is?'

'We were told she was staying with your daughter.'

The man scratched at his tousled hair. 'Janice?'

'Yes, sir. I presume she is your daughter.'

'Of course she bloody well is.'

'And we understand that Nellie has been staying with her.'

'First I've heard of it.'

'So she's not here then?'

The man leaned forward. Pollard could smell his sour breath. 'Listen. I don't know this Nellie Gwynne. If she's a friend of my daughter, *I've* never met her and I can assure you she's not staying here. Now, can I get back to bed? I've got to be up in a few hours to work another shift.'

After the front door was shut the two detectives dashed back to the car. The rain was heavier than ever and they were dripping wet.

'What do we do now, sir?' Gordon asked, as the car windows rapidly steamed up.

'I don't bloody know. I just knew this would go badly the minute we left Colllinghurst.'

'We could ask at the pub,' the DC suggested.

'I suppose so. Might just as well, while we're here. Although I doubt we'll have any luck.'

They drove back to the village, Gordon frequently wiping the condensation off the windscreen with his hand. They pulled up outside The Railway. Pollard turned to the DC. 'You go and ask. I'm staying here. It's bound to be a waste of time.'

Gordon got out of the car and walked up to the pub. He tried the door but it was locked. He pulled the sleeve of his raincoat back and looked at his wristwatch. Rain spattered the face. Ten-forty-five. He banged on the door.

'Go away! We're not open yet.' A voice drifted from inside.

'It's the police,' Gordon shouted. 'We need to speak to you.' There was a pause of a few moments while rain dripped off the brim of his trilby. Then the noise of bolts being slid back and the door opened. The landlord peered out.

'Bloody hell! You look like a drowned rat. Come in, for Christ's sake.'

Gordon stepped over the threshold.

'Can I get you something? A brandy or a hot drink?'

Gordon took off his hat and shook his head. 'It's tempting, but I'd better not. The guvnor's waiting in the car.'

'Fair enough. What can I do for you?'

'We need to speak to your barmaid.'

'Nellie?'

'Yes.'

'Oh. I haven't seen her for a couple of days. Not since her boyfriend was found dead.'

'I see.'

'Can't really blame her. Was quite a shock.'

'Well that's the thing,' Gordon said.

The landlord cocked his head to one side and gave the policeman a quizzical look.

'I'm not sure I should tell you this. But I suppose it will come out sooner or later. It wasn't his body.'

'What?'

'The body she identified. It wasn't Sidney Barrett.'

'Who was it then?'

'I'm sorry. I'm not at liberty to tell you.'

'But she was sure about it. I saw her after she got back from identifying the body. She was really cut up.'

'Well she was mistaken. The fingerprints on the victim showed it was someone else.'

'I don't understand. How come she got it wrong?'

'That's what we wanted to talk to her about.'

'I see. Have you tried her house?'

'Yes, we were there earlier. And we went to a friend's. No one has seen her.'

The landlord shook his head slowly from side to side. 'I'm sorry I can't be more help.'

'Well if you do see her, can you let us know?'

'Of course. Now are you're sure about that drink?'

'No. Thanks anyway.' Gordon put his hat back on and made his way to the car. Once inside he told Pollard what the publican had said.

'Said it would be a waste of time. She's obviously buggered off without telling anyone. Bet she knew we'd be after her. Come on. Let's get back to Sussex.'

Five minutes after they'd left, Bert, the landlord, opened up the pub for the lunchtime trade. His first customer was the owner of Bow Bridge Marina, his blond hair darkened by the rain and smeared across his scalp. He took off his waterproof and hung it on a hook by the door.

'Filthy weather, Jim,' Bert said.

'You can say that again.'

'What can I get you?'

'A whisky – and make it a double.'

The landlord frowned. 'Bit early for spirits, isn't it?'

The yard owner scowled. 'Normally yes. But I've had a bit of a shock.'

Bert pushed a glass up under the optic. 'Oh yes?'

'Some lowlife has stolen one of my boats.'

Handing him the glass he said: 'That's a bugger.'

'Worse than that – it's *LIZA*.'

The landlord looked blankly at him.

Jim took a gulp from the glass and smacked his lips. 'The one Sid was living on – the lad they found dead.'

Bert stared at him. 'I don't believe it. The police were here just now, talking about him.'

'Why, what did they want?'

It wasn't him that was killed.'

'Bloody hell! I thought that girl, Nellie, identified him, didn't she?'

'Apparently she got it wrong.' Bert said.

'I don't understand.' A puzzled frown crossed Jim's face.

'Neither do I. And that's not the only thing.'

'Oh?'

'She's missing too.'

Jim drained his glass. 'You'd better give me another.'

'Are you sure?' Bert asked.

He considered for a moment. 'Perhaps not. Better make it a pint of bitter.'

When the landlord had pulled the pint, placed it in front of him and put the money in the till, he sat on a stool behind the bar. 'Are you going to tell the police about the boat?'

Jim supped from his glass. 'I suppose I should. I was going to wait and see if anybody along the river had seen it.'

'Odd that the girl has disappeared at the same time.'

The yard owner drank some more beer and looked thoughtful. 'If it wasn't Sid that they found dead, then he's still out there somewhere.'

'I suppose he is,' the landlord agreed. 'Hey. What if *he's* taken the boat?'

'Mmm. That's a thought.'

# Chapter 20

*In the mid-nineteenth century, brewer Ralph* ***Fremlin*** *did not approve of public houses. Instead, he produced bottled beer for the home trade, believing it could be consumed in moderation more easily, delivering bottles door-to-door with a horse and cart.*

**'ARE YOU** sure we should be doing this?' Nellie asked.

Sid let out a big sigh. 'Of course I am, love. I *had* to get away. You didn't have to come with me, you know.'

She snuggled up to him. 'I'd go anywhere with you. You know that.'

'Here. Let go of my arm or we'll hit the bank!'

Nellie moved a little way away. 'Sorry! It's just… I love you.'

'I know.' Sid smiled and twisted the wheel, correcting their course.

Barrett had been desperate to get away. He knew it was only a matter of time before the police came after him. They had set off in *LIZA* the previous evening, just after dark, heading downriver towards Maidstone and Allington Lock. Here, Barrett knew, the freshwater river ended and the tidal Medway began. He was aware that the craft was not meant to be used in a seaway but felt confident that, if he was careful and avoided any strong tidal flows, he should be able to navigate the rest of the river and eventually find his way into the estuary. He'd told Nellie that they would head up the Thames and find somewhere to stay. But he had another plan. One he wasn't going to share with her – for now. He knew he wouldn't be safe staying in the country but figured that if he could get to Europe he could disappear. He had an idea that if he picked the right time, when the sea was calm, he could cross the channel to France. But, for now, the goal was to get to Allington, and through the sea lock.

There had been a fretful moon, with thin cloud obscuring it from time to time, and he'd motored slowly, keeping to the centre of the river, avoiding craft moored at the sides. When they reached Teston lock he was relieved to find that the last boat through had come up river so the lock was full of water and it was only a matter of minutes before they were underway again. They passed under Teston Bridge and were into the countryside. Navigation was almost impossible here, as trees crowded the river, deepening the shadows, so he decided to moor up for the night. Once the boat was secure, he closed the curtains and lit the oil lamp. He was too rattled and Nellie was too excited to eat much but he forced himself to heat some baked beans and toasted bread under the grill. They shared a bottle of brown ale that Nellie had got from the pub.

Sitting either side of the little table they each picked at their food. 'We're going to have to be careful,' he said. 'It won't be long before Jim realises the boat is gone.'

Nellie looked alarmed. 'How long do you think we've got?'

'Well, I know he had a lot of paperwork to do so he'll probably spend most of his time in the office. Plus he usually makes straight for the pub at the end of the day. *But* he might decide to take a stroll along the bank.' He shrugged. 'So there's no way of telling. Hopefully he won't notice tonight so, if we get away early tomorrow, we'll be well on our way before he sees that the boat is missing.'

He didn't sleep much, his mind churning. The events of the last couple of days filled his thoughts and in the morning he was up as soon as it became light enough to see. He crept out of his bunk, leaving Nellie sleeping in hers. Starting the engine he set off down the river. It was less than four miles to East Farleigh and, for a while, he enjoyed the solitude as the boat motored along. Nellie poked her tousled head out of the cabin as they were approaching the lock.

'Morning sleepyhead,' Sid said, forcing a grin.

She yawned. 'What time is it?'

'Just after five.'

'Bloody hell.'

'Language! Listen. If you can take the wheel while I do the lock gates we should get through quickly, then you can go back to bed.'

'Okay.' She stepped into the cockpit and kissed him on the cheek. He put his arm round her and pulled her close to him. 'Thanks for coming with me.'

Again, luck was on their side. They were through the lock in no time and Nellie went back to her bunk. Travelling down the river, chugging along at a steady five knots, he was able to concentrate on nothing but the journey for long periods but, every so often, he was brought up short by the enormity of what he had done. He shuddered and shook his head. He couldn't undo the past – he could only move forward.

It was so early there were no other boats moving on the water. A pair of pristine white swans drifted past, swimmingly majestically by the bank with a line of mottled grey cygnets following behind; a coot shot across the river in front of *LIZA* and disappeared into the reeds; a pair of mallards paddled furiously, wings flapping, until they took off, quacking noisily. Under other circumstances he would have enjoyed taking photographs of them.

For a while, the banks remained tranquil, just meadows and trees, dotted with the occasional dwelling. On the left, the railway line ran parallel. An early commuter train rattled noisily by, the wheels clickety-clacking on the rail joints. It was close enough for him to see figures in the carriages. Then it was gone and the only sound was the burble of the boat's engine. He had taken the precaution of filling two five-gallon containers with fuel so knew it would be some time before he would have to buy any more. By then he should be well away from the Medway, Jim, the boatyard owner – and the police.

As he got closer to Tovil more houses and businesses appeared on the banks with boats tied up alongside. His anxiety level started rising but still, his was the only craft out on the river. They passed under the footbridge and were soon in Maidstone proper. A sharp bend in the river brought the Bishops' Palace into view. A little further on his nose picked up the malty tang of roasted barley and hops, coming from the Fremlins Brewery. He passed by the collection of industrial buildings. Tied up alongside were a couple of Thames sailing barges sitting low in the water, piled high with wooden barrels. He smiled. He knew these flat-bottomed craft could safely navigate the tidal waters of the Medway so felt more confident that *LIZA* could follow in their wake. Soon the buildings along the banks dwindled and they were back in wooded countryside. The cabin door opened and Nellie appeared, holding a mug out to him.

'Where are we?' she asked.

Sid took the mug. 'Thanks for the tea.' He took a sip, steering the boat with one hand. 'We're well on our way. Already through Maidstone.'

She sat down on the seat across the stern of the cockpit. 'That's good. When do we get to that lock where we meet the sea?'

'You mean Allington. That's where the tidal part of the river begins, but it's a long way from the sea.'

'Oh.' She drank from her own mug.

'We can't go through that lock on our own. It's not like the others, it's much bigger. There will be someone there to open the gates for us. I just hope Jim hasn't raised the alarm yet.'

Nellie's eyes widened. 'Do you think he might have done?'

Sid looked at his watch. 'I doubt it. It's not yet six o'clock. He's never in that early. I should think we've got a good chance of getting through and well on our way before he notices.'

She sat quietly for a while as the boat slid past the craft moored along Ford Wharf boatyard. 'Didn't you say something about getting the tides right?'

'I did. We have to be there between three hours before high tide and two hours after.'

'And will we?'

'Yes. I've timed it so that we should get there just after slack water. Then we'll have the tide with us, but not too strongly, when we've gone through the lock.'

She reached out and squeezed his arm. 'You're so clever.'

He shook his head. 'I'm not so sure about that.'

~o~

Russell sat in his office feeling frustrated. The promised search warrant had not materialised. Apparently there was some sort of complication in court and the magistrate who was supposed to be signing it had been busy all morning. He decided to go to see Stout once more to find out if it had been issued at last. Just as he was walking along the corridor to the Super's office, Pollard came bustling into the station and tried to push past him.

'Hold on,' Russell said, grabbing his arm. 'What's your hurry?'

'I need to speak to the Superintendent – straight away.' He shook the DI's hand off and marched on. Russell followed him as he stormed into Stout's office.

'What the hell…?' The Superintendent's eyes blazed.

'I need to speak to you,' Pollard announced.

'This had better be good.'

'Our witness has disappeared,' the DS stated baldly.

'Say that again,' Stout growled.

'Nellie Gwynne. She's not there.'

Stout reached for his cheroots, not taking his eyes off the sergeant. 'Explain.'

'We went up to Wateringbury, like you told us to. She wasn't at home and the landlord of the pub where she works hasn't seen her for a couple of days. What do I do now?'

'What about the boatyard?' Russell had been standing quietly in the doorway.

'What's that?' Stout demanded.

Russell stepped into the office. 'The yard where Sidney Barrett lives on a boat. If he's not dead, and she's his girlfriend…' He left the sentence unfinished.

'Well?' The Super stared at Pollard. 'Did you ask there?'

The wind went out of the DS's sails. He hung his head and wrung his hands. 'No, sir.'

'No sir? Why the hell not?'

'Didn't think of it,' Pollard mumbled.

'For Christ's sake! I told you to track down the girl and find out why she lied. It should have been simple enough, but once again you've cocked up. Now get out! I want to have a talk with a *proper* detective.'

'But…'

'Out! Now!' Pollard turned and slunk out of the office. If he'd had a tail it would have been between his legs. Stout looked at Russell. 'Take a seat inspector. I think we need a serious discussion.' Russell sat while Stout busied himself with his cigar. Once it was going to his satisfaction he looked up and said: 'Tell me your thoughts.'

The DI considered, staring into space for a long while. His body was still but his mind was whirring like a slot machine. Images of Floyd's bedroom; the warehouse where the body was dumped; the fleeting glimpse of a figure running into the woods, they all tumbled through his mind. His conversations with Nettie's father and Edna Button; what Mrs Floyd had told him about her boys. What if? Suddenly his thoughts slotted into place.

CLUNK, CLUNK, CLUNK.

A row of gold bars lining up in the machine. Jackpot! He focused on Stout, excitement in his face. Leaning forward the words came tumbling out.

'We're pretty sure that the victim is Flossie Floyd's stepson, Daniel, not Sidney Barrett. But we don't know who killed him. Doesn't it seem strange that the two should have been so easily confused? The height, the build, the distinctive Elvis tattoo. *What if they're brothers?*' His eyes sparkled.

'I'm sorry, you've lost me.'

'Flossie Floyd had another son. There was a falling out and he went off. Although they were only stepbrothers I've been told that they were so similar that they could have been twins.'

'But the name – Sidney Barrett?'

'He must have changed it when he moved away.'

Stout frowned. 'I still don't understand.'

'Look.' Russell tapped on the desk with his forefinger. 'Nellie Gwynne deliberately wrongly identified the body. If, as I'm starting to feel certain happened, Sidney, or whoever he is, told her to, it can mean only one thing.'

'Which is?'

'*He* killed Floyd.'

It was Stout's turn to sit in stunned silence. He sat, his cigar forgotten as it smouldered in the ashtray. He stared at the DI. Finally he spoke. 'He murdered his brother?'

'We don't know that. It could have been a fight that got out of hand, so possibly manslaughter. Either way, we need to find him.'

'You're right, we do. What a mess. I shouldn't be saying this to you but if Pollard had done his job properly this wouldn't have happened.'

'I can't comment,' was all Russell said.

'What do you suggest we do?'

'I'd offer to go to Wateringbury to make enquiries but, as you know, I've got my own investigation to follow. There's no point in sending Pollard there again; I think we need to find Barrett as soon as possible. Why not contact the local force and get them to ask questions?'

'Good plan. I know the Super there. I'll get on to him right away.'

Russell nodded. 'About the warrant…'

'Oh yes. I'll do that too – try to track down the magistrate.'

'If you would, sir. I'd like to search the place before any more evidence goes missing.' Russell was just getting up to leave when he paused. He turned to the Super. 'It was Barrett at the gatehouse.'

'Sorry?'

'We thought it was Daniel Floyd who ran away into the woods. But it couldn't have been – he was dead.'

# Chapter 21

*A **meerschaum pipe** is made from the mineral sepiolite, sometimes found floating on the Black Sea. When smoked, meerschaum pipes gradually change colour – shades of yellow, orange, red, and amber from the base on up.*

**IT WAS** nearly midday before Stout finally called Russell into his office. 'Sorry, Sonny. I've only just got hold of the magistrate. If you drop by the court you can pick up the warrant.'

Russell was just walking out the door when he turned. 'What about Barrett?'

'Not good news I'm afraid. The local boys went round to the yard and discovered that the boat he'd been living on has disappeared.'

Russell's eyes widened. 'When did it go?'

'They don't know. Apparently Jim, the boatyard owner, only noticed this morning. They found him drowning his sorrows in the local pub. He *said* he was going to report it, but hadn't got round to it.'

'Then Barrett has got away?'

'So it would seem. They've put out an alert along the Medway, west to Tonbridge and east to Maidstone. They're confident that someone will spot the boat before it gets very far.'

A bluebottle buzzed lazily round the lightbulb.

Russell looked thoughtful. 'Isn't there a lock near Maidstone where the tidal river begins?'

'Yes, that's right. At Allington.'

'So theoretically he could go through the lock and head out towards the Thames estuary?'

'Theoretically, yes.' Stout looked down at the paper on his desk. 'But I understand that the boat, LIZA, is only suitable for use on the non-tidal part of the Medway.'

'Yes, she'll be a river boat – flat bottomed.'

'So I understand.'

'Let's hope they find him before he tries it then.'

~O~

Nellie discovered how clever Barrett was when they reached Allington lock. As the boat approached the gates they could see a sign proclaiming:

**LOCK CLOSED**
**NEXT OPENING**
**7am tomorrow**

'What!' he exclaimed. 'That can't be right.' He manoeuvred the boat to the side, grasped a ring set in the quay wall and sounded the boat's horn. After a few moments a youth appeared on the towpath leading to the lock. The lad was about 12 or 13 years old, tall and as thin as a beanpole.

'Can't you read? Lock's closed!'

'But it's high tide now,' Barrett protested.

'Sorry mate. You've got it wrong. Tide's going out now.'

'I don't understand...' As the boy turned to go Barrett called out. 'Hold on. 'We really need to get through.'

'Not my problem.'

'Can't you just open the lock for us?'

''S'not my job – my dad's the lock keeper.'

'Where is he?'

'You're too late. He's gone to the café for his breakfast.'

'Listen.' Barrett beckoned to the lad who sidled reluctantly over to the side.

'If I make it worth your while, could you let us through the lock?'

The boy's eyes narrowed. 'How much?'

'Half a crown?'

'You're joking.' He started to turn away again.

'No wait. How much do you want?'

'Ten bob.'

'What?'

The boy folded his arms. 'Take it or leave it.'

Nellie tugged at Sid's sleeve and spoke for the first time. 'Go on, give it to him.'

Grimacing, he reached into his pocket and pulled out a ten-shilling note. He held it out. In one swift movement the boy bent down and snatched it from his hand. 'Ta. Don't blame me if the tide's running fast when you get through,' he said, laughing, and walked away.

After a few moments, when the only sound was a duck quacking back up the river, there was the whine of machinery and the gate on their side creaked open. There was just enough room between the lock wall and the gate on the other side for Barrett to manoeuvre LIZA into the lock. No sooner were they in than the machinery whined again and the gate closed behind them. Then the paddles were opened and the water level started dropping rapidly. Barrett held on to a chain, hanging from the lock wall.

As they plummeted lower and he had to hold the chain further down it became slimy with weed and it was as much as he could do to hold on and stop the boat being sucked towards the further gates. The water boiled and swirled – the boy must have opened the paddles fully as a punishment. Finally the water settled and he was able to ease his grip on the chain. The seaward gate opened. Putting the engine in gear he moved the boat cautiously forward. They had only gone a few yards into the river when the flow caught the hull and the boat started turning side on.

Nellie let out a little squeal. 'Sid! What's happening?'

'It's the tide,' he said. 'It's pushing us sideways.'

'Do something! It's scary!'

He increased the engine revs and slowly *LIZA* turned into the stream. If they hadn't both been so alarmed, and had had time to turn around, they would have seen the youth, standing by the lock, guffawing.

'Bloody idiots!' he said out loud. 'Fancy goin' down the river in a boat like that.' He'd have something to tell his mates when he got to school. *And* he was ten shillings the richer.

Barrett didn't have time to think about the money as he wrestled with the steering, trying to keep the boat moving in a straight line. The engine was going almost flat out and they were barely keeping up with the tide. He knew the speed limit was supposed to be five knots but the way they were racing past the banks he reckoned they were travelling at nearly double that. And, to add to his alarm, the banks seemed perilously close, with huge mounds of glistening mud on either side. Nellie said nothing, just clung on to his arm. When he risked a quick glance he could see that she was as white as a sheet, her eyes wide with horror.

Somehow he managed to steer a course down the centre of the river, narrowly avoiding the treacherous banks. He knew if he hit one at this speed the boat would be almost certain to capsize and he didn't reckon much to their chances in the swirling water. The river twisted and turned and in no time they were barrelling past Aylesford Priory. He was becoming increasingly fatigued with the effort of controlling the craft and was starting to think that only divine intervention would save them from disaster. But then, whether he was so weary that he was steering the boat intuitively, or the river was widening and the speed of flow was lessening, things seemed to become easier. He gave Nellie a weak smile and her grip on his arm relaxed.

'I think it's going to be all right,' he said. 'I reckon we're through the worst of it.' This could prove to be a case of famous last words.

~O~

Russell had rounded up a couple of constables and was just going to tell Barrow that they were good to go when Wickstead called out to him.

'Sonny, I've just had the hospital on the phone. Nettie has come round and is starting to talk.'

'Thanks. That's great news. Now we'll find out what happened.' He told the PCs to wait for further orders and set off with Barrow for the hospital. As they drove along the high street he said: 'Stop here, would you? I want to get some flowers.' Barrow brought the car to a halt; Russell got out and went into the florists. He was back in a few minutes bearing a large bouquet. He smiled sheepishly. 'It's the least I can do for the poor girl.'

When they arrived at the hospital they were greeted by the stern-faced matron who looked the detectives up and down. 'If you're here to see Miss Sharpe I can allow you only five minutes. She's still very poorly and I don't want her to get tired out. Understand?'

Russell nodded. He wouldn't like to cross swords with this harridan. They were ushered into the side room where Nettie was half-sitting in bed, propped up by several pillows. Her head was swathed in bandages, the face beneath as white as the material but a smile lit up her face when she saw who it was.

'Nettie,' Russell said. 'I brought you these.' He held out the bouquet.

'Thank you, sir. That's really kind.' Her voice was as faint as her complexion was pale. Russell looked around the room. There were already several arrangements of flowers in vases on the window sill and cabinet. His face fell. Nettie noticed him looking. 'Don't worry, yours are the best. Sit down so I can talk to you.'

He and the DC pulled up chairs either side of the bed. 'How're you feeling?' Russell asked.

'I've felt better, to be honest. I've got a thumping headache but they say it will go in time.'

'Do you feel up to telling us what happened?' The DI looked concerned.

'Yes,' she said weakly. 'But I'm not sure how much help it will be.'

'The case is currently bogged down, anything has got to help. We really need to know where you were when you got hit over the head.'

'I was at Sowsden Manor.' She looked embarrassed. 'I know I shouldn't really have been there.' The two detectives exchanged a glance. 'I just had a feeling…' Nettie stopped to catch her breath, 'that something wasn't right and wanted to have a look round. I sneaked into the walled garden, through the gate on the main road. Luckily no one was around so I was able to get in unnoticed. At first I found nothing out of the ordinary and was beginning to think that I'd got it wrong, my instincts had let me down.' She stopped again and took another breath, the effort of talking taking its toll. 'Then I noticed that the vegetables in one of the beds didn't look right – they were decidedly sickly.' She grinned weakly. 'I know about these things as dad is a keen gardener.'

'Go on,' Russell encouraged and patted her hand.

Nettie frowned. 'I remember pulling up leeks and carrots… and thought it strange how easily they came out of the soil. Then it occurred to me that they'd already been lifted, then just pushed back in. I guess that had damaged the roots, so they were basically dying. I knew I was on to something and got a spade and started digging.'

'And you found a body,' Russell said.

'How did you know?'

'Instinct. I don't want to tire you but can you tell us what happened next?'

'I dug down, only a couple of feet, and the spade hit something. I knelt down and scraped the earth away with my fingers and found a hand…'

Russell couldn't contain his excitement. 'Whose was it?'

Nettie looked miserable. 'I don't know. That's when something hit me hard on the head and everything went black.'

'Have you any idea who hit you?'

'No, I didn't see who it was and I didn't hear anything. They took me completely by surprise.'

'Can you remember anything else?'

'Not really. I was vaguely aware of being picked up or dragged, then being bumped along in some sort of confined space. The next thing, I was waking up here. Sorry.'

'Don't worry, you've had a really bad time. I'm just glad you're on the mend.'

'I hope so. I want to get back to work.'

Russell grinned. 'There's no rush for that.'

She smiled back. 'I just wish everything wasn't so hazy.'

'So you don't know what happened – how you were found?'

'No, I've asked, but nobody would tell me.' She sank back into the pillow, looking even paler, if that were possible.

Russell looked concerned. 'Are you sure you're up to this? Would you like us to go?'

She gave a little shake of her head and winced. 'No, it's all right. I'd rather know.'

'If you're sure…'

The nod she gave was barely perceptible.

'Right, well, we were down at Pett Level when a call came in. Apparently Johnny Weeks' Ford Popular had been found dumped down a farm track off the Pashley Road.'

Nettie leaned forward a little. 'I remember now,' she breathed. 'I borrowed it.' Russell thought he could just discern a frown under the bandages. 'But that's strange. I thought I left it in a layby just up the road from Sowsden.'

'We think whoever hit you must have found it.'

'And the keys would have been in my pocket. But where did you find me?'

Russell was reluctant to tell her but knew she would rather have the truth. 'I'm afraid… you were in the boot.'

Her eyes widened and she let out a little gasp. 'No wonder I felt bounced about.'

'I was really concerned. You were in quite a state when I found you.'

'The doctors say I'll be okay. Apparently the injury I received is less serious than they first thought.'

'Plus you're fit and you've got youth on your side.'

She smiled. 'I suppose so. I just wish the headache would go.'

Suddenly the door opened and Jaqueline Jacques stood glaring at them. 'I said five minutes! You've overstayed your welcome. Now scoot. Miss Sharpe needs her rest.'

The two men said a hasty goodbye and did as they were told. As they were walking along the corridor Russell stopped.

'Sir?' Barrow said.

'I've just had a thought. We don't have any idea what Nettie was hit with. It would be useful to know before we search the walled garden. Let's go and see if John Crooks can tell us.'

They headed for the mortuary. The pathologist was sitting on one of the chairs in the anteroom, his head wreathed in smoke. His teeth were clamped round the stem of a Meerschaum pipe and he was puffing furiously.

Russell spluttered and waved his hand from side to side, trying to clear the air. 'For goodness sake, John, that stinks to high heaven. How do you put up with it?'

Crooks took the pipe out of his mouth and pointed towards the door with it. 'It's better than the stench we get in there sometimes!'

'I guess you're right,' Russell conceded.

'Anyway, what can I do for you?'

'We've just been to see Nettie.'

'How is she?'

'Improving, although it could be a long haul, I reckon.'

'That was quite a blow she received.'

'That's what I wanted to talk to you about.'

'Oh?'

'I know it's not your department but I wondered if you could say what was used to hit her.'

The pipe had gone out but Crooks didn't make any attempt to relight it. 'You're right, it's *not* my department.'

'That's a shame.'

'But… I just happened to be there when she came in and I had a chance to look at the injury.'

'Any idea what caused it?' Russell asked.

'Not definitively, I'm afraid. But I can say it was something heavy and flat.'

'Like a spade?'

'Quite possibly.'

'Thanks, that's a great help.'

~o~

After picking up the warrant from the courthouse they drove back to the station to collect Beaumont and Lees.

'Right lads. See if you can find a couple of spades in the store.'

Beaumont frowned. 'But sir, I thought we were going to a garden. Surely there'll be spades there.'

'Yes there will.' Russell tapped his nose. 'But I don't want you using them, we're going to collect them and give them to Lewis to examine.'

'Fair enough,' Lees said. 'We'll see what we can find.'

They were back shortly, grinning and each carrying a spade which they stowed in the boot of the Wolseley. They set off for Sowsden Manor and Russell turned in his seat and explained what they were going to do.

'I want you to dig up a vegetable bed. It's possible that there's a body buried there.' There was a gasp from one of the constables. 'But I suspect that it's been moved so I want you to sift through the soil and look for anything that might have been left behind.' He turned to Barrow, driving the car. 'You and I are going to have a look in that garage we couldn't get into before.'

'But didn't Dearborne say that Peters has the only key?'

'I'm hoping that he'll be there with it, if not we'll just have to find some other way to get in.'

As they passed the drive by the gatehouse Russell was apprehensive. He was annoyed that it had taken so long to get the warrant. Evidence could have been removed or destroyed. He would have been even more vexed if he'd known that a bright red sports car had come out of the drive and gone roaring down the road not long after they had passed the entrance.

The Wolseley pulled up outside the gate to the walled garden and the policemen piled out. Beaumont retrieved the spades from the boot and they went in. Russell marched up to the nearest glasshouse and walked inside. Peters was bending over, intent on something on the bench. He looked up, saw the policemen and scowled.

'Inspector Russell. What can I do for you?' His voice was far from friendly.

The DI held out the warrant. 'We've come to search the garden.'

Peters' scowl darkened. 'Why? What for?'

'We have reason to believe that an assault was carried out here.'

'*Who* was assaulted?'

Russell wanted to play his cards close to his chest. He didn't want to give the other man any advantage. 'I'm not at liberty to give out that information. We may also need to take away certain items.'

Peters was starting to look rattled but he kept his voice even. 'This is an outrage. I'm going to speak to the Chief Constable.'

'Feel free, sir. What we propose is completely legal and this,' he waved the warrant, 'gives me full authority.'

'Well don't expect any cooperation from me.'

'I don't – sir. In fact, I'd be grateful if you kept out of our way.' He turned to the others. 'Right, come with me, I'll show you where to dig. Barrow, put your gloves on, find all the spades you can and put them in the boot of the car.' Then turning back to Peters he said: 'Sir, when I've shown the men what I want them to do, I'd like you to open up the garage behind the tennis pavilion.'

'What? Why?'

'Just do it, will you please?'

Peters grunted and followed them out of the glasshouse. When they reached the vegetable beds Russell held up his hand. 'Wait a minute, this doesn't look right.' The bed where he'd seen the sickly vegetables had a clear space in the centre. He turned to Peters. 'What's happened here? Yesterday this bed was full. It's too early to start harvesting. What's happened?'

Peters gave a creepy smile. 'Ah, someone made a mistake and sprayed for carrot fly but the mixture was too strong. I decided to dig all the affected vegetables up and prepare for another crop.'

'I see.' Although Russell was far from convinced he made no comment. Instead he spoke to the constables. 'Right, I want you to dig over that cleared patch. Go down two or three feet and see if you can find anything.' He glanced at Peters but the man's smile remained fixed. 'Now, sir. Let's go and look in the garage.'

The horticulturalist led the way out through the other door. Russell followed him. As they walked Peters said. 'You're making a big mistake, Inspector. I've got nothing to hide.'

'We'll see about that.'

When they reached the garage Peters produced a key from his pocket and opened the padlock. 'There, help yourself.'

Russell pulled the handle and the row of doors slid easily along the track revealing the interior. He entered the garage. To his dismay there was just one shrouded vehicle and a space next to it with discarded canvas on the floor. He lifted the sheet on the vehicle to reveal a shining grey Bentley. Dropping the cloth he turned back to Peters. Russell was sure he could detect a shadow of a smirk on the man's face.

'Satisfied?' Peters asked.

A pigeon cooed in a nearby tree. Russell rubbed his chin. 'I'm baffled, sir. I understood from your head gardener that you were storing a car for a friend.'

'Correct.'

'So where is it?'

'Where's what?'

'Your friend's car.'

'Oh.' Peters looked blankly at the detective. 'He collected it.'

'I see.'

'So it wasn't your wife's MGA?'

'My wife's MGA? Of course not.' He sounded indignant. The indignation sounded real. 'What makes you think that?'

Russell just stared at him for a moment. 'Can you tell me what colour your friend's car is?'

'Colour?'

'Yes.'

Racing green, I think.'

'Are you sure?'

'Pretty sure – why?'

'No reason. Perhaps you'd furnish me with an address for this *friend*.'

Peters sighed and shook his head. 'I'm afraid I don't know.'

'That's a little odd – if he's a friend.'

'Well, I say a friend – more of an acquaintance really. You see I met him in the pub and it started to rain. His car was one of those sports jobs – without a roof. I suggested he put it in the garage and collect it when the rain stopped.'

'I see. So how did this *acquaintance* get home?'

'Oh, er, another friend took him.'

Russell knew the man was thinking on his feet and making it up as he went along but he was a convincing liar. 'Are you sure about that – sir?'

'Of course I am,' Peters blustered. 'Now if that's all, I've got work to do. Haven't you got criminals to catch, or something?'

The DI ignored him, refusing to rise to the jibe.

'By the way, have you found Daniel Floyd yet?' Peters asked.

'Didn't you know?'

'What?'

'He's dead.'

Peters' jaw dropped – his eyes widened. 'Dead? I don't believe it! How?'

Russell was enjoying the man's discomfort. 'It was his body that was found in the Morris Traveller.'

'But I thought the body belonged to that chap from somewhere up in Kent?'

'Sidney Barrett.'

'That's him.'

'No, we think *he* was the one who killed Floyd. Now if you'll excuse me, I need to check on my men, then break the news to Mrs Floyd.' Russell marched back into the walled garden, Peters trailing in his wake. The two constables were leaning on their spades. They'd taken off their tunic tops and rolled up their shirtsleeves.

Russell was pretty sure that body – if indeed it had been there – would have been moved. But he hoped they might find something. 'Anything?' he asked.

'Just this, sir,' Beaumont said, holding out a small grubby object.'

Russell took it from him. He rubbed off the dirt to reveal an earring. It was a clip-on with a pearl drop – showy but sophisticated. Peters peered over his shoulder. 'Do you recognise it, sir?' Russell asked him.

The horticulturalist shrugged. 'Afraid not. Could have come in with the compost – we buy it in bulk you know.'

'Not your wife's then?'

Peters snorted. 'Certainly not. Never seen her wearing anything like that.'

Russell just nodded. He turned to Barrow. 'Right, let's go and find Mrs Floyd.' Then to the other two policemen: 'Carry on. See if you can find a sieve. I want to know if there's anything else, however small.'

As they were walking away Barrow said quietly: 'He was a bit quick to deny that the earring belonged to his wife.'

'I noticed that too. Don't believe a word of it.'

~o~

'Mrs Floyd. Could we come in please?' They'd had to wait some time before the housekeeper had finally come to the door. She opened it a crack and peered out suspiciously.

'Oh, it's you. What do you want this time?'

'If you'd just let us in?'

'I suppose so.' She opened the door further and walked down the corridor, letting the detectives follow behind. The house smelled of lavender furniture polish. They reached the kitchen and she turned towards them, arms folded tightly against her bust; lips set in a thin line. 'Well. What *do* you want?'

'It might be an idea if you sat down Mrs Floyd.'

She pulled herself up. 'I'm fine standin', thank you.'

Russell knew when he was beaten. He took his hat off and held it in both hands. 'I'm afraid we've got some bad news.'

'You've found Daniel.'

'Well, in a manner of speaking.'

'What do you mean by that?'

Mrs Floyd. Daniel's dead.'

'What? How?'

'He was killed.'

'Who by?'

'I really think you should sit down.'

Automatically the woman pulled a chair out from the table and slowly lowered herself on to the seat. 'I don't think I'm going to like this.'

Russell walked round to the other side of the table and sat opposite her. 'This is rather difficult. 'I'm afraid the body that was found in the boot of the car in Nottery belonged to your stepson.'

The housekeeper's hands flew up to her face. 'I don't believe it.'

'I'm sorry but it's true.'

She slowly lowered her hands and clasped them in her lap.

'I've got some more bad news.' Russell's voice was quietly measured. 'I think he was killed by your son.'

'I don't understand.'

'I need to ask you something.' She stared at the detective. 'Did the boys both have the same tattoo?'

'Yes, it was Elvis,' she snorted. 'Wasn't very good.'

'And did one of the boys have a scar on his leg?'

'My son – my real son did.'

'But not Daniel?'

'No. My lad had a nasty accident on 'is bike. It 'ad some of them metal pedals. 'E were going too fast, came off the bike and somehow the pedal scraped all down 'is lower leg – blood everywhere.' She looked alarmed. 'Have you found him?'

'Mrs Floyd. I don't think you told us your previous married name.'

'It was Lane.'

'Not Barrett?'

'No. Why would you think that?'

Russell glanced at DC Barrow, who was standing to one side of the housekeeper. 'We think we've found your son, but he's changed his name.'

'What do you mean?'

'A lad, fitting his description, has been living on a boat in Wateringbury in Kent.'

Mrs Floyd gave him a puzzled look. 'What makes you think he killed Daniel?'

Russell had no concrete evidence that Barrett *had* killed his stepbrother; he was just relying on his gut instinct. He couldn't tell the woman that. 'I'm afraid the evidence points towards him,' was his noncommittal reply.

'But why?'

'It may not have been deliberate; may just have been a fight that got out of hand.'

She said nothing, just stared – stunned.

'We really need to find him.'

'I thought you said 'e was living on a boat some place in Kent?'

'That's right. He was.'

'*Was*?'

'The boat's disappeared. We think he's taken it and gone with his girlfriend.'

'*Girlfriend*? What do you mean?' This was too much for the poor woman to take in.

Russell explained as gently as he could about Nellie Gwynne and her deliberate misidentification of the body. 'Would you be prepared to come down to Collinghurst to confirm that it is your stepson, Daniel Floyd?'

At this, her face crumpled and big fat tears rolled down her cheeks. She rummaged in her housecoat pocket, brought out a large handkerchief and buried her face in it.

~o~

'Right,' Russell said to Barrow as they walked back towards the kitchen garden. 'You go and see how Beaumont and Lees are getting on. I want to find out more about this.' He took the earring out of his pocket. 'I think I know someone who might be able to identify it.'

He strode through the walled nursery. The two PCs were still sifting soil but there was no sign of Peters. Going out through the road gate he got into the police car. In a few minutes he was turning into the drive of Edna Button's elegant house.

'Inspector Russell. How nice to see you again – do come in. I hope you've come to tell me that you've found Rosie. I knew she'd just been off on one of her jaunts.' She spoke over her shoulder as she led the way into the drawing room.

'I'm afraid not. We still haven't found her.'

'That's a shame – please sit down.' She held her hand out towards one of the armchairs and took a seat in the other.

'I'd like to show you something.' Russell held out the earring.

As she took it from him she let out a little gasp. 'Where did you find this?'

'You look like you recognise it.'

'I do. It's Rosie's.'

'How can you be sure?'

'Because I gave it to her.'

'I see.'

'You haven't told me where you found it.'

He took it back from her. 'No. I'm not sure if I should.'

'Oh? Why?'

Russell sat quietly for a moment. He knew it wasn't prudent to share information with a member of the public, but he liked this woman. He'd warmed to her when they first met and liked to think that she was trustworthy. He made a decision.

'Listen,' he said, his voice low and earnest. 'This really must not go any further.'

She nodded solemnly. 'I understand.'

'We found it buried in the walled nursery at Sowsden manner.'

Her hands flew to her face; her eyes wide. 'Oh God! Do you think she's dead?'

Russell shrugged. 'We can't be certain but it's starting to look that way.'

'If she is dead, do you know who killed her?' She was sitting perfectly still her complexion chalky white.

'I can't say.'

'Do you mean you won't say?'

'No, I really don't know. I have my suspicions but need more evidence.'

'Could it have been Daniel Floyd?'

'I don't know,' Russell replied. 'And we can't ask him.'

'What, not until you find him?'

'Oh, we've found him.'

'You have?'

'We have, but he's dead.'

'No!'

'It was his body that was found in the car.'

Puzzlement crossed her face. 'I don't understand. I'd heard he was the one who committed the crime.'

'We were led up the garden path – given a deliberately false identification.'

Her brow furrowed. 'It doesn't make sense. How could that happen?'

'I think I've said enough. I'd be grateful if you keep this to yourself – for now. I think it will come out into the open very soon, but meanwhile I'd like it kept quiet.'

Her face softened. 'I quite understand. I appreciate you telling me.' She leaned towards him and placed her hand on his. 'You can trust me to be discreet.'

She was so close he could smell perfume or scented soap. He found it quite unnerving. She let go of his hand and sat back in her chair. He inwardly breathed a sigh of relief. Isobel Bailey was the only woman for him. 'Thank you,' he said. He started to rise. 'I'd better go. Thank you for identifying the earring.'

~O~

'Sorry, sir, we couldn't find anything else,' Beaumont said.

'We sieved every bit of soil – and there was nothing,' Lees added.

Russell was twisted round in the passenger seat of the Wolseley as they were leaving Sowsden Manor. The two constables sat in the back, still in their shirtsleeves, their hands and arms blackened with soil. There were muddy streaks on their cheeks and foreheads. They both looked exhausted. 'I know you did your best. At least we found the earring.' As he turned to face forward the radio crackled into life.

*'Calling all cars, calling all cars. Anyone in the vicinity of Pashley Road. There has been a car crash.'*

Sonny picked up the microphone. 'DI Russell here. We're a few minutes away. Will attend.' Barrow swung the car off the A21on to the B2099 and put his foot down. 'Any more details?' Russell asked.

*'Negative. A member of the public phoned it in. You'll be the first on the scene.'*

After a mile or so a man stood by a Land Rover flagging them down. Barrow braked hard; Russell put his hands on the dashboard and braced himself. There was something lying in the road. As the car rolled to a halt they could see it was the body of a deer.

The man had a broken shotgun over his arm. As he got out of the car Russell said: 'You're Mr Clements, aren't you? The farmer who found the abandoned car in his lane a few days ago?'

'That's right. Most of this is my land. I was just going to check on some sheep when I saw this poor blighter. He had broken legs so there was nothing for it but to put him out of his misery. Shame but there it is.' He shrugged.

Russell felt a wave of irritation and spoke brusquely. 'I understood there'd been a car crash.'

The man seemed dazed, lost in another world. He didn't answer at first. Then he shook his head and focused. 'Sorry?'

He was obviously in shock. Russell addressed him more gently. 'The car?'

'Oh, of course. It went through the hedge.' The DI looked where he was pointing. There was very little sign of damage. Clements saw him looking. 'Tough things, these native species. It's bounced back up. I didn't realise at first, then I smelled petrol.' He put his shotgun in the back of the Land Rover and pushed through the hedge. Russell was close behind, followed by the other policemen. The ground fell away and there was a car, the bonnet wedged at an angle between two trees. But not just any car – a red sports car.

Russell gasped. 'I don't believe it!'

'It's an MG,' Barrow announced.

Russell sniffed the air and felt a rising panic. 'We've got to get whoever is in there out. With the petrol leaking it might go up at any time.' He and Barrow scrambled down to the driver's side, the two constables did the same on the other.

Barrow started heaving at the door. He grunted with the effort. 'It's jammed! We need a lever or something to get it open.'

There was a shout from the other side. 'We've opened this one!' Lees said. The two detectives scrambled round and between them they got the passenger out of the car. It appeared to be a woman, wrapped tightly in a bedsheet. They laid her on the ground and loosened the fabric. The exposed face was streaked with soil, the nostrils clogged with mud, the closed eyelids crusted with dirt.

'Oh God!' Russell said. 'It's Rose Peters.' His worst fears had been realised.

Barrow held his fingers to her neck. He shook his head, sadness filling his eyes. 'She's dead, sir.'

Beaumont clambered back in the car. 'The driver's stuck,' came his muffled voice. 'He's alive, but in a bad way.'

'We've got to get him out.' Russell's voice had an edge of urgency.

'But what if he's seriously injured? We could make it worse,' Barrow said.

'We'll just have to risk it. I reckon the smell of petrol is getting worse.' He turned to Lees. 'Go back to the car and call for the fire brigade and ambulance. Tell them to hurry.' The PC scrambled up the bank while the others tried to get the driver out.

'It's no good,' Beaumont said. He was sprawled across the passenger seat, arms outstretched, trying to free the man as gently as possible. 'He's wedged under the steering wheel.'

'The fire brigade will be able to cut him out, won't they?' Barrow asked.

'Yes they will,' Russell agreed. 'Though I'm getting really worried about the petrol leaking.'

'But sir. If it was going to catch fire, wouldn't it have so by now?'

'That's a point. We don't know how long it's been here.' He turned to the farmer. He'd been standing a little way behind them in a trance, still looking shocked. 'Mr Clements? Any idea?' The man didn't reply immediately so Russell shook his arm gently and looked him square in the eyes. 'Sir?'

After what seemed an age the farmer finally focused on the policeman. 'Sorry, what did you say?'

'The car. How long has it been here?'

'I don't know for sure. I had to go back to the farm to phone after I'd found the deer and smelled the petrol. I don't know when the car went off the road.'

'How long did it take you to get to the farm?'

'Not long. Five minutes?'

'And five minutes to get back here?'

'I imagine so.'

'And how many minutes before we turned up?'

Not long – you were very quick.'

'Luckily we weren't far away. So the car has been here for at least a quarter of an hour?'

'Must have been.'

Russell turned to Barrow. 'Seems you were right. Let's wait until the brigade gets her. Best to leave it to the experts.' He paused. 'I wonder who the driver is?'

Beaumont had wriggled out of the car and was brushing down his tunic. Barrow took his place and leaned in through the door. After a moment his head appeared, a look of amazement on his face.

'Sir! It's Dearborne, the head gardener!'

'Well I'll be…' Russell was lost for words. They stood there without speaking for some moments, turning the events over in their minds. A rook cawed somewhere overhead; an unseen creature rustled through the undergrowth. Then Lees came scrambling down the bank, carrying a blanket.

'I thought we could cover the lady up – until the ambulance arrives.'

'Good plan. I'll help you put it over her,' Russell said. As they were doing it they could hear the distinct sound of a clanging bell in the distance.

It was only a few more minutes before the uniformed figure of a burly fireman came bursting through the hedge. He slipped and tumbled down the slope, his black leather helmet rolling down in front of him. He got up grinning. 'Sorry about that. Right. Anyone still in the car?'

'Yes, the driver,' Russell said. 'He's trapped under the wheel and we can't get his door open.'

'Bring a jemmy,' the firemen yelled. Another uniformed figure appeared through the hedge, brandishing a serious looking length of iron rod. He slithered down the slope and handed it to the first officer. He wedged it in the gap in the door, leaned heavily on it and with a sound of tearing metal, the door sprang open. He lost his balance and landed on the ground again but was soon up on his feet and, with the help of his companion, managed to force the steering wheel up sufficiently so they could extricate Dearborne. They lifted him as gently as they could and put him down on the ground. The firemen knelt beside him then looked up at Russell.

'He's unconscious but alive, just, though I suspect he's got a number of injuries. I don't think we ought to move him any more. Leave it until the medics turn up.'

Meanwhile other firemen had appeared dragging a hose, ready to douse the car if it caught fire, although there was still no sign that it would happen. Another clanging bell sounded and soon a couple of ambulancemen carrying a folded stretcher had joined them. The scene was starting to get crowded when Crooks, the pathologist, arrived at the gap that had now been made in the hedge.

'Bloody hell!' he boomed. 'How am I supposed to get down there? Someone give me a hand.'

'John,' Russell said. 'What are you doing here?'

Crooks chuckled. 'I heard there'd been a car crash and thought there might be a stiff. I hitched a lift with these guys.' He nodded towards the figure shrouded in the blanket. 'Looks like I was right.'

Russell shook his head sadly. 'You're incorrigible. Stay there and we'll bring her up to you. We need to get this poor chap out first.'

With the help of the firemen the ambulance crew lifted Dearborne on to the stretcher where he was secured with straps. Then, with difficulty, they manoeuvred him up the slope, through the hedge and into the ambulance. Soon it was on its way, the sound of the clanging bell fading as it rushed back to the hospital. A second ambulance had arrived and the exercise was repeated with the body of Rose Peters.

'Could you put her down here for a moment please?' Crooks asked. When they'd rested the stretcher he turned to Russell. 'I think you were right to fear the worst, Sonny,'

'I'm afraid so, John. Not the outcome we'd hoped for.'

'Who'd have thought she'd end her life, killed in her own car?'

Russell shook his head. Thoughts tumbled through his mind. 'It doesn't make sense, John. Nettie was sure she'd found a body buried in the vegetable bed. And I was convinced it was Peters' wife. I didn't want it to be true. At first I was certain that she had just gone off and would come back unscathed but as time went by I just knew something had happened to her. Now I'm completely confused.'

While Russell had been talking, Crooks had knelt by the body, getting down on his knees surprisingly easily, considering his bulk. He peeled back the blanket they had laid over her then gently teased away the sheet that wrapped her. He took his time giving the body a close examination. Russell waited patiently, knowing the pathologist couldn't be hurried when he was concentrating on his work. After what seemed an age he looked up.

'Sonny? You were right.'

'What do you mean?'

'The signs all indicate that this was most likely the body that young Nettie uncovered.'

'How can you tell?'

'Judging by the state of her – the mud and dirt – I'd say she's spent some time buried in the ground.'

'So she didn't die when the car went off the road?'

Crooks shook his head. 'I'll need to examine her in the lab but I'd say she's been dead for several days. In fact, I'd stake my reputation on it.' He held his hand out. 'Right, now help me get up. You can give me a lift back to Collinghurst.'

# Chapter 22

*The* ***BSA Bantam*** *is a two-stroke motorcycle produced by the Birmingham Small Arms Company. Production began in 1948. Exact figures are unknown, but over 250,000 were built and some estimates place the number closer to half a million.*

**BARRETT WAS** finding it easier to control *LIZA* as they made their way along the twists and turns in the river but Nellie thought he looked tense.

'Why don't you take a break, Sid? I'm sure you could do with a cuppa.'

Now that she had mentioned it he could feel the tension in his neck and shoulders. 'Yeah, but I really think we should keep going while we can.'

She gave his arm a squeeze. 'Come on, ten minutes won't make much difference.'

'I suppose you're right. I need to put more fuel in the tank, anyway. We'll have to find somewhere to tie up. Keep your eyes peeled.' The river wound its way past houses in Snodland and Wouldham and then they were in open countryside with just fields and marshland on either side.

'What about there,' Nellie said, pointing ahead towards the right bank. There was what looked like an old wooden jetty, long disused. Barrett reduced the engine revs and steered towards it. As they drew closer he could see it was in a poor state with missing timbers, and those that were left looked decidedly rotten.

'I just hope it's strong enough.' His voice was gloomy and there were worry lines across his young brow.

'Let's give it a go, anyway,' she said brightly. 'If it's not, we can always look further down.'

As *LIZA* bumped into the stage the woodwork shuddered, but stayed firm. Breathing a sigh of relief he threw a rope over one of the upright timbers and made the boat fast. Once he was sure it was secure he switched off the engine. The quiet was almost deafening. Barrett stood for a while, rolling his shoulders and moving his head from side to side, trying to undo the knotted muscles.

'Why don't you stretch your legs? I'll put the kettle on and we'll have a cup of tea in a few minutes.'

'Okay. I'll see if the jetty will hold my weight.'

He climbed up on to the structure and walked slowly along the patchwork of timbers, stepping carefully over the rotten boards and managed to reach the bank without mishap. He turned and waved to Nellie. She smiled and waved back before disappearing into the cabin. Then he set off. His footsteps crunched through the sparse grass and stones along the riverside footpath. The wind soughed softly. Birds called from the muddy banks: the mournful cry of curlews and the insistent piping of oystercatchers.

He realised that for the last few hours all his concentration had been on getting the boat this far without mishap but, as he strode on, darker thoughts crept stealthily into his head; the enormity of what he had done weighed down on him. He hadn't meant to harm Daniel; it was just a scrappy scuffle that got out of hand.

He thought about the meeting in the derelict warehouse.

He'd ridden his motorbike down to Collinghurst with the idea of reconnecting with his family. But it was a stupid idea. When he'd telephoned his brother the reception he received was less than lukewarm and Daniel had been reluctant to meet. But he'd managed to persuade him and at first was delighted when he saw him push open the door into the warehouse where they'd played as kids. He had to admit his brother looked rather good in his drape jacket and skinny jeans, his dark hair styled into an impressive quiff. His delight was extinguished when he saw the thunderous look on his brother's face.

'What are you doing back here?' Daniel had growled.

'Don't be like that.'

'Like what? Why should I be pleased to see you? What do you want, anyway?' Barrett reached out to touch his brother. With a snarl, Floyd flicked his hand away. 'Well? Why are you here?'

This wasn't how Barrett had planned it on his trip down to Sussex. He hadn't expected his brother to welcome him with open arms but he thought he would at least give him a hearing. As his second-hand BSA Bantam had bumbled down the road at a sedate thirty-five miles an hour he'd rehearsed telling him about Nellie, and how they planned to marry. He was even going to ask if he would be his best man. Now he realised he'd made a wasted journey.

'I see now there's no point in talking to you. You're obviously not going to listen.' He started to turn away. Quick as a flash Floyd reached out and seized his arm. 'How dare you! You turn up here and don't even have the guts to stay and talk.'

Barrett tried to shake his brother off but his grip was vicelike. 'Let go of me,' he hissed through gritted teeth. 'You're not interested – I don't know why I bothered.' With a wrench he freed his arm and turned again. As he was walking away he felt something hit him sharply in the middle of his back. He spun round. 'What the…!' Floyd had a length of bicycle chain wrapped round his hand and wrist. Without thinking Barrett lunged forward and grabbed it in his gloved hand and pulled hard. His brother was taken unawares and the chain slithered out of his grasp, drawing blood.

'You bastard!' Floyd plunged his other hand into the pocket of his drape jacket and pulled out a metal object. Barrett recognised it straight away, lunged forward again and grabbed the knuckleduster. Floyd stood for a beat, his eyes widening and his hands forming into fists. He saw red and went for his brother, roaring like a bull. In the few seconds before the attack, Barrett had slipped his fingers through the knuckleduster and before his brother could put his hands round his throat, he'd swung his arm and caught him a hefty blow on the side of his temple. Floyd staggered but remained on his feet. Then Barrett watched as his brother put his hand under his jacket and, with mounting horror, saw him produce a large knife with a wicked-looking blade. Suddenly he lunged, covering the few feet between them in a split second. Barrett didn't have time to turn out of the way and anticipated the pain as the blade plunged into his body. But it didn't – something happened. Maybe he'd misjudged it; perhaps the blood from the gashes caused by the chain had made his hand slippery, but Floyd lost his grip and the knife twisted round as their bodies crashed together. His eyes filled with horror and he slipped to his knees then slowly crumpled on to his side. Barrett staggered back, echoing the horror as he saw of the handle of the knife, protruding from his brother's chest.

'Oh God!' he cried. He dropped to the ground and put his fingers to his brother's neck. With a feeling of dread he realised he could find no pulse. He shook Floyd's shoulders and even slapped his face but the lad remained lifeless. He began to sob and panic started rising in his breast. What the *hell* was he going to do? He sank back on his heels.

After while he sat up and put his head in his hands. 'Think,' he told himself, 'no one knows I'm here. I can just disappear again.' Somehow an aura of calm descended and automatic reflexes took over. He looked around and took in the fact that there was a Morris Traveller parked in the warehouse. He ran across to it and grasped the handle on the back doors. He twisted it and opened the doors to reveal just an old, threadbare carpet, which he pulled out. Returning to the body he wrenched the knife out of his brother's chest and dropped it in the dust. Then crouching, he lifted the lifeless form, carried it to the car and placed it, almost reverently, in the back. He picked up the carpet, he draped it over the body, concealing it from view. Now for the knife. He picked it up in his gloved hand, wondering what to do with it. He looked back towards the car and saw the wooden flap beneath the floor. Opening it he could see a spare wheel with a rag wedged in beside it. He pulled out the oily piece of material, wrapped the knife in its folds and thrust it in beside the wheel as far as he could push it, then closed the flap and the back doors. The initial feeling of calm was starting to dissipate as it dawned on him what had happened. He looked down at his hands and slowly turned the palms upwards. The gloves were shiny with his brother's blood. Horrified, he tore them off, threw them to the ground and ran from the building. Jumping on his motorbike, he kick-started it into life and left the scene.

Barrett was suddenly shaken out of his reverie by a loud commotion. Two ducks, alarmed by his presence had taken off from a pool close to the path, with a whirr of wings and loud quacking. He stopped and looked round. The jetty and the boat were out of sight. He hadn't realised he'd walked so far. Nellie would be worried so he set off at a trot to return to her.

# Chapter 23

***The Seahorse Inn** is an ancient hostelry in the quaint town of Nottery Quay. It dates from the 12th century but was rebuilt in 1420 after being sacked by the French.*

**AS SOON** as they got back to the station Russell made for the Superintendent's office. He knocked on the door and was invited straight in.

'Sit down Sonny. I assume you've got news for me.'

Astonished at being addressed so informally, it was a few seconds before he could speak. Stout looked expectantly at him. 'It's not good news, sir,' Russell began. 'We've found Mrs Peters.'

'Alive?'

'I'm afraid not.'

'I heard there has been a car crash.'

'Yes, but that's not how she died.'

'Oh?'

'She *was* found dead in the car, but John Crooks thinks she died sometime before that.'

'I see. So you were right to have your suspicions.'

'So it seems.'

'Tell me what you've found out.'

Russell explained about the search in the walled garden, the discovery of the earring and the car missing from the garage, as well as finding that the driver of the car was the head gardener.

'So Dearborne probably killed her,' Stout stated. 'We'd better let Peters know what's happened to Rose.'

'I'd rather leave it for a while, sir.'

'But for heaven's sake. The poor man has just lost his wife.'

'I know. But I'm not convinced that Dearborne is responsible.'

'What do you mean?'

'It seems too simple to blame him. Yes, I'm sure he's not without blame but I've got a feeling that Peters has played a much bigger part.'

Stout sighed, rested his elbows on the desk and put his head in his hands. 'Not another one of your feelings....'

'If you could let me have a little more time before speaking to Peters I'm sure I can make a watertight case against him. Lewis is at this moment conducting tests on the spades we collected from Sowsden, Crooks is examining Mrs Peters' body and hopefully, we'll able to talk to Dearborne soon.'

'I think we should let him know his wife is dead, but we won't say any more.' The Superintendent looked at his watch. 'I suppose a few more hours won't make much difference. I'll give you until midday tomorrow to get the evidence against him together.'

'Or arrest him.'

Stout's eyes narrowed. 'We'll have see about that. I'll need concrete proof before I give you permission to do anything so drastic.'

~O~

He sat in his office for as long as he could, pushing papers around and getting increasingly frustrated. Finally, aware the day was slipping away, Russell decided to see if he could gee things up. His first port of call was the forensics lab. He pushed the door open and could see the half dozen spades that Barrow had collected piled up on the table, with Lewis leaning over, studying one of them intently. He looked up.

'Hello Sonny. What can I do for you?' He grinned. 'As if I didn't know.'

Russell returned the smile. 'I hate to put pressure on you but I'm up against it. Stout has given me limited time to produce some evidence. Have you turned anything up?' he asked.

'I thought it wouldn't be long before you started chasing me. I'm afraid I can't give you anything definite,' he said, shrugging.

'That's okay. I know you'll be doing your best – I just thought I'd ask. I'll leave you to get on with it.'

Lewis held up his hand. 'Hold on. I might not have anything for certain but… I think we've found what was used to hit Nettie.'

'Really?' Russell's heart leaped.

'Look at this.' He handed the DI a magnifying glass. 'Look closely where the shaft of the spade fits into the handle.' Russell took the lens and studied the area Lewis had indicated. Caught under the edge of the metal were a few strands of blonde hair. 'I think there are skin fragments, and possibly blood, but I need to do some tests. Plus I'll need hair samples and Nettie's blood type to compare.'

'So if they match, then we can be certain that this was the weapon used to hit her. When will you know?'

'Sonny, I understand that you are anxious to find out but I can't work miracles, I'm afraid. Hopefully I'll have something definite by mid-morning.'

Russell sighed. 'Fair enough. I'll go and see John Crooks but I expect he'll say the same.'

He found the pathologist in the mortuary. Thankfully the Meerschaum was unlit on a side table, but the smell of death hung in the room like a threatening cloud.

'I wondered how long it would be before you started chasing me,' Crooks boomed. 'And before you ask, I don't know how she was killed or the time of death, so you can bugger off!'

'Nice to see you too, John. Sounds like I've touched a nerve.'

'Yes, you have! I don't like being put under pressure. You know that.'

Russell stood his ground and set his jaw. 'John, I'm not asking a lot, just a rough idea.' He looked beseechingly at the pathologist. 'Please?'

Crooks harrumphed and raised his eyebrows. 'Well, as it's you. I wouldn't do it for anyone else, you know.'

'I know you wouldn't and I appreciate anything you can tell me.'

Crooks stared at him. 'As I said, she wasn't killed in the car crash; she was bumped off some considerable time before that.'

Russell didn't ask, just looked expectantly.

A ghost of a smile crept across the pathologists face. 'About a week – is that what you want to know?'

'Thank you.'

'And, as to the cause of death? My best guess is strangulation.' He held his hand out like a traffic policeman. 'But, I won't know for certain until I've opened her up. *Now* you really can bugger off. I'll be working late so come and see me again in the morning.'

Russell left Crooks and made his way into the main hospital. Dearborne was in a side room, off the intensive care ward. PC Beaumont was sitting on a chair outside, thumbing through a magazine. When he saw the DI he stood up quickly.

'Afternoon, sir.'

'Has he said anything yet?'

'I'm afraid not. They had to sort out a badly mangled leg and a couple of brokwen ribs and they're concerned about internal damage so he's under sedation. Sorry.'

'Not your fault, lad. I just thought I'd ask. How long are you here for?'

'Another hour then Lee takes over.'

'Right you are. Please ask him to let me know as soon as Dearborne comes round.'

Frustrating as it was, there was nothing Russell could do about it – he would just have to wait until the morning and hope more information had come to light by then. When he arrived back at the police station the desk sergeant called to him.

'There was a telephone call while you were out, Sonny.'

'Oh, who from?'

Wickstead's eyes sparkled and Russell detected a smile beneath his walrus moustache. 'It was the delightful Miss Bailey. She asked if you could ring her back.'

In his office he dialled her number and she answered almost immediately. 'Sonny! I haven't seen you for ages. Are you ignoring me?'

He sighed. 'Of course not. It's just been rather intense lately. I'm so sorry if you're feeling neglected.'

'I am a bit. I don't suppose you're free this evening?'

'As a matter of fact, I am. There's not much more I can do here until the morning.'

'Oh goody. I thought you might like to treat me to a meal at The Seahorse Inn.'

'Crikey, that's a bit posh, especially for a weekday.'

'Is that a no, then?' She feigned disappointment.

'Of course not. You deserve to be pampered and I could do with something to take my mind off work.'

'I hoped you'd say that.' She giggled. 'Seven pm?'

'Fine.'

'I'll book a table.'

'I'll meet you there at six-thirty and we'll have a drink first.'

# Chapter 24

*If a cargo vessel wishes to travel empty or partially empty to collect a cargo, it must travel* ***in ballast****. This keeps the vessel in trim, with the propeller and rudder submerged. Typically, this will be achieved by flooding the ballast tanks with sea water.*

**AFTER BARRETT** had returned to the boat he just couldn't dispel a feeling of depression and hopelessness. Nellie had tried in vain to shake him out of it but had finally given up and retired to the cabin in a sulk. So he stood alone at the wheel, steering the boat, as they motored past Cuxton. The river had widened on the approach to Rochester and had become busier, with more craft of all sizes moving about. *LIZA* started to feel rather small and he began to wonder if he had been too optimistic. Perhaps he should rein in his ambition and travel up the Thames, as Nellie thought they were doing. But he'd set his heart on going abroad. Sure it couldn't be that difficult to cross the channel?

He'd studied the map. He reckoned if he hugged the coast, travelling past Margate and round the North Foreland, he could easily get to Dover. Then it couldn't be more than twenty-five miles of open water before reaching Calais. He understood there was a network of canals which would take him right through France and was sure he'd be able to pick up work here and there.

The thought of being in waters more suitable for *LIZA* lifted his mood and made him feel more confident.

Rochester Castle came up on the starboard bank, then they were going under the road and rail bridges. The river took a sharp turn to the right and almost immediately a turn to the left bringing the dockyard into view. There were several menacing looking naval ships moored alongside, towering over *LIZA*, with figures moving about on deck. Suddenly he felt very vulnerable. It seemed to take an age to pass them, with his anxiety ramping up and cold sweat trickling down his back. He breathed a sigh of relief when he'd finally left them behind. But his return to near calm was short lived. The craft that they had passed going up river, although larger, had so far kept to their own side. The wash from their wake had made his little boat rock, but not alarmingly. This was about to change.

As they passed Upnor Castle the river again took a sharp turn to the right. Barrett knew that the rules of the river meant that he kept to the starboard side, passing traffic going in the other direction on the port, or left-hand side. So it was a huge shock when he turned the corner to see a large coaster coming straight towards *LIZA*. Panic surged through him. Whoever was steering was completely oblivious to his little cockleshell of a boat. The gap between the oncoming vessel and the bank looked microscopically small. It was too late to alter course and pass on the wrong side of the coaster so he had no alternative but to try to squeeze through the gap. He felt like closing his eyes as the rusty hull grew ever closer and towered above him but he held his nerve and steered straight ahead.

By some miracle the two craft passed, inches apart, without a single scrape, but it was not over yet. The coaster was obviously in ballast and riding high. The propeller was barely in the water and as they slid past the stern, Barrett could feel *LIZA* being dragged towards the foaming undertow it created. He pushed the throttle forward as far as it would go, the engine screaming, and fought with the wheel, as his little vessel bucked and rolled from side to side and the thrashing propeller of the larger craft threatened to drag them in. He really thought it was the end. Then, as fast as it had begun, it was over. The coaster carried on her merry way and *LIZA* was left rocking in its wake. He eased the throttle right back and stood at the wheel, shaking with relief.

'What was all that about?' Nellie had appeared in the open cabin doorway, her face ghostly white. 'I was almost thrown out of my bunk!'

'Some bloody idiot on the wrong side of the river. All over now, thank God.'

'It felt really dangerous.' Nellie had come up beside him, staring with frightened eyes.

'Nothing I couldn't handle,' Barrett said, his grim smile at odds with his churning stomach.

'When do we reach the Thames?' she asked. He didn't answer straight away and her eyes narrowed, suspicion clouding them. 'What?' she said.

In for a penny, in for a pound, he thought. 'We're not going up the Thames.'

'*What*!?'

'We're going to France.' She just stared, her mouth gaping. Taking the opportunity he outlined his plans, playing down the dangers of crossing the Channel. When he'd finished she was very quiet for some time. Finally she spoke.

'You're determined to go through with it, aren't you?'

He nodded solemnly, looking straight ahead, concentrating on steering the boat.

'Well if that's your decision, I trust you.'

He smiled and gave her a kiss. 'Thank you. It'll be an adventure. Now, can you get the map? I need to find our way out into the estuary.'

~O~

Russell entered the bar of the Seahorse Inn and looked round. He saw that Isobel was already there, seated in one of a pair of high-backed armchairs, next to the giant's fireplace. She beckoned him over. He bent down and kissed her before taking the other chair.

She pushed a glass towards him. 'I hope you don't mind, I've got a bottle of Chablis Premier Cru.' Seeing his raised eyebrows she chuckled. 'Don't worry, it's on me. I got paid today for a diamond bracelet I'd reset.'

'In that case…' he picked up the glass, breathed in the aroma then took a drink. 'I always knew you had taste.'

'Flattery will get you everywhere.' Her eyes sparkled. 'Now, tell me what's been keeping you away from me. Must be something pretty big.'

He looked round to check that no one was eavesdropping. 'Well actually, it all revolves around the body that was found in the back of the Morris Traveller.'

'That I persuaded Duncan to tell you about.'

'And I wasn't there.'

'And Bonny Parker ended up having a heart attack. How is he, by the way?'

'On the mend, though I doubt he'll be coming back to work any time soon – if ever.'

'Oh?'

'He was close to retirement anyway.' Russell looked

thoughtful. 'Funny, I miss him in a strange way – used to enjoy sparring with him.'

'Haven't you got another detective to do that with now?'

'Sergeant Pollard?' Isobel took a sip from her glass and nodded. Russell snorted. 'The sooner he goes back to County, the better. He makes Bonny and Clyde look like Holmes and Watson.'

Isobel laughed. 'You really don't like him, do you?'

'That's an understatement. The man causes chaos wherever he goes.'

'Anyway, you were going to tell me about the case.'

'Right. As I said, the body in the car was at the beginning.' He paused, looking thoughtful. 'No, actually, it began before that.'

He told her about Nettie and how she'd uncovered a body in a vegetable bed at Sowsden then someone had struck her over the head. 'We're pretty sure it was the body of Rose Peters but when we went to look it had gone, only to turn up in a car that had crashed.'

'Who was driving?'

'Dearborne, the head gardener.'

'What he's got to say about it?'

'We don't know. He was quite badly injured and is heavily sedated. I'm waiting to hear when we can talk to him.'

'So whose body was it in Duncan's car?'

'That's the odd thing. We, or rather Pollard, assumed it was someone called Sidney Barrett, when it was actually his brother, Daniel.' Russell explained about Flossy Floyd's son and stepson and how they looked like twins, with identical tattoos. 'I can't be sure but I think that Sidney killed Daniel, possibly by accident and is now on the run.'

'Presumably you're keeping a watch at railway stations and the ferry ports?'

Russell laughed. 'We would be, except we think he's made his escape by boat.'

'Really?'

'Yes, he's somewhere on the Medway.'

'Doesn't that lead into the Thames, then the Channel?'

'It does, but he's in a flat-bottomed craft with no keel. It's only really suitable for non-tidal waters.'

'You're assuming he knows that.'

'By all accounts he's a bright lad so I expect so. Also, we've heard from the lockkeeper at Allington where the tidal part of the river starts. He says that he hasn't seen the boat that Barrett stole go through the lock, so he's probably holed up on the river somewhere. It's only a matter of time before we find him.'

'And what about Rose Peters? Do you know who killed her?'

'That's where it gets complicated. It *could* be Peters himself. I don't trust the man, he's just too clever. Or it could be Floyd, *or* Dearborne. Hopefully we'll have a better idea when we're able to interview him.'

'Wasn't the other chap, McDonald, missing too?'

'Him!' Russell guffawed.

'Went off and drowned himself, so I heard.'

'*Pretended* to drown himself, I reckon. It's been several days and the body hasn't turned up.'

'Perhaps it never will.'

'Possibly, but I think he staged his own disappearance. He had money problems, had been fired from his job and I think is wife is a bit of a harridan, despite her meek appearance. No, I reckon he's gone off somewhere and taken on a new identity.'

Just then a waiter came up to them. 'Excuse me, sir, madam. Your table is ready. If you'd like to follow me to the dining room.' He picked up the ice bucket and bottle of Chablis and led the way.

~o~

Douglas McDonald lay back on the single bed, his hands clasped behind his head and grinned. It might only be a little attic room but it was warm and bright and there was a distant view of the sea from his window. The overwhelming burden of responsibilities had been lifted from his shoulders and he felt almost weightless with relief. Earlier, his new friend, Mary, had introduced him to the owner of the hotel. He was more than relieved to find someone to replace Danny, who'd been called up to do his National Service, and had asked no awkward questions. The tasks he was to undertake were well within his capabilities and although the pay was less than he was used to, he had a roof over his head and could say goodbye to his past. And as for Mary… They'd got on so well he could see their friendship developing into something more. But there was no rush, he had all the time in the world to create a new life. He would just have to remember that from now on his name was David Gilmore.

~o~

Navigation became trickier as they rounded St Mary's Island. Barrett wished he had a proper Admiralty chart instead of a road atlas. Even though it was large scale there was very little detail beyond the coast. He felt panic rising – there appeared to be no obvious channel. What direction should he take? As if reading his thoughts, Nellie asked:

'Do you know where you're going?'

He looked at her. Her normally cheerful face was serious and strained. He glanced around and thought quickly. 'Easy, we just follow the other boats.'

'Ooh, you are clever.' A sudden lurch as LIZA rose and fell over the wake of a passing vessel made her lose her balance. She stumbled and fell heavily against the cockpit coaming.

'Are you okay?' he asked, anxiety making his voice go up a register.

'I think so. I didn't know it was going to be as rough as this.'

'Perhaps you'd better put on a lifejacket. There's one in the locker.'

'What about you?'

'Oh, I'm okay. I've got the wheel to hang on to.'

'If you're sure…'

'Perfectly. Go and put the lifejacket on.'

She disappeared into the cabin and he stood, bracing his legs against the swell. If it was like this now, what would it be like in the Channel? He struggled to push the thought out of his mind and concentrate on steering a straight course.

~O~

Russell and Isobel sat in the dining room of The Seahorse Inn. The table was covered with a crisp white linen cloth and candlelight reflected off the polished cutlery. With oak beams crowded together overhead and venerable old oil paintings in gilded frames on the walls it was both an intimate and timeless room. Frowning Isobel reached across and took Russell's hand.

'Are you okay?'

'Yes, sorry.'

'You seem a bit distracted.'

'I suppose I am. This case has got me baffled. I just need a break – something tangible so I can make sense of it.' He squeezed her hand. 'I'll try to put it aside for now. Tell me about your work – this diamond bracelet for instance.'

Just as Isabel was about to speak a waiter appeared with their *hors d'oeuvres* – whitebait for Isobel and spring vegetable soup for Russell. 'I hope you don't mind me having fish,' Isobel said.

'Of course not. Just because I'm a vegetarian I'm not going to force my views on you.' He smiled. 'Anyway, you were going to tell me about your work.'

Again, before she could start the waiter returned. He bowed obsequiously. 'I'm sorry to bother you but there's a telephone call for you, Inspector Russell.'

'How the hell…?'

'I'm afraid it's urgent.'

'You'd better go,' Isobel said.

Russell put down his spoon. 'I'm really sorry. I'll be back in a minute.'

The waiter led the way to the reception desk. Russell picked up the handset lying on the counter. 'Yes?' he said, tersely.

'Really sorry to bother you, Sonny.' It was Wickstead, the desk sergeant. 'I've just had a call from the hospital. Dearborne is conscious. I thought you'd want to know.'

'Oh, right. Thanks.'

'DC Barrow is on his way with the car. He should be with you in a few minutes.'

'How did you know I was here?'

There was a chuckle down the line. 'Miss Bailey let slip she was taking you to The Seahorse tonight. I'm sorry to spoil your evening.'

'Not to worry. Thanks for letting me know.' He put the receiver down. This could be the break he was hoping for. If Dearborne could talk he might find out who killed Rose Peters. He made his way back to the dining room.

'Who was it?' Isobel asked.

'It was the station. I'm afraid I'm going to have to go.'

Isobel's face fell. 'Oh.'

'I'm so sorry. You stay here and enjoy your meal. I'll make it up to you – promise.' He pecked her on the cheek.

'You'd better…'

Russell stood outside the Inn waiting for his transport to arrive. It was just turning from dusk to dark and the few street lamps illuminating Seahorse Street were coming on, lighting up the road between the ancient houses. After a few moments he heard a car and saw the headlights flickering up and down as it bounced over the cobbles.

In ten minutes they were pulling up outside Collinghurst General. Inside the hospital they walked down the corridor towards the ward where Dearborne was being treated. PC Lee, keeping watch outside the room, sprang to his feet when they approached. 'Sorry to bother you, sir. But I thought you ought to know.'

'Quite right. Have you spoken to him?'

'No. The matron told me he was awake.'

Russell couldn't help grinning. Perhaps Josephine Jacques wasn't the dragon he at first thought. They entered the room. Dearborne was propped up, supported by several pillows. A clean white bandage was wrapped round his head and one leg was coated in plaster, held up at an angle by a cable suspended from an overhead frame. A nurse was leaning over, holding a thermometer. She looked up.

'Matron says you can have five minutes. You mustn't tire him.'

'Thank you. We won't.'

Russell pulled out one of the metal-framed chairs and sat down. Barrow took his place on the other side of the bed.

'How're you feeling?' the DI asked.

Dearborne looked at him, his eyes wary beneath the bandages. 'Sore and a bit groggy.'

'That's the painkillers, I expect.'

The gardener nodded, then winced.

'Do you remember what happened?'

'Yes. I was driving Mrs Peters away from Sowsden. A deer ran out in front of the car and we crashed.' His eyes narrowed. 'Is she all right?'

'You know she's not,' Russell said quietly.

'I don't understand.'

'Yes you do. She was already dead when you set off. And don't pretend to look surprised. We know.'

Already pale and weak, Dearborne seemed to fold in on himself.

'Do you want to tell me about it?' Russell asked.

'I didn't kill her.'

Russell was inclined to believe him – just an instinct, but these so often proved accurate. 'So who did?' he asked.

'I can't say.'

'Can't or won't?'

Dearborne just looked down at his hands, folded on the bedclothes. Said nothing.

Russell leaned closer. 'Listen. You're going to be charged with aiding and abetting but if you don't talk, you're facing a full-blown murder charge.' He let that sink in. 'So I suggest you tell us who was responsible. Was it your boss, David Peters?'

The gardener looked up, horrified. 'No, no!'

'But he knows.'

'Yes.' The voice almost a whisper.

'So come on. Who did it?

Dearborne appeared to consider, then make up his mind. 'I might as well tell you as he's well away by now. It was Daniel.'

The two detectives looked at each other. Barrow started saying: 'You don't know, do you?' Dearborne looked perplexed.

Russell stopped the DC from saying any more. 'Nothing you need worry about.' He started rising. 'We've taken enough of your time. I expect you need to rest.'

As they walked back down the corridor Barrow said, anxiety in his voice, 'Sorry if I put my foot in it, sir.'

'Don't worry, lad. You weren't to know. I wanted to keep him in the dark.'

'Did you believe him?'

'That he didn't kill Mrs Peters? Possibly. That it was Floyd who did? I'm not so sure. He doesn't know that he's dead – thinks he's on the run. I want him to believe that for the time being.'

'What about Peters? Are we going to see him?'

'I don't think so. He's been told about his wife. Was quite shocked, apparently. But, how real the shock was I don't know. I'm convinced he's a jolly good actor, as well as a consummate liar. Hopefully there will be more evidence in the morning, then we'll confront him.' He looked at his watch. 'If we go back to the Seahorse now, I should be just in time for my dessert.'

~O~

As they'd crossed Whitstable Bay, Barrett had been finding it increasingly difficult to keep on course. The sea was more troubled, with waves coming at an angle to the boat making it slew, first to one side, then to the other. In addition, *LIZA*'s high freeboard meant she was constantly being pushed by the freshening wind. Earlier, he'd managed to top up the fuel tank, but the constant motion meant that he'd spilled petrol onto the cockpit floor and the fumes were making him feel nauseous. Poor Nellie was already feeling seasick and had retired to the cabin, to lie down, with a bucket next to her. It wasn't working out quite as he'd hoped.

# Chapter 25

*Puce is a dark red or purple colour and is the French word for flea. It is said to be the colour of bloodstains on linen or bedsheets, even after being laundered.*

The next morning Russell was sitting at his desk, hands clasped behind his head, whistling the opening of the Adagio from Beethoven's seventh. Aggie, curled up by his feet, stirred at a knock on the door.

'Come in,' the DI said.

'Hello Sonny. I've got some news for you.' It was Lewis. Aggie wagged her tail. She liked him.

'Good news, I hope.'

'I think so.' The forensics man sat down. 'We were up late last night, going over those spades. As you'd expect, there were a number of different sets of fingerprints on most of them but we discovered something very interesting.'

Russell sat up. 'Go on.'

'A particular spade, the one I showed you, with the hair and skin fragments, has only got one set of prints on it.'

'Dearborne's.' Russell stated.

'No.'

'Floyd's then.'

'Nor his. They don't match any we have on record.'

'So it can only be one person. David Peters.'

'That's what I thought,' Lewis agreed.

'So it *was* him who whacked Nettie.'

'It seems likely, but I'll need his prints to be sure.'

'We're going over there this morning. When I've spoken to John I've a feeling we're going to have enough to charge him, if not with murder, then certainly conspiracy.' Just as he was speaking, the phone on his desk rang. He picked up the receiver. 'Hello?'

'Sonny!' The pathologist boomed loudly enough for Aggie to prick up her ears.

Russell put his hand over the mouthpiece and grinned at Lewis. 'Talk of the devil! Then removing his hand: 'John. What can I do for you?'

'Can you get over here now? I've got something I think you ought to see.'

~o~

Crooks seemed in a much better mood than the day before. 'I'm pretty sure I've found out how she was done in,' he said.

Russell glanced across at the form on the stone slab, shrouded in a rubber sheet, and gave an involuntary shudder.

Crooks chuckled, his tummy wobbling. 'Don't worry, you're not going to have to look at the corpse – she ain't a pretty sight, not been sewn back up yet. Come over here.' He led the way to a bench at the side of the room where an Anglepoise lamp cast circle of white light. He reached into an enamel dish and held up a small object. 'Do you know what this is?' It appeared to be a curiously shaped bone, no more than an inch across.

'No, I don't. But I'm sure you're going to tell me.'

'It's a hyoid bone,' Crooks said triumphantly. 'The only bone in the body not connected to any other. It's held in place by cartilage and muscle and connects the floor of the mouth and the tongue.

Its name is derived from the Greek *hyoeides*, meaning shaped like the letter *upsilon*, that is, U-shaped. Not to be confused with *epsilon*, which is a different letter altogether.'

'That's all very interesting, John. But what's its significance?'

'It tells us how she was killed.'

'And how was that?'

'Strangled. I thought that was the case as there were pressure marks and slight contusions on her neck, but this confirms it. Difficult to see without a microscope that it's been fractured. Classic sign when someone's had their throat squeezed.'

'Right.' Images buzzed through Russell's head: Peters, Dearborne, Floyd. Which one did it?

His thoughts were interrupted by Crooks. 'And before you ask, I can't tell you who it was. If it was recent, they *may* have flakes of skin or tissue under their fingernails. But as I estimate that she has been dead for over a week, they would have washed their hands by now – several times – removing any trace of evidence.'

'That's a shame.'

'But, I didn't get you over here just for a Greek lesson. *I* can't tell you who finished her off, but *you* might be able to.'

'How?' Russell was perplexed.

'Fingerprints! Whoever did the deal pressed so hard he left an impression of his thumb in her throat. First thing we noticed before slicing her open.'

'That's great news.'

Crooks held his hand up. 'Don't get too excited, it's very faint. However, I've sent it over to Lewis, and if anyone can make something of it then he can.'

'High praise indeed, coming from you, John.'

The pathologist raised an eyebrow. 'You know where flattery will get you... Now, bugger off and let me get on with my work.'

Walking back down the stark corridor towards the entrance Barrow asked: 'Is he always as rude as that, sir?'

'Always. But I don't take it to heart – it's mainly bluster – and I put up with it because he's exceedingly good at his job.'

'Do you think we're any closer to finding out who killed Mrs Peters?'

'Possibly. If we're to believe Dearborne it's down to Daniel Floyd or Peters himself. I'm banking on the thumbprint giving us a clue. Meanwhile, I think we've got enough to bring Peters in. We'll pick up a constable then we'll go and get him.'

~o~

As they travelled down the drive they could see that the Land Rover was parked outside the Manor House. 'At least we know he's here and not over at the nursery, sir,' Barrow said.

'That's something. But I can't say I'm looking forward to this.'

'Why's that, sir?'

'He's good friends with the Super, and *he* definitely won't be pleased.' Barrow parked the car and, as they got out, Russell said: 'We won't bother Mrs Floyd we'll go straight to the walled garden. I expect he'll be there.' As the three policemen walked in through the doorway the horticulturalist could be seen in the glasshouse, busy at the bench. He was so engrossed that they were almost upon him before he looked round. The initial look of surprise on his face was almost instantly replaced by one of sadness. So sudden was the transformation it was like a switch being thrown.

'If you've come to tell me my wife's dead, I already know. One of your constables came round yesterday evening.'

'No, we haven't. I'm afraid we've come to arrest you in connection with the death of your wife.'

As if another switch had been thrown, his features changed again, arranging themselves into a look of indignation then anger. 'You cannot be serious! Can't you see I'm grieving? How can you possibly think that? She was killed in a car – her car – being driven by Dearborne. That's who you should be arresting.'

'He's under police watch in hospital. But we know that your wife wasn't killed in the crash. She'd already been dead for several days.'

'I don't believe you.'

Russell decided enough was enough. 'You may not believe it but the evidence is stacked against you.' Then turning to PC Beaumont: 'Put the cuffs on him and read him his rights.'

'Now listen! The Chief Constable is a close friend of mine. Just wait until he hears about this.'

'He'll hear about it soon enough and realise what a duplicitous man you are.'

'How dare you!'

'Constable. Take Mr Peters to the car.'

~o~

As soon as they arrived at the police station Russell instructed Beaumont to escort Peters to the interview room. 'And before anything else, take his fingerprints and get them straight to Lewis.' When they'd gone he said to Barrow: 'We'll leave him for a bit, see if he gets rattled.'

He'd just sat down in his office when Sergeant Wickstead put his head round the door. 'Sorry, Sonny. The Super wants to see you – immediately. I don't think he's in the best of moods.' He gave a wry smile, his bushy eyebrows lifting.

'I can guess what he wants. I suppose I'd better face the music.'

'*What the hell are you playing at*?' Stout thundered. His eyes burned as brightly as the cheroot when he put it in his mouth and sucked hard on it.

'Sir?' Russell affected innocence.

'Bringing Peters in. The Chief Constable is going to be down on us like a ton of bricks as soon as he hears about this.'

'I'll take that risk, sir.'

Stout banged on the desk with his fist. 'It's not you taking the risk – it's my neck on the block! Why on earth have you done it?'

'I've strong reasons to believe that it was Peters who killed his wife.'

'What?! I thought that Dearborne admitted it was the Floyd boy who did it.'

'I think he was lying to cover up for his boss.'

'You think? Is this another one of your *feelings*?'

'No, sir. The evidence is stacking up against him.'

Stout took another hard drag on his cigar. 'What evidence?'

'Lying about the car in the garage for one thing...'

'For crying out loud. That's hardly evidence for killing his wife. Especially as the car turned up with the gardener at the wheel. Have you even considered that *he* is the murderer?'

'I don't think he is.'

'There you go with your bloody thoughts again. What else have you got?'

'There was the vegetable patch.'

Stout snorted. 'And what does that prove?'

'Nettie – WPC Sharpe found a body buried there.'

'Listen.' Stout took one more drag on the cheroot and stubbed it out viciously in the glass ashtray. 'The poor girl suffered a nasty blow which was bound to have muddled her head. She quite possibly dreamt the whole thing up.'

'Then how did she end up in the boot of Weeks' car, not far from Sowsden?'

'That doesn't have to be anything to do with Peters. It was probably the gardener – or the dead boy Floyd. Yes, probably him.'

'That would be most convenient,' Russell said quietly.

'*What did you say*?'

'I said it would be convenient. Then we could wrap up the case and Peters will walk away innocent.'

'But he is!'

'I really don't think so.'

A livid puce was starting to rise from Stout's collar, colouring his neck and turning his already florid cheeks bright red. Russell could sense an almighty anger was about to erupt when there was a loud rapping on the door. '*Go away*!' the Super shouted.

The door opened and Lewis appeared.

'*I said GO AWAY*!'

'I think you'll want to hear this, sir,' Lewis said mildly.

'It had better be good.'

'It is.'

Stout seemed to calm down a little in the presence of the forensics man. 'Go on then,' he said, wearily.

Lewis was holding an evidence bag in one hand. 'I wasn't sure before but now everything points to Peters.'

'This had better be good,' Stout muttered.

'I've just made the connection, thanks to John Crooks.'

'Well, what is it? Spit it out.'

'This.' He held up the bag.

'What on earth is it?' the Super asked.

'It's a bandage.'

'I don't see what that's got to do with the case.'

'It came off David Peters' hand.'

'I still don't understand.' Stout was starting to lose patience again.

Russell grinned. '*I* do. It was the dog bite, wasn't it?'

'That's right. John changed the dressing and quite fortuitously hung on to the old one.'

'I still don't see the significance,' Stout persisted.

'I've had a chance to examine the clothes that Mrs Peters was wearing. There was blood on the collar of her blouse.'

'There was bound to be,' Stout said. 'She was in a sodding car crash.'

'But it wasn't hers. By John's reckoning she'd been dead for over a week, so it couldn't be fresh. I've run some tests and it's definitely the same group as Peters'.

'But surely that's the same as hundreds of other people?'

'Not so. It's AB negative, very rare.'

'But even so...' Doubt was beginning to appear in Stout's manner.

'I agree that on its own the evidence against him would be flimsy at best. But with this...' In his other hand he was holding a sheet of paper.

'And what's that?'

'Fingerprints. We've just managed to get a match for the prints on the spade, *and* the thumbprint on Rose Peters' neck.'

Stout heaved a sigh. 'Don't tell me – it's David Peters.'

'I'm afraid so. It's quite conclusive.'

'Sounds like you could be right, Inspector.' Russell nodded but kept his counsel. 'But how does Dearborne, the gardener, fit into it?' The Super asked.

Russell rubbed his chin. 'I don't know for certain but I suspect that Peters has some sort of hold over him – or has been paying him to help in the cover up.'

'And the Floyd lad?'

'I don't think he had anything to do with it. It seems like he wasn't around very often.'

'And you think *he* was killed by his brother?'

'His *stepbrother*, Sidney Barrett, yes.'

'Deliberately?'

'My feeling is that it was an accident that went wrong – a fight that got out of control that ended up with Barrett going on the run. We won't know for certain until we catch up with him.'

'How is that search progressing?'

'The Kent police are still searching for *LIZA*, the boat he stole, along the Medway, so it's only a matter of time.'

'Good, good. And what about the other missing person – Douglas McDonald?'

'I'm afraid there's been no news. 'We circulated a description with a photograph, but no one has seen hide nor hair of him.'

'I thought he'd walked into the sea and drowned?'

'Well, his body certainly hasn't washed up. If you want my opinion I think he faked his suicide so he could disappear without trace. I believe he'd had enough of his old life and wanted to get away and start afresh.'

~o~

When Peters was questioned by Russell and DC Barrow, Stout insisted on sitting in. The horticulturalist's face lit up when he saw him come into the interview room but soon fell when the Super averted his eyes and refused to acknowledge him. As Russell anticipated, Peters had a ready answer for every question, putting all the blame onto Dearborne and Floyd. After an hour when he'd emphatically denied being involved with the death of his wife, he was sent back to the cells.

'I think you handled that really well, Sonny,' Stout said. 'You're quite right about him being duplicitous. He once told me that he wanted to be an actor. It seems he might have made a good one. But I'm sure you'll get the better of him. We'll let him stew for a while then bring him back up later for another grilling.' He grinned. 'Talking of stew and grills, I realise I've missed my lunch.' He looked at his watch. 'The pub will be open. Can I buy you a pie and a pint?'

This was such a rare offer, Russell could hardly refuse. 'Thank you, sir. I'd like that. I'll just get Aggie. She likes the pub too.'

He turned, before he could see Stout's reaction and started walking back to his office. He was just about to open the door when Wickstead called out.

'Sonny, I've just had an officer from the Margate lifeboat on the phone. They've rescued someone from the sea. A young woman was clinging to a capsized boat not far off the coast.'

'Why have they let us know?'

'Apparently it shouldn't have been there as it's not a sea-going vessel.'

Russell's heart leapt to his throat. 'Don't tell me, it's called *LIZA*?'

'Afraid so.'

'And just one person rescued?'

'That's all. She's in a state of shock and suffering from exposure. They reckon she only survived because she was wearing a lifejacket. When they picked her up she kept repeating: "Sid, where's Sid?"'

Russell had been looking forward to a drink but this news had put a dampener on his mood. He was just about to go and tell Stout when the phone rang again. Wickstead held his hand up.

'Someone for you. I think this might cheer you up a bit.'

The desk sergeant passed him the handset. 'Hello. Who's calling?' he asked.

'Is that Inspector Russell?'

'It is. What can I do for you?'

'It's about the poster for the missing man – Douglas McDonald.'

'Oh yes?'

'I think I've found him. Well he looks like the man in the photo – though he's using a different name.'

'Can you tell me a little more?'

'Yes. I run a small hotel in Eastbourne and I think I've just given him a job.'

## THE END

# Blood on the Tide

**A DI Sonny Russell mystery**
**Chris O'Donoghue**

**WHEN A** gruesomely mutilated body trussed up in a distinctive fashion washes up on a lonely stretch of the south coast in the 1950s, DI Sonny Russell is soon struggling to unravel an intriguingly knotty puzzle. And as more bodies, similarly tortured, appear he begins to realise that, for some at least, the war is far from over.

A trail of intrigue leads him to Europe where he befriends a French detective and together they set out to track down the villains.

Blood on the Tide is a story of the sea and boats, murder and Nazis that begins in a sleepy coastal backwater and takes the reader through post-war France and Germany.

*'The writing is concise but vivid and authentic – clearly carefully researched. It would make a great film with its evocation of the sights and sounds, cars, boats and trains and way of life in the 1950s.'*

*'The pace doesn't falter at any point and the book is hard to put down.'*
*'A post war murder mystery with a difference. I was swept along with the characters in this wonderfully, intelligently written book.'*
*'Chris O'Donoghue expertly conjures up the atmosphere of Britain in the 1950s. He has a feel for place and an eye for the telling detail.'*

*'I'm a big fan of Simenon and I'm sure anyone who is will enjoy this tale of the quirky DI Sonny Russell who is a vegetarian and lives in a railway carriage.'*

*'Like the best books in this genre you will not want to put it down until all the loose ends are tied up.'*

# Blood on the Shrine

**The second DI Sonny Russell mystery**
**Chris O'Donoghue**

**SNOWED IN** on a Buddhist retreat DI Sonny Russell isn't peaceful for long. A monk is found dead in the shrine room and two men also staying at the centre quickly arouse his suspicions.

Meanwhile his sidekick, DC Johnny Weeks meets a small time crook who, thinking he is trustworthy, asks the policeman to participate in a daring train robbery.

The action begins in Russell's sleepy corner of the South-East, travels to Eire and has its denouement in France, skilfully engineered by Russell's wily old friend, Inspecteur Bruissement.

Blood on the Shrine is a story of Meditation and friendship, deception and intrigue, which tests DI Russell to his limits.

*'It grips the reader from the beginning. Not only does the author continue from his previous book, Blood on the Tide, but a new tale is intricately woven throughout with familiar characters including Sonny's dog, Aggie.'*

*'I really enjoyed this sequel to Blood on the Tide and especially loved the way that the new plot became interwoven with a continuation of Chris's last storyline.'*

*'It's a neatly-crafted work that carries on from Chris's first novel and carries the reader at a brisk pace to a climax that leaves plenty to expand on in his next book, Blood on the Strand.'*

*'A book that once you've started you will put off all other jobs to carry on reading. Can really picture all the characters and think it could make a really good TV series.'*

*'A really cracking read, so full of atmosphere, ties up the loose ends from Blood on the Tide nicely, bring on book three.'*

# Blood on the Strand

**The third DI Sonny Russell mystery**
**Chris O'Donoghue**

**IN A RAGING GALE** a heavy crate is washed up on the beach near Compass Point. DI Sonny Russell and his sidekick DC Johnny Weeks happen upon it while braving the weather near Sonny's home. Puzzled, they go to get help to recover it, but when they return it has gone. So begins a thrilling and dangerous search for stolen Nazi plunder. It leads the detectives, ably assisted by an eager young policewoman, Nettie Sharpe, on a twisting trail that encompasses Hastings fisherman, their iconic net huts, ruthless foreign criminals and the shady side of antique dealing. BLOOD ON THE STRAND is a story of intrigue and drama, set on the sleepy south coast in the post-war mid-fifties.

*Chris O'Donoghue has kept up the suspense and action in this, his third Sonny Russell story. Sonny and his sidekick Johnny Weeks are joined by a WPC to solve the riddle of stolen Nazi treasure.'*

*'Great to return to familiar characters and see them evolve, as well as meeting new ones. Some unexpected twists and interesting plot.'*

*'Another good Sonny Russel mystery from Chris O'Donoghue. I recommend this series of books, proper 50s police detective work.'*

# Blood on the Cards

**The fourth DI Sonny Russell mystery**
**Chris O'Donoghue**

**A TRAVELLING FAIR** brings fun, laughter and excitement - but when one comes Nottery Quay it brings gruesome death too. The resident fortune teller is found with her throat cut in a damp and dirty WWII pillbox near the Royal Military Canal. The owner of the fairground comes under suspicion but, when a second body is found, DI Sonny Russell begins to have his doubts. Falling foul of his bombastic boss Superintendent Stout yet again, he is taken off the case and replaced by the bumbling duo Bonnie and Clyde. However, assisted by his French opposite number, Inspecteur Guillaume Bruissement, and his ever faithful sidekick DC Weeks, he pursues his own investigation. So begins a gripping tale which criss-crosses Sussex and Kent and ends in a thriller chase along the canal, with disastrous consequences...

*I've been enjoying the DI Sonny Russell series and this book doesn't disappoint. The feel of the time is present and the story was nicely engaging. I've grown to love the characters and you can't help rooting for them. A great read.*

*This is the 4th book in the "Blood on the" series and is a gripping read. Held my attention till the end as I did not cheat and read the last chapter halfway through the book. No skim reading, good twist at the end with the clues being in the story if you pay attention. Cannot wait for book number 5.*

*Have read the three earlier books and enjoyed this fourth book in the series just as much as the others. Especially interesting when you live in the area in which the series is set. Hope there are more stories to come.*

*A real page turner with good characters and some plot twists, I think this may be my favourite of the Sonny Russell series.*

# Blood on the Dunes

**The sixth DI Sonny Russell mystery**
**Chris O'Donoghue**

**A LONG-BURIED SKELETON** emerges from the shifting sands at Camber during a raging storm.
A badly injured man is found in a derelict warehouse at Nottery.
A mixed-race boy goes missing from a children's home in Peasmarsh.
Could these seemingly random occurrences possibly be connected?

At first, a puzzled DI Sonny Russell can see no link but, as more horrific events unfold, he begins to detect a troubling pattern.

Blook on the Dunes is a story of fractured relationships and fraught decisions, made years before, that come back to haunt those involved and others who were left to suffer the consequences.

*Chris O'Donoghue trained in industrial ceramics at Bournemouth Art College and worked at Poole Pottery and Cranbrook Pottery in Kent before setting up on his own in Rye. He later specialised in model making and sculpture.*

*When much of the kind of work he did began to be made in the Far East, Chris, having always loved the outdoors, decided on a change of direction and started gardening. His design ability led him to create three medal-winning gardens at the Chelsea Flower Show.*

*A lifetime's passion for the sea, crime novels, the simple pleasures of the Fifties and railways – he is well known on the model railway scene – led him to combine all three in this, his fourth published book.*

The first six DI Sonny Russell mysteries

**BLOOD ON THE TIDE**
**BLOOD ON THE SHRINE**
**BLOOD ON THE STRAND**
**BLOOD ON THE CARDS**
**BLOOD IN THE GARDEN**
**&**
**BLOOD ON THE DUNES**

are available from Amazon
or direct from the Author
chrisodonoghue.blogspot.co.uk
www.chrisodonoghue.co.uk

The seventh DI Sonny Russell mystery
**BLOOD ON THE NILE**
will be published soon